BAD

THE TREE OF DREAMS
And Other Stories

The
TREE OF DREAMS
And Other Stories

BY

MIKA WALTARI

G. P. Putnam's Sons
New York

CONTENTS

THE TREE
OF DREAMS

Translated by Lily Leino

1

MIDSUMMER Day was raw and rainy, and we were all sitting in the kitchen that afternoon. The children were washing the dishes for once. My wife was playing solitaire at the cleared table and you sat by the window, silent. I tried not to look at you too often lest my glances disturb you. Perhaps also because of the others. We were speaking of love. I suppose I really began it, to amuse you or to make you aware of me.

"Love beautifies a woman amazingly," I said. "I know that from experience. I once loved a girl. It was a long time ago and only for a short while, but she had such a crush on me that she swore she didn't know how she had lived without me. She was so infatuated, in fact, that she compared me to a god."

"Oh, that was your childhood friend," my wife remarked, slapping cards onto the table. "No, I'm not going to win this game either. I'm cold. What a midsummer!"

"I'm not saying this in any conceit," I maintained. "Quite the contrary. I know only too well what I am." But that was not the truth. How should I know what I am? Because my whole body began to tremble at the mere sight of you from the attic window, knowing that you actually had come with the others, and recognizing you as you all waited for the rowboat on the other side of the river.

"I mention this only as an example," I assured them, "because she visibly grew more beautiful. Her eyes sparkled and even her skin became clearer. And all because she was in love. I don't doubt that she really did love me sincerely, but just the same, scarcely a month after telling me all this, she was married to another man."

"But—" you began breathlessly. I loved your air of breathlessness. With a flip of my hand I stopped you. You didn't have to say anything.

"There was nothing illogical, false or wrong in it," I said defensively. "You see, before that she hadn't attracted any attention where she worked. Of course, she was pretty enough to have some of the men walk her home, and she would go out now and then, but it was love that made her sparkle. One of the directors noticed her then. It was wartime, and the man was on work leave but could be sent elsewhere any day. He proposed and wanted an immediate wedding. That was easily arranged in those days. Naturally the girl wanted to get married, just as every woman does. In her defense, I must confess that she frankly sought my advice."

"And you?" you asked. Because of the rain the dusk had come early. I saw how the pupils of your eyes expanded with the darkness, until your eyes seemed black. It made me catch my breath.

"I?" I continued, although it was difficult for me to speak. "Naturally I said, 'By all means get married now that you have the opportunity. The very fact that you're asking me proves that you've already made your choice. But let's not meet anymore, at least not like this.' That's what I told her with a feeling of relief. Nothing would have come of our affair anyway, except unpleasantness and guilt."

One of the girls hung up her dish towel and said sagaciously, "That's how women are."

"No," I replied, "that's how love is." My throat was tight, I had difficulty in breathing and I couldn't look at you.

You said nothing. But from some depth a memory rose to the surface and I felt a compulsion to continue. "Whenever I remember her, I remember the cranberry tree."

"They grow beside outhouses," someone remarked in disgust. "Filthy things. Backyard love." That, too, was true.

My wife swept up the cards and rose abruptly. "Let's go outside, girls," she said. "It's not raining so hard anymore. It's stifling in here."

You rose obediently, for you were our guest in the country

for the first time. And the last, although neither of us probably suspected that then. You were still somewhat shy with us. You tried to smile and I detained you. "Don't go yet." To the others I said, "You all go ahead. We'll come along after a while."

The rain had turned into soft mist. The kitchen had grown dark and your eyes were black as you looked at me. You must have been afraid of me, but you sat down obediently nevertheless.

"You must never think of me as an evil and cynical person," I said quietly. "I merely mentioned that experience because it popped into my mind. Because I wanted to tell it to you, too. Especially to you. One occasionally has such impulses. But it was all true. Of course, it could have been told another and perhaps a prettier way."

I rose and stepped across the floor in the darkening room to the table. The walk was years long. Frightening steps.

I sat beside you at the table, near you but separated by a chair.

"It could be told another way," I repeated. "She actually was a childhood friend—if a fifteen-year-old boy can be called a child. And she was fourteen when we first met. As the adage has it, a person always returns to his first loves. It's true, too. Whenever something remains unfulfilled, it must be fulfilled later in life. If one happens to meet again, and has matured meanwhile, and is receptive at that particular moment."

The dusk deepened on that raw midsummer night. You turned your head. "Why did you use the plural?" you asked. "Have you really been in love so many times?" There was no sarcasm in your words. You spoke like a child, in amazement.

"What about you?" I demanded. "Why should you say that to me—you of all people? You're not even thirty and already you've been divorced twice."

I wounded you deliberately, but you merely said, "Let's not talk about me."

"A person matures along with his loves, if he ever does," I said. "Good lord, love itself is only a tiny drop of joy in the sea of despair that it creates around itself. It's terrible to love, because one always unwittingly hurts others.

"What of it if one hurts oneself?" I continued. "My suffering is my own and so is my guilt. I'm an impossible, a hopeless person. But believe me, I've never destroyed another person's life."

I stopped to consider whether that was true. "At least, not deliberately," I amended. "Except, of course, my wife's. And my own."

I raised my hand quickly to forestall your comment. "Don't misunderstand this, either. Naturally we have our happy days and will continue to have them. But every woman basically craves security. How can I give anyone a feeling of security when I continually surprise even myself?

"Believe me," I said, trembling, "if I've ever had happiness or luck or success, I've invariably destroyed it. Smashed it to bits. It's like a sickness in me, and I can't do anything about it. That's why it doesn't pay to envy me. But I've never deliberately ruined anyone else's life."

Having said that, I lightly touched your hand with my own. You were startled. You shifted in your chair, your neck became rigid and even your face stiffened.

"How strangely a person returns to his first love," I said quickly. "My childhood friend could serve as an example of that, too. But one could also cite it as an example of eroticism. How the first youthful erotic experience colors one's whole life, determining the erotic approach and the limits of ecstasy and gratification. One could tell it like that, too, touchingly."

I grew silent for a moment, then added quietly, "You see, she is dead, and has been for many years. But if I had never met her again after our youth, I would probably go to my grave knowing that something in me was eternally unfulfilled.

"I'm insatiable," I exclaimed. "Bottomless. I can't help it. I've hated myself for it, despised myself, until I've begun to understand that in order to develop, a person must learn to recognize himself. Not approve of, but recognize.

"Bitterness is the worst poison," I continued. "If it would corrode only the person himself, but in time it also corrodes his surroundings, and the person can do nothing about it. But love can melt bitterness, although only for a short while, and perhaps only now and then. Damn it, my surroundings ought to be grateful that I've been able to fall in love a few times and through love been liberated from my horrible self."

Then I hastened to contradict myself. "No, I don't want to be cynical because that isn't the truth, either. I'm selfish, glacially selfish. It's best for you to know that lest you expect too much of me. I do know how to talk, that I do. But words are always just an approximation. And usually how one says something means more than what one says. That's why lovers develop their own foolish language in which words are merely secret symbols of something that only the two of them know."

I recalled something and felt constrained to smile. "Once before the wars in my dark days—I'll tell you about them some other time—I met a couple who had sunk to the denatured alcohol stage. The woman was positively grimy. But you should have heard the man once say affectionately to his wife, 'Oh, you damn whore!' The way he said it, with brusque masculine gentleness, made it the finest declaration of love I've ever heard."

"How repulsive!" you breathed.

"No. Beautiful," I insisted.

"Why do you talk to me about such things?" you asked as though begging for mercy.

I didn't touch you. I didn't dare. "You should know. If you don't, it's useless telling you."

Just then I could have taken you in my arms and easily thrown everything overboard. I knew it and that's why I didn't try, although my whole being lusted for your lips, for you. I rose and thrust my hands into my jacket pockets.

"Let's go," I said.

The damp rain of midsummer night was soft as mist on my hot face. At the bottom of the hill a light shone from the window of the sauna chamber and the girls moved there as though on a lighted stage. As we approached I heard them laughing and talking animatedly. I calmed down.

At that very moment I heard a bird whistle, then warble and again change its song. A nightingale was singing in the reeds on the sauna shore. I could hardly believe my ears.

"A nightingale," I murmured, and the happiness of my youth welled up in me. This could no longer be a coincidence. Beyond the years, past death, the nightingale in the reeds sang of an old love on the threshold of a new.

We stood beside each other in the dusk, in the cold drizzle of a midsummer night. The nightingale whistled, warbled and changed its song ceaselessly. It sang near us, only a few steps away, but the gray bird was not visible in the dusk.

The warm light of life spilled from the sauna window into the damp evening. "My dead darling," I said, "why have you returned to sing to me? Is it an omen?"

I don't know why I said that. Certainly it wasn't pretense, for I felt Marvi's presence too strongly. It was as though her spirit had spread like a veil over the living scene and me.

I had the same feeling on many a night after you had left, when the sun had set and the moonlight touched the red walls of the house with a ghostly light. And the nightingale sang night after night in the reeds by the sauna shore.

During weekdays I often thought of taking out Marvi's few letters and reading them again. I knew that they were hidden somewhere among numerous other papers. I had not been able to destroy them. I should have sorted them all, but it was left undone for a long time. That usually happens when life flows along its familiar channel.

After all, nothing really had happened, although I knew that without a word or a touch, infinitely more had occurred between us than if I had slept with you. To you, too, and not only to me. Love is like that. Yes, that's what love is like.

2

Once, much later, we lay in bed together. The sun had circled the window to afternoon. You whispered in my ear, "Oh, my darling." Words, only words.

I asked, "Why do you act as though you had never loved anyone before? I know everything about you. Or perhaps not everything, since no one can know everything about another.

But I do know a lot, more than you may think. So why are you like this to me?"

You pressed your fingers against my lips. "You always talk so much. Why talk unnecessarily?"

"I was born to play with words," I explained. "It's my profession. My calling, if you will, although I'm not usually so snobbish. But perhaps it's not even that. I just want to find out about myself, and you. So why?"

You thought hard, wrinkling your forehead. "I don't know. It's really silly, and they'd make fun of me if they knew. But don't laugh. I feel as though I had never been in love before. Perhaps there's something in me that no one else has been able to find."

Well, I certainly didn't love you because of your intellect. I reached for the bottle beside the bed. The sun had gone by the window, the ice cubes in the bucket had melted. "Do you want some?"

You merely shook your head on the pillow. "I don't either," I said. "I haven't the strength to lift the bottle. That's bad. I never thought I'd slip so far. But actually I've said many times that I surprise even myself. Well, you at least are not thinking of dear old England."

You looked at me inquiringly. Your eyes were blue-gray, and in the bright light the pupils had contracted again. You were tired. Your face was naked, for to me you dared reveal your naked face. That alone indicated that you really loved me, in your own way and with no false illusions.

I related the old tale about the English princess who married into the German court. Some time later her mother wrote to inquire how she was adapting herself to the unpleasant aspects of marriage. To which the girl replied, "I just shut my eyes tight and think of dear old England."

You laughed at the timeworn story, then stretched. "No, I'm not thinking of dear old England."

"Only of clothes and dressmakers," I said teasingly. But you didn't bother to reply. You only smiled knowingly.

"Try to remember that you're fifteen years younger than I," I warned you.

"You're not old," you reassured me, as a woman on the threshold of thirty reassures a man my age. "Don't imagine such a thing."

I didn't have the strength to argue. "Let's talk," I suggested. "Or are you asleep already?"

"No, no, I'm not asleep." You rubbed your eyes with your fists like a sleepy child. "Why should I waste a second in sleep when we can be together like this?"

"Let's talk, then," I said. "Let's steal time, we relentless thieves. But is it actually stealing to give another something that no one else has been able to accept? That's what you have done for me, and that's a lot. That's a tremendous lot, my darling. One has to mature to that through terrible years. I'm so glad that I didn't meet you when you were a young girl. I doubt whether you would have liked me. Perhaps I wouldn't have liked you, either."

Hands behind my head, I reminisced. "Do you remember the first time we really kissed? We were both drunk, of course, even you. It probably wouldn't have happened otherwise. My hand accidentally touched your bare skin. That's not like me. Believe me, that hasn't happened before. That touch burned me. Your skin was cool but it still burned me, and I knew that I would never be at peace until you were mine."

You looked reproachfully at me, but I shook my head stubbornly. "I'm not claiming that I can't live without you. That would be stupid. Naturally a person can go on living. Perhaps not as well, but living nevertheless. We mustn't exaggerate. We must try to say to each other only what we really mean."

I continued, "Then I knew that I would never be at peace until you were mine." I suddenly stroked your shoulder. "That's the worst part about me—it isn't enough that I possess the body, I must have everything—you, even your thoughts, so that I really know you. So that we alternately say just what the other has been thinking. That, too, is love."

You smiled. "Shall I pour you a drink?"

"That's too easy a thought transference," I said. "But go ahead and pour if you have the strength. I suppose I was thinking of it in passing."

You reached across me for the bottle. I felt you against my body. I knew your beauty. But beauty alone no longer sufficed for me. I took a drink from the glass and lighted a cigarette.

"I mentioned touching you," I continued. "I suppose that touch bound me to you. Well, shall I tell you some more about my childhood friend Marvi? When the nightingale sang, she returned to my memory after many years. She returned from beyond the grave to tell me that she too had helped me to mature. Just as I released her from my touch and prepared her for another man.

"For another man," I repeated slowly. "You too are prettier than before, and your eyes are sparkling. Is it possible that I'm doomed to that same accursed task?"

"Never," you exclaimed in alarm. "Never. You mustn't think of it." You looked at me, just looked at me dreamily, then shook your head. "You don't want me to say never," she concluded, stroking my temples. "All right, I won't say it. I'll just urge you not to torment yourself, darling. Why do you always torment yourself needlessly? If you must talk, tell me about your childhood friend."

I thought back, and the memories no longer hurt. Neither was there any bitterness. They were only beautiful, those distant memories, even those of my boyhood. I scarcely recognized that boy anymore.

"I attended a boys' school," I began, "and didn't even have any sisters. It probably wasn't good for me. Undoubtedly it helped make my physical awakening so painful. To me girls were alarmingly tempting creatures when I first began to notice them. How pathetic boyhood timidity is! It compels one either to crawl into a shell, or to go overboard in talkativeness. I suppose my first kisses were just the clumsy games of puppyhood, groping and curious. I didn't love any particular girl. I was just in love with love and afraid that no one could ever love me. I was so round-cheeked and childish."

"You poor thing," you said, caressing my neck, as your eyes darkened.

"Don't," I begged, drawing away. "I spent the summer in a town where the heath was warm in the evenings and the pine

trees were tall and copper-colored in the sunset. I was fifteen
and terribly alone. I was working during vacation, and every
morning before seven I would pass an endless line of women on
the road making their way to the woolen mill. A thousand girls
passed me every morning. It was a town of erotic hunger. I
sensed it in the way I always sense things around me. But I
won't talk about them. Besides, I had a friend, a girl whom I
shyly kissed. But in a way it didn't mean anything, for she too
was just curious. And a kiss, even the most unsuccessful, was
like an incredible gift to me. Perhaps I wasn't so unpleasant
after all. Perhaps someone actually could care for me."

"You poor thing," you said again, extending your glass. I
filled it absentmindedly. In my memory I recalled the resinous
fragrance of the heath and the bitter-damp evening smell of the
cranberry tree in the yard. You swallowed the drink and your
shoulders shook.

"Bad?" I asked and then continued. "It was a hot summer.
The road exuded warmth in the evening. I sometimes saw
Marvi on the road. Her hair was blond and she always walked
with her chin in the air. She had an erect figure and the firm
breasts of a girl. Her complexion was clear, and she was not as
suntanned as many of the others that summer. My God, how I
adored her before we had even exchanged a word! Much later
she confessed that she had noticed me watching her on the road
and had feared that I would speak to her, because she would
have had to toss her head and snap at me. She wouldn't have
dared do anything else. And how she tossed her head, haughtily,
as though she were proud of being pretty. But actually it wasn't
that. She was at least as uncertain of herself as I. It was just an
indication of timidity, that habit of tossing her head.

"I knew her name," I went on. "I even knew something about
her home. In a moment of daring I had walked through their
courtyard. Several families lived there. It was an untidy yard
and beside the steps grew a cranberry tree. I plucked a leaf and
crumbled it in my fingers to catch its fragrance. It made me
feel as though I owned something of her, although I didn't even
know her then.

"Naturally my friend knew her," I continued. "They attended the same school, although Marvi was in a lower grade. My endless questioning annoyed her. 'You won't get anywhere with Marvi,' she teased me. 'Marvi's stuck-up. She doesn't go around with boys.' But I suppose every woman is a procuress at heart, or perhaps it was only the cruel curiosity of the teens, but once when she had joined me on the road she stopped to talk to Marvi. She disregarded my presence until Marvi's glance forced her to introduce us. Marvi shook my hand casually but her eyes were round with fear. As I suppose mine were. For the life of me I couldn't say anything that made sense, and so the opportunity passed. But at least I had met her. I had the right to tip my cap, stop and chat if I dared. It never went beyond the cap-tipping stage, however. I never dared even smile, and neither did she. We were both deadly serious when we greeted each other. She even paled in nodding to me. How amusing we must have been! A fifteen- and a fourteen-year-old. But perhaps it wasn't so laughable after all.

"Are you asleep," I asked, "or can you listen to some more?" Your hair shone disturbingly soft against the pillow. Your neck was slender and so was your face. You opened your eyes a little and said apathetically, "Go on."

I was telling it more to myself than to you. "This is probably boring, but it's essential if you're to know me. One Sunday toward the end of summer the building contractor with whom I was living took me along to inspect a large municipal building. There was a certain dark girl—a big girl compared to me. All of nineteen, I learned later. She remained behind to talk to me, showed me around the yard and then suggested, 'Let's go into the woods.' "

"Ahaa!" you exclaimed, raising yourself onto your elbow. I had to laugh.

"It wasn't quite so dangerous. We just went into the woods, she sat down on a hummock, sighed that it was hot and opened the top button of her blouse. I kissed her and she held me tightly, kissing me back in a way that was completely new to me. It was shocking and revolting, and I felt no desire for her moist lips. She smiled and raised my clumsy hand to her bosom and in confusion I opened still another button of her blouse.

Again I felt as though I had been given a bounteous gift, although afterward I realized that I hadn't even liked her breast. It was big and soft. Still I felt humbly grateful that something like that could happen to me. Actually, this is quite a ridiculous tale."

"What then?" you asked. "Did the big girl hurt you?"

"Don't be silly," I retorted. "I probably would have run away in fright. Her eyes were dreamy for a moment, then she yawned, buttoned her blouse and said, 'We'll have to get back. It must be late.' Actually, it wasn't so late. On our way back, by the big barn, she casually asked how old I was. When I told her, she lost all interest in me, and we never met again. But I still remember her warmly, for she gave me a priceless gift."

"I hate that girl!" you snapped.

"Why? It didn't mean anything," I assured you. "It was just experience, valuable experience for a timid fifteen-year-old. But surely you don't hate Marvi."

"I don't know," you said. "I don't know yet. I just hate the explorer in you, your cold-blooded curiosity. How can you do something like that unless you love the other?"

"Don't be childish, darling. There are men who never get beyond that stage. I mean, they only learn how to sleep with a woman, that's all. Perhaps they're satisfied. They experience lust, all right, but no gentleness, no beauty. I've been guilty of it myself, why deny it? But it leads only to the heart's death, and that to me is the worst that can happen to a person. Someone else, of course, might consider it happiness.

"There's no such thing as happiness," I went on. "There are only fluctuations, peaks and troughs of waves, the infinite rolling of the sea. There's joy and there's ecstasy, even though they're bought with lies and despair. But happiness there is not. Believe that, darling."

And so I again unwittingly brought tears into your eyes. I kissed your naked face, your nearness. "Don't," you pleaded. "I can't any longer. Don't."

"It is getting late," I conceded. "I see that the sun has already passed the window. But I'll finish the tale since I began it. I was going to tell you about physical contact. You see, my experience gave me courage, and the next time I met Marvi on the road I stopped to talk to her. I even smiled. I asked her to go with me to the dance, and after some hesitation she promised. I waited for her in the courtyard by the cranberry tree. We both danced uncertainly and soon left the floor. I didn't take her directly home. We walked to the other side of the railroad yard, to a grove. There was moonlight, of course, on that August night. No, the place is no longer there, but I remember it clearly. I tried to make conversation about everything that interests teen-agers, because I was so afraid that she would get angry. I wouldn't have hurt her for the world, but I had dreamed about her all summer and so I timidly put my arms around her.

"I can still feel how she stiffened, but she didn't resist. She let me kiss her lips, the lips that knew even less about kissing than mine. Some fifteen years later she confessed that I was the first boy she had ever allowed to kiss her. She was wearing a white dress that could have been made over from her confirmation dress. I fumbled with it until I had opened it and she, child that she was, thought that that was the way it should be. My bashful hand found her white bosom, and it was the most beautiful thing I had ever experienced. I didn't dare kiss it, I didn't even dare move my hand. Both of us just stood there, frightened. Suddenly she started, tore herself loose, and with her back to me began fixing her dress.

"The moonlight dazzled my eyes, and my love dazzled me. That moment I felt that nothing bad or wrong could ever happen to me. 'Marvi, dear Marvi,' I whispered. But she kept her back to me and sniffled. Then I, who always manage to spoil everything, foolishly stooped to pick up a small stone merely as an excuse to say something to her. I circled around her and showed her the stone on my palm. 'Marvi,' I said, 'I'm taking this stone as a souvenir, so that I'll never forget this moment.' At that she burst into tears and ran away. I didn't dare call her by name, for the town was already asleep. I caught up with her only by her front steps under the cranberry tree.

"She had calmed down by then. Tossing her head, she said with such anger that I was horrified, 'I hate you! I hate you, and I'll never let you speak to me again. Don't even try to greet me. If we happen to meet I'll turn my head away.' That was the first time that my world turned upside down because of a woman. Believe me, I didn't have the slightest idea why she was so angry."

"You poor boy," you said, a woman's wisdom in your voice. "You really believed what she said."

"Of course I did." Even decades later it made me angry. "I'm basically a serious person. One of my shortcomings is that I believe whatever is said to me. You know how easy it is to hurt me. But not even you could guess why she was so disturbed. No, not because I had touched her breast. Not at all. You see, as we kissed, she probably felt something of what I myself did, and that's why she was so terribly hurt when she thought I needed a stone to remind me of something she could never forget. For the first time she had overcome her timidity and pride. For the first time she had stiffly allowed someone to touch her. It was as though she had been branded with a hot iron, she told me years later in a true confessions style. But to me it had seemed only a fleeting game that required a tangible reminder. So thoroughly can people misunderstand each other.

"I could only assume that I had unwittingly wronged or shamed her," I continued. "A terrible feeling of guilt came over me, and yet I didn't regret it. Even if she never wanted to see me again, I knew that I could never forget her. A blissful feeling still enveloped me, like a poem welling up in a person. I felt happy and unhappy simultaneously. It was the most beautiful experience of my youth. And as an erotic experience it was far more soul-stirring than anything that happened later.

"And so, darling, when I kissed you for the first time, it meant more to me than if I had possessed you. Actually, darling, I possessed you already when I accidentally touched your bare flesh for the first time. You understand, don't you—it was something I hadn't experienced before, something decisive, like that first embrace of my youth. It marked me, just as Marvi once marked me. Now do you understand why I've had to tell you this?"

You looked at me with smiling eyes and slowly shook your pretty head. "Oh, you! You always have to talk about things that are self-evident. Besides, it wasn't accidental, in case you still think that. After all, I am I. But now I'm hungry."

"Food, always food," I lamented. "The most trying thing about love is that one has to undress and dress at the most peculiar times. But of course you must have food."

We dressed. Leaning back in an easy chair, I watched you put on your face. Evening lipstick. Miss Dior fragrance. And silvery blue eye shadow on your lids. As you looked into the mirror you lifted your upper lip in a grimace and admired your teeth. Beautiful, even, gleaming white teeth. You were radiant.

As you rose to go out I said, "Listen."

You made a questioning sound. "You probably know that I love you terribly," I said.

"Silly," you murmured and ran your hand over my cheek. We went down to eat.

3

They were probably the heaviest steps of my life, the steps that led me to you. Undoubtedly you realized it. Much, much heavier than those that forced me away from you. Even though your smile was bright and my happiness limitless when we met, I realized that everything had its price. I was not meant to be a betrayer.

That's why agony and restlessness again seized me as they had so many previous times. Sleep fled and I lay awake nights with my only companion the burning oven that was my head. For me there was no home in the cold universe. I felt that the world itself was too small for human lust—merely a tight enclosure beyond which the distant stars flickered. I thought of time, too, and of flight in time. I thought of the furrowed gigantic pillar in the chapel of the Barcelona cathedral, and of Mount Eryx in Sicily and the well of Aphrodite. The marble mosaic floor that had come to light in the ruins of a Norman fortress, where the bodies of those who arrived from many lands to die for love were buried. Aphrodite of Eryx was the wealthiest Aphrodite of the Mediterranean. The earth in her yard is still layered with soot and ashes.

All these things came to my fevered mind in the early hours of the morning. On some nights restlessness compelled me to walk around. I moved carefully, lest I awaken someone. At my desk I leafed through books, searching for the faces of those long since dead who still lived in cloth, wood or stone. Their eyes stared restlessly into mine, their faces as vivid as when they were alive.

But of course a person doesn't awaken to the past with living eyes. Only for your sake would I have wanted to believe in return and immortality, to feel your lips once more in another life. To make love to you in another life, because this world deemed it theft.

No, the vivid faces of the departed did not console me. I fingered the marble cube that I had picked up from Aphrodite's floor. The memory of your eyes, your lips, your limbs, scorched me.

What a horrible spell, I thought. Why did I have to meet just you? After all, I had been fairly happy. Or was it my own emptiness that had made me seek you out? I should have heeded the formidable bird with brown arrows on its back that followed me from bush to bush in the orchard on the last day of autumn.

I wondered, too, whether I was still only a child, once more greedily gulping down human life to nourish myself. For everything has an end, even lust. Especially lust. There is nothing more sickening than the death of passion. When even the dearest face becomes strange and ugly under a penetrating gaze. When one can count, in cold terror, every sign of deterioration, everything peculiar, distorted and calculating that one can find. In every face—even yours.

That is what I thought about during the murderous hours of early morning. And nothing in itself explained anything, because the reasons were twined like rope of many fibers. They could be fingered separately, each fiber could be cut, but together they were woven into a bond too strong for a mortal to cut. You were stronger than my will.

The piece of marble fell from my fingers and rolled onto the blue rug. As I stooped to retrieve it, I remembered how as a boy I had picked up the stone in memory of Marvi. Good Lord, it had been in my pocket the entire fall semester! I became sixteen. At that age a person lives and grows rapidly. Some time that winter I emptied my pockets and threw away the stone with other trash. It no longer meant anything to me, or so I thought. Whole new worlds were bubbling in my mind. If one girl didn't care for me, it didn't pay for me to waste my thoughts on her. Youth is an amazingly practical period. Its wounds heal quickly. If she felt contempt, perhaps hate, for me, why should it concern me? After all, I would never have to meet her again.

Instead of senselessly tormenting myself, I began to rearrange my desk drawers. Letters that for years had been tied into bundles came into my hand. But Marvi's few letters had to be somewhere apart. Finally I found them in a folder among some useless papers. I didn't even remember that her photograph was tucked in among the letters.

I recognized her restless handwriting on the envelopes, the handwriting of a lonely person. She had written them in pencil, at night after leaving me, or while waiting for me. Good Lord, had I wronged her, too? I didn't know. I knew only that apparently we were fated to meet, in order to free ourselves of each other.

I looked long at her picture. She was smiling, and there was none of the harsh, nervous stiffness that had marked her when I met her again. Only a gentle smile. She had had the picture taken at my request, so that I would have something to look at during her absence. Once I had been happy about that photograph. Now I merely looked at it quizzically and nothing stirred in me anymore. That was how Marvi looked during the weeks in which we loved each other.

She was then thirty. Presumably it is true that only when a woman approaches thirty can she accept love as well as give it. Before that everything is groping, excitement, blindness, uncertainty. And so many people never ripen to love. They probably don't realize it, however. At most they are aware of a vague dissatisfaction for which they compensate with such pastimes as color photography, card games or collecting. Or perhaps they do realize it but are trying to make the best of it, these dependable, conscientious, honest people. Fortunate people. Enviable people.

For love is a beast. Love is a siren. Love is worse than dope. One can die of love. A person can easily lose his nerve and sense of proportion because of it. The most scrupulous and stable person is in the greatest danger if love disastrously comes his way. Or must a person possess a basic flaw to attract love? Some gap, some mental decay? I thought of all this with Marvi's letters in my hand.

In my fevered and hypersensitive condition I could smell the acrid odor of the cranberry leaves in my fingers. I could not free myself of it although I had freed myself of Marvi.

No, I didn't read the letters then. Not yet. Some reluctance restrained me. I merely arranged them in chronological order according to their postmarks and tucked the photograph between them. I tossed them into the pile that I intended to take to the country for perusal, as though I needed to replenish myself with my former self. I knew full well that I was undergoing a change. Whether it was growth or decay I didn't know. I knew only that it hurt grievously.

I returned to my bed as quietly as I had left it. Cranberry tree. Backyard. Mental decay. I dozed off, my head full of smoldering ashes.

4

We were sitting in a restaurant, you and I. Only a few people were there, but even they disturbed me. You were sipping white wine. I wasn't drinking then. I just had to meet you, to see you again, even though among people and across a table. The white wine became you. Naturally you had done your utmost, but I intended to remain firm.

"Some night you'll crack," I said, "after you've sorrowed and lusted enough. I mean that I could never be happy anyway, no matter what happens."

A forlorn look came into your eyes. "Such long eyelashes," I said hastily. "By the way, I came across Marvi's letters recently. Remember?"

"Why do you always talk so?" you demanded. You were sullen and hurt.

"I haven't seen that dress before. It's attractive," I remarked placatingly. You touched the dress and smiled, looking into my eyes. I looked back smolderingly. "Nevertheless, you would be even lovelier if your only garment were the white wine."

You leaned toward me and smiled again. How you smiled! "You should know."

"Lead me not into temptation," I pleaded.

You shrugged and stiffened. "Thine is the power," you said submissively. I had wounded you. One always wounds when loving.

"Forgive me," I begged. "I'm impossible today. I'm impossible always. I suppose you know that by now."

It was true. Whatever we said, strangeness lay between us. The strangeness of people, of clothes, of the table. Only when two people are alone is it comfortable to love. That is why loving is so hopeless; the most hopeless thing there is. But in our case it wasn't that kind of strangeness. We both knew what it was; there was just no point in talking about it.

"May I have another glass of wine?" you asked.

"Of course. But let's return to Marvi's letters."

"Would you let me read them?" you broke in. "Since they seem to be so important to you."

"No, I wouldn't. Such things aren't done. I didn't even reread them. When I do, perhaps I'll burn them. Then I'll finally be free of Marvi. You see, a drop of her apparently still remains in my blood, otherwise I wouldn't think of her as often. For your sake, of course. Another glass of white wine, miss.

"I was in a mental institution when we met again after many years," I began, studying your expression. You didn't cringe. There was only a quiver in the corner of your eye.

"Didn't you know that?" I asked in feigned amazement. "How strange. You really don't know very much about me."

"What a shame," you said slowly, tilting your head. Your smile said that you knew at least as much about me as anyone else. Even more. That was most important to you: knowing something that no one else knew. I hadn't been able to hurt you, after all. You were too confident of your knowledge.

I regretted my confession. "I wasn't there very long. Only about six weeks. It was during the war, when I had exhausted myself to the breaking point. Or had been exhausted, however you want to put it. I wasn't as weary as I am now. In fact, I worked quite fast and I suppose they wanted to take advantage of it. At any rate, I had to take over an extra assignment that had to be done at night for security reasons. I completed the task, but lost my sleep. An unnerving trip that I had to undertake about the same time finished me.

"After that I couldn't sleep more than an hour or two each night, and then only with the aid of sleeping pills. The old momentum carried me forward for a few weeks, but no one can go on forever. Naturally, I began to drink. Stiff as a log, I could sleep several hours, but of course I suffered the consequences the next night. Finally the doctor sent me off to a mental institution and I went gladly. I wouldn't have had a vacation otherwise. Insomnia is a civilian complaint."

I thought back to those weeks. "That was my first real period of sleeplessness. It all started from that. I had always had spells of insomnia, but it became a sickness during the war, and since then it has struck almost every year. Sometimes in darkest winter, sometimes at the end of a hard assignment that leaves the brain grinding nothing. Nowadays I get over it in two or three weeks, for I know how to take care of myself. I used to take the insomniac's hypomanic excitement seriously, but now I know that it isn't normal; it's a sickness. The worst of it is that a person actually feels happy in that condition. The brain works faster, ideas fly, one has to be busy every moment. Or to prattle. But it's a sickness just the same."

I looked you in the eye. "Just as on those rare occasions when

I feel happy I know that I'm sick. Unfortunately. I'm a melancholy person, so happiness for me spells sickness."

"Don't say that," you protested. "You mustn't say that." You glanced at the table.

"Another glass of white wine, miss," I ordered. "Go ahead and drink, sweetheart, if it helps matters. It probably won't hurt you. I'll take you home."

The waitress removed your lipstick-stained glass and brought a fresh drink. You had on your evening makeup with the silvery blue eyeshadow. You were beautiful but shy, and the makeup allowed you to conceal your face from the world. Only to me did you dare show your naked face. I knew by that that you loved me. You submitted defenselessly to me, and I repaid you by hurting you. One should never belong to another so completely, for it leads only to suffering and destruction.

" 'You mustn't say that,' " I mimicked you. "You women are crazy when you're in love. Marvi didn't find any flaws in me either, although the doctor gave me the old-fashioned Sulfonal cure that twisted my tongue and even my eyes but still didn't help my insomnia. When the head nurse was in a good mood she would make me some strong coffee at four or five in the morning just to pass the time.

"A stupid drug," I recalled. "It used to be used because it wasn't habit-forming. Actually, I suppose, a person could use anything as a narcotic if he wanted to. Even milk."

"Don't tease," you laughed. "You're just joking."

"Like hell I am. If you drink enough milk, the body's fluid balance is disturbed and you find yourself in a state of stupefaction similar to epilepsy. At least, when you drink white wine you know what you're getting. Sweetheart, you're not becoming tipsy before my very eyes, are you?"

You laughed at me, your eyes slits. Your mouth was that of a tiger. "You were going to tell me about Marvi." Then you became serious, opened your purse and studied your reflection. "Maybe I am getting drunk," you conceded and put on some more lipstick. You deliberately gave yourself a wider, more ruthless mouth.

"That two such drunkards had to meet," I marveled. "Perhaps that's all it is—the gratitude that one has found one's own kind. But don't be afraid. You're not so bad as I, and won't be even after fifteen years. But be careful."

"Only that," you said sadly. "Of course it's only that. What else did you think?"

"Mumm Cordon Rouge," I said. "The champagne of melancholy, of tears. The driest champagne in the world—so dry that it squeaks between the teeth. Don't forget that. Let's not cry tonight."

"Tell me about Marvi," you urged. "You're always talking, anyway."

"It wouldn't work," I explained. "Believe me. If one of us were sober at times, the other would begin drinking, and that would be the end of it. We'd sail straight to hell, both of us."

"Darling, oh my darling," you pleaded. "In hell, could we be together, just the two of us?"

I shook my head. "Now you're being silly."

You leaned toward me, reaching out your hand. "I'd like to have a little girl by you," you said slyly. "I've always wanted a little girl. I'm a woman, don't forget."

"That's the damnable part of it. Fool that I was, I thought that you were grown up. Miss, another glass of white wine, please. Now in God's name don't start crying! You know how mascara smarts. People are looking at you. Now don't pretend."

I changed the subject. "About Marvi. I had heard about her over the years. I knew that she had left school and gone to the Institute of Social Sciences to study journalism. I suppose she had a flair for writing, but she was too shy to succeed in that field. Then she studied foreign languages and became a correspondent in a business firm. She was doing well at that when we met again.

"Actually, we had met briefly even before the war. Once on a train, I remember, when we talked easily and I noticed that she had the same erect figure and the same way of tossing her head. I also couldn't help noticing that she was brazenly wearing a brassiere. And why not? She had every reason to be proud of her figure. Although she made sure that I saw her engagement ring, I had a feeling that she wasn't completely oblivious to me."

You pinched my arm on the table and your eyes darkened. "Tell me about Marvi. Tell me what there is to tell, but don't gloat."

"Sorry, I was just getting into it. My mood was the basis for it, of course, and the fact that I was home with my family. No one can stand seeing another person deliberately driving himself toward a mental breakdown, much less understand it. That's why we were cruel to each other, my wife and I, wounding each other ceaselessly. The fault was mine, of course. Still it was as though sandpaper were being rubbed over bare skin. No woman can stand that, not even the most understanding. That knowledge in itself made me ill."

I stopped to ponder the matter. "Perhaps, after all, my insomnia represented a hysterical person's characteristic refuge in illness when the pressure has grown unbearable. However that may be, I happened to meet Marvi on the street one evening. Why just her? I would have greeted anyone who was kind just as enthusiastically. 'Marvi,' I must have shouted, 'for heaven's sake come and have a drink with me!' She tossed her head, smiled, and glanced at her watch. 'For five minutes,' she said. I don't think she even drank, just sat and watched me. And smiled as only Marvi could smile. She was no longer shy or afraid. But I just kept on drinking and babbling about everything, to keep her with me so that I wouldn't have to be alone. We sat there until closing time, when I suggested, 'Let's go to your place.' She looked frightened. Her landlady was a nervous elderly spinster who would throw her out. But in my condition, what did I care about disturbing other people?"

"Sometimes you can be very stubborn," you conceded.

"You see," I explained, "a person in such a nervous state generates electricity that catches others up in it. Marvi was swept along without even realizing it. And so we went to her room, she fearfully and on tiptoe. I still remember that room well. The wardrobe, the desk, the threadbare remnants of a once elegant bourgeois home. There was even an Oriental rug on the floor."

"And then?" you prompted.

"We kissed. We caressed each other. She was experienced, too, a grown woman. I must have told her that I had never been able to forget her. I suppose I cried, too, in my drunkenness. But then something inexplicable happened. My mind cleared suddenly, and I found myself kneeling before her. I had opened her blouse, and the beauty of her bosom made me speechless. Beauty so dazzling, so achingly fair that it permitted no impure thoughts. It stayed my drunken hand and halted my tongue. I couldn't even think of touching her, but only rested my forehead on her breast. It was as cool and inviolate as it had been when I had first placed my hand on it as a boy. 'Marvi,' I said, 'I don't deserve anything so beautiful.' I was drunk, of course. And then—"

"And then?" you probed.

"Then I fell into her bed and slept like a log. For the first time in weeks I slept until morning without waking once. Until at last her alarm clock rang and awakened her, lying beside me fully clothed and tremblingly wondering how she would get me out of the apartment without the knowledge of her landlady. That was impossible, of course. We heard her moving about and coughing in the vestibule. Besides, I had to go to the toilet. Seizing the bull by the horns, I straightened my tie, combed my hair and stepped into the vestibule to greet her with a smile. Then for the first time I mentioned that Marvi and I were childhood friends. She was an elegant old Swedish lady, and we became almost friendly. At least, she later told Marvi that she thought me very human. Well, I suppose that's one thing that can be said of me, don't you think, dear?"

"At the very least," you conceded generously. At any rate, I made you laugh in that fiendish situation.

"She didn't serve us coffee that first time, so we had some coffee substitute in a little café before she went to work. I had an interview that same morning, so it worked out well. I jotted down her telephone number—it was the least I could do. She was quite unhappy and ashamed of the whole affair. Everything could have ended there, with neither of us being obligated in any way, except perhaps to smile if we should meet on the street. Naturally I sent her flowers, and to the landlady also, along with a few humble words.

"But alas, already then there was a drop of Marvi's blood in me and I wanted to know everything about her—her aloof body, her thoughts, everything. No, I don't remember whether I was even in love with her. It's just that I was so desperately lonely, and her beauty glowed in me. Only a little. You don't have to be jealous. She was a spring, a clear spring, a muddy spring, a spring at the root of a cranberry tree. Dearest, am I getting drunk or are you? I guess talking so much is intoxicating. Normally I don't talk this much. Now I just have to, to you. It's better to talk than to cry.

"Tonight you're a brilliant listener," I praised her. "Miss, make it another one, please."

"Closing time," the waitress said amiably. She was tired but nevertheless tried to smile. It was good to have someone smile at us, even though she could not have understood.

"All right. The bill, then, please." You stared at me with unhappy eyes. "Don't be afraid, I'll take you home. I'll thrust you in through your front door. You won't be able to go anywhere else tonight."

"I've had enough," you said, shaking your head. "No more white wine for me."

"Don't lie. I know you. But I'll see you to your door. Once you get into bed, it'll pass. You always sleep so soundly."

"Bed," you drawled, as though savoring the word. You smiled, and once again your mouth was that of a tiger.

"I hate time," I said. "When I'm with you, I hate time. It flies by too fast, like a bullet straight to the heart. That's what it is to me. By the way, I've forgotten to tell you that I want you, terribly."

You looked at me, your mouth a bitter red. "Then why are you so merciless?" you demanded. "Thine is the power, thine is the power, thine is the power. How many times do I have to repeat it?"

The bill came. As we left, people stared at us. "Let's go," I said, and began reciting senselessly, "In bidding farewell to one's love. Tell me, do you love another? I have never loved another.

Felicità sta sempre all' altra riva. Mind the rug, darling. Shall we walk? Your head will clear. Both our heads will clear."

You pressed against me as we went down the lobby stairs. "I'll never get over this. I don't want to."

"I only bring you misery," I thought aloud. "You were cheerful once, even happy. You had your work, your family, your friends, the whole world. I've brought you only misfortune."

"No, no, no." You sealed my lips with your hand. "You only bring happiness, nothing bad, nothing sordid. If only you allow me to meet you now and then."

The electric lanterns of night. The unnatural glow of neon lights. In the taxi no word was spoken. You merely squeezed my hand tightly in your bare hand. How naked a human hand can be! In the street outside your building I said, "Please wait a moment while I see the lady safely inside." The taxi driver sighed and twisted himself into a more comfortable position.

Before the elevator I said, "Wipe your lipstick off."

You clung to me as one drowning person clings to another. What am I? I thought. What do you think you see in me? What have I done to you? I saw mortal fear in your eyes.

"Sleep well," I said. The door separated us like the lid of a coffin.

In the taxi I sighed, "Let's go." Dark buildings. The unnatural glow of neon lights. My city. I took a handkerchief from my pocket and wiped my mouth. No stain. You were considerate, adorably considerate. Suddenly a ridiculous memory pushed its way through years of bitterness. Once somebody had wound her hairs carefully around my sleeve buttons to make sure that they were noticed. But who? For the life of me I couldn't remember who had done it. Was that what had happened with Marvi? Did I remember only the beautiful things? Had the unpleasant things sunk to the bottom of my mind into complete oblivion?

5

My work didn't progress. One siege of depression followed another at alarmingly brief intervals. Letters remained unopened for weeks. It was agonizing to answer the telephone. Time rumbled ahead like a tormented streetcar. Time pounded nerve-rackingly in my head. I was able once again to drop off into a dull sleep. I slept late, very late in the morning, because I had no desire to face another agonizing day. I thought, I have nothing to look forward to anymore. Why should I ruin your life? It would be better not to meet—better for you, perhaps for me as well, and certainly better for the other people.

But at night after turning off the light I lay awake, wide-eyed, staring into the darkness. It's dangerous to do that. I remembered the tingle of your touch too well, and so I fled to Marvi. Marvi was dead, but her gossamer being enveloped me and penetrated me. In the darkness her eyes mocked me and smiled at me, as though she now understood matters better than I. There was nothing evil or cloudy in her eyes, merely goodness as they smiled at me in the dark.

How her eyes radiated love on those dark December mornings! Soft snowflakes melted on her cheeks. Many mornings we would meet in a brightly lighted café before she went to work. I needed her. I needed her desperately, her warmth, her vitality. It was as though I were devouring her in order to replenish my own fading strength.

Years later I looked back on those weeks at the mental institution as the happiest period in my life. After the horrible pressure I was free, at least for a brief breathing spell. That meant a great deal during wartime. It was as though a giant machine had spewed me to one side temporarily. I needed human warmth, I wanted beauty to sustain me and help me live without cracking up.

Marvi, too, must have felt herself pathetically alone in a world of people. And when the tempest caught her up she probably didn't even want to resist. Not anymore. The tension of our first childhood contact drove us together. As I remember it, she wasn't even surprised when I called and told her that I was in a mental institution. She was merely happy that I called and promised to come and see me. She did come. I had a private room in which I could receive visitors undisturbed. That's how it began.

I remembered it all in the dark: the ancient wooden building, the slippery linoleum floors with their worn spots, the creaking rattan chairs, the off-key piano in the patients' recreation room, and the fat old head nurse who always smelled of camphor. There was the tall youth who sometimes came into my room to talk and borrow books, until one day he became restless, wandered from room to room with trembling mouth and tears of agitation in his eyes and finally collapsed in the dreadful unconsciousness of an epileptic fit.

There was also the black-haired boy with leechlike dark eyes and strangely flushed cheeks who begged matches of everyone, claiming that his night lamp had been disconnected and he couldn't read. But he wouldn't accept a flashlight. Only matches would do. No one gave him any but he got them somehow and one night tried to set fire to his mattress.

After the first few disturbed days and sleepless nights I remained secluded in my room. I needed no other companionship, for I had Marvi. She came every day to visit me.

My doctor was not opposed to it. He just gave me Sulfonal in increasingly larger doses. On his rounds he would sit opposite me at the table and ask questions aimlessly while watching me with shrewd eyes. He let me talk, the words tumbling over one another, my tongue thick from the drug. Hypomania, he diagnosed.

Seeing that whenever my wife came we only agitated each other, he freed her of the unpleasant duty. It was a relief to both of us when the doctor suggested that my wife discontinue her visits. In my condition I was a stranger to her, although in my hypersensitive state even that fact seemed an affront. I was alone, forsaken. No one cared for me. Disgusting self-pity is in itself an indication of sickness.

But Marvi swallowed it whole. Love is blind. She noticed nothing different or exceptional about me but accepted me as I was. Of course, extreme tension creates its own spell. My morbid fervor contaminated her, touching her with its unhealthiness.

I told the doctor that I had never been as happy as in the institution. He merely smiled knowingly and urged me to go out more and to cultivate other interests. I bought several paintings during those weeks. Somehow I needed their beauty, color and form. The doctor discussed them knowledgeably with me. He himself collected antique silver. Everyone has his own psychological compensation.

I had Marvi. Naturally I couldn't conceal her visits from the doctor. Not that they could have been concealed. He thought that she was good for me. One day I asked him whether I might visit Marvi that evening and stay out late. He smiled. "It's all right with me if you stay out late but you don't have to say where you'll go or what you'll do. In fact it's better if I don't know."

We had planned that visit for a long time, Marvi and I. We longed for each other. Hungered. Our passion welled up from the depths of our togetherness. A glance, a touch, an embrace no longer sufficed.

She had told me about her engagement. Some management trainee at the factory had begun taking her out evenings to the factory's social club. Invisible barriers separated the townspeople. Marvi's curiosity was satisfied by those parties at the club, by meeting the engineers' wives and being invited to homes that previously had been closed to her. She undoubtedly believed herself to be in love with the man since she accepted his proposal. But she was reluctant to have him touch her, and perhaps her very aloofness was a challenge.

After a while the man began to demand that she submit to him. After all, they would be married in a year when he had completed his training. Marvi finally consented, probably to convince herself that she actually loved him. She felt ill after the first time. The man talked her into sleeping with him a few more times, even though it was revolting. In fact, the man himself began to seem revolting. She was afraid that she might have a child and would be forced to marry a man whose very touch made her cringe. To her great relief she learned that she was not pregnant, and immediately thereafter broke her engagement. The feeling of relief was, however, accompanied by a feeling of incompetence. She feared that she might be abnormal, that she would never know how to love.

Not that she regretted submitting to her fiancé. Quite the contrary. Only then had she awakened to the direction her life was taking. If it hadn't happened, she might have married a man who was a stranger to her and committed herself to a life from which there was no escape. She shuddered to think that she might have had children by such a man.

But she wrapped herself tightly in her pride, began to work harder and to study languages. During the following years she gladly accepted invitations, learned to smoke and drink, and to kiss her escorts good night at the door. She even submitted to caresses to convince herself that she wasn't different from others, but once at home she had to wash her mouth, brush her teeth many times and clean the skin that a strange hand had touched.

"That's why your touch was like a revelation," she explained, her face pale, her hands pressed together. "I was prepared to force myself once more. After all, you were terribly drunk. I thought that I'd despise you afterward. But it wasn't anything like the other times. There was nothing cruel or greedy in your touch. No, it was beautiful. Really. I could never have believed that a touch could be beautiful."

That's how she explained it to me as we sat in my room in the institution, the air full of acrid cigarette smoke and the walls glowing with the paintings I had bought. Imagination. Infatuation. She was pale as she spoke, but she had to explain. She had to clarify for herself what it was and how it had happened to her.

"It was beautiful for me, too," I assured her. "So beautiful that it hurt, despite my drunkenness. I slept as though I had finally achieved peace of mind after years of waiting."

I thought back to our youth. "Marvi, do you remember when I was fifteen and touched you? What did you really think of me?"

"I suppose I thought you were terribly bold," she said slowly, "and that you were just toying with me. I was afraid of you. And insulted by the stone. But perhaps it was just pretense. At any rate, something happened to me, and it was as though I were locked up inside after that. I supposed I've remained locked up all these years."

That's what she said, as I remember it. She definitely did say "locked up." Perhaps a mere touch can do that to a shy person. Perhaps it can also set free. Again I remembered how my hand unwittingly touched your cool skin. Even though you yourself made it possible, as you later admitted. You were more experienced than I. A woman.

I lay awake in the dark with my eyes open. My body was tingling all over. I can't free myself of you, I thought, I simply can't. So why should I torture myself and you?

6

After lengthy temptation, I once again sat in an empty room in the middle of the night with the warmth of sherry in my veins, staring at a telephone. My inhibitions melted slowly in the sherry's glow. Only the click of a dial, a ring, and then your voice. No more was needed. I sat staring at the telephone for an hour or two, and somewhere deep within me I knew perfectly well that I would call you. I had known it when I ordered the first drink. A large glass, I told the waiter.

There's probably nothing bleaker than a strange room in which one sits in the middle of the night with a drink within reach staring at a telephone. A transients' room, the presence and breath of strangers still around one.

Then—your voice, your breathlessness over the phone. You came, in the middle of the night, at my first request, and disregarding the warnings that were shouted to you at home. You had no more pride than I. And when you were with me, and I felt the warmth of your neck under my lips, everything was incredibly simple and clear, as though nothing bad had ever happened. The spell returned. I loved the bleak room because of you.

Over my shoulder you glanced at the bottle on the table. "Dry Sack?" you asked.

"Dry Sack."

Your eyes were dark with emotion. "Bless Dry Sack for bringing you to me," you said. "Anything, anything at all if it brings you to me.

"If you only knew how terrible these weeks have been," you whispered. "I thought I'd never see you again."

"So did I," I admitted. "I'm a coward. But Dry Sack has more courage." I released your hand and poured myself another drink. The warmth of the sherry shimmered in my blood.

"Go ahead and drink if you must," you said. "I'm going to take a bath. Is there hot water at night? The telephone ringing so suddenly and so late and the sound of your voice made me break out in perspiration."

We didn't say much more than that then. Sometime much later you opened your eyes drowsily and asked, "What day and what century is this?"

"A little girl at the gates of heaven," I murmured. "She can afford to wait, a hundred, even a thousand years. She's had to wait before now. Time hasn't the same meaning there as it has on earth."

"Earth?" you asked. "Where's that? I'm sitting on top of a cloud."

"I was just dreaming," I explained. "She was wearing a little red skirt. I wonder if it was you or Marvi?"

"Don't. Your beard is scratchy."

I rubbed my chin. "I wonder what day this is. I know the year and the month, the country and the city. I think."

"What difference does it make?" you asked, beginning to cry. "It doesn't make any difference anymore." The tears rolled down your naked cheeks. You wept decorously and without sniffling. Your face became wet.

"No, it doesn't make any difference," I conceded. "We've

spoiled everything again. Shall I ring for a razor? I'm sorry if it hurt you."

You clutched me with both hands. "No, don't. It doesn't scratch badly. In fact, it feels good."

I reached for the bottle again. It was empty. So be it. I leaned back, hands under my neck. "I suppose I could get some pajamas."

"No, don't," you pleaded. "It's just a waste of time."

"Just think," I said lazily, "there are people for whom time hangs heavy. Although that's nothing. Have you heard what a real dipsomaniac is? A man who drops into a tavern for a beer before bedtime and wakes up in Hong Kong three months later with a six-inch beard on his chin."

"Why couldn't we wake up in Hong Kong?" you suggested. "I'd love to wake up in Hong Kong with you."

"With empty pockets, dirty, ragged, and the hangover of the century?"

You put your arms around me and pressed your cheek against my shoulder. "If only you were poor, dirty and in the gutter, perhaps then I could keep you."

Suddenly you looked happy again. You began to study yourself and observed, "I have heavy arms. Can you really love me even though I have such heavy arms?"

"They're not heavy, they're very tempting," I assured her. "Besides, I'd love you even if you were so fat that I'd recognize you only by your eyes. But never fear, it'll pass in time. Everything always passes, and then I'll be rid of you. . . . If you only knew how your pupils dilate until your eyes are absolutely black. You're a terrible woman, really frightening. I'm not the lover for you."

"It's just difficult for you to begin," you said consolingly. "I'm like that myself. If you only knew how afraid I am that I don't know how to make love."

"You! You were born to make love. That's a gift in itself. I've never met a woman with such a natural flair for it."

"That's not so; you're just saying it to please me," you sighed happily. "Once you slept with your head on my arm. A century ago, or was it two centuries? Your head was terribly heavy."

"Sometimes it weighs all of a ton," I said. Then I remembered something. "Once after I'd worked all day, straining my mind, my weight went up two whole pounds since morning, even though I didn't eat anything."

You looked dubious but ready to believe even that if I said it was so.

"That's not quite true," I amended hastily. "I wondered about it myself until I realized that the scales were out of order."

You were silent again. Your eyelashes were fantastically long, your cheeks had narrowed, your face was naked in my arms. How beautiful you were!

"No, I'm not a good lover," I repeated stubbornly. "Actually, people know very little about love. Like the doctor who took care of me at the mental institution. After I had been with Marvi that night he asked me if I'd had fun. I had to tell him that nothing had come of it. He nodded sympathetically and assured me that the Sulfonal was to blame. But I told him that I never succeed the first time. One has to familiarize oneself with the other first. Even a body has to familiarize itself with another body. This was something new to him. He removed his glasses and began wiping them in interest. I suppose even you were amused by me in the beginning, although you were very tactful. I like you because of that, too."

"Don't say that. I was so frightened that I trembled like gelatine," you said. "I was delighted that you were afraid, too."

"As a matter of fact," I remembered, "Marvi too was glad that nothing came of it."

"You're always talking about Marvi," you grumbled.

"We had anticipated it too long, that's why we were so tense. Actually, it could have been calamitous if everything had gone smoothly. As it was, Marvi had to overcome her inhibitions and stop thinking about herself. A woman loves with her whole body, and if she is responsive to love only a little is needed to bring her undreamed-of bliss. Good Lord, I felt myself completely inept, but Marvi literally blossomed. It was an even greater miracle to her than to me. She wept for joy, and there was nothing defensive or forbidding about her any longer. She herself said, 'My body is like water.' "

You stretched yourself gracefully. "Fortunately your Marvi is dead, otherwise I might have to kill her. I feel as though I didn't have a bone in my body."

"What about your head?"

You touched it. "Not in my head, either. I wonder if I even have a head left. I love you."

"I can't understand why you do."

"Because you're just what you are. You move your hand thus and so. You turn your head a certain way. And when you speak or think you sometimes wrinkle your brow."

"So it's only physical," I said wistfully.

"Also physical," you corrected me. "Aren't you glad that you have a body?"

"Yes," I admitted. "For the first time I'm completely happy that I have a body. Even though it is only a poor miserable one."

"I love your poor miserable body," you said and kissed my cheek. "Besides, it isn't miserable. Don't insult it without cause."

"I've tried to be good to you. I have nothing more to give you, you know that."

"No one was ever good to me before you," you assured me in all seriousness. "I never even knew how good a person can be to another."

"You just think so. You're infatuated, you poor misguided woman. You don't know very much about me."

"I know enough," you whispered. "I know just enough. No matter what you did to me, you couldn't destroy that."

Perhaps it was true, perhaps only infatuation. "We're no different from the others," I said bitterly. "Many have experienced the same thing, in one way or another. Misunderstanding at home, too much alcohol, an illicit relationship. Contemptible. Unworthy. Looks ugly on the books. And still its supposed to open up a new land, a sea of ecstasy into which no one ever has dived as we have, unconditionally and with no thought of tomorrow. No, don't think that we're any different from other people."

"Don't think of it, darling," you pleaded. "Don't think of it right now." You tried the bottle, reaching over me gracefully. It was still empty.

"Let it be," I said. "It wouldn't help anyway. Have some tea instead, with French bread and butter. You need it."

"No," you said and felt your waist. "I reduce beautifully when I'm with you. I feel so light, as though I actually were a little girl on top of a cloud."

"Two pounds a day," I calculated. "There could be worse ways of reducing. But it wouldn't work; you'd get nervous."

"I'm not cranky yet," you insisted. "Don't be afraid. Not until the third day." You began counting on your fingers. "Wait, what day is this?"

"I don't know." I was tired.

"Three plus twenty-seven," you counted. "How much is that?"

I honestly didn't have the strength to count. "Never mind," I said. "I don't know. It's exhausting me."

You touched my temples and chest with your fingertips. "Is that really you?" you said in wonder. "Can it be true? I thought that I'd never meet you again."

"Who did you think it was?" I demanded. "Although what does it matter? You yourself know what you're doing, adult that you are."

You pressed your palm to my mouth. "Again? It doesn't pay. There are no others, there never have been. You should know that. You're only torturing yourself."

"Infatuation," I said. "You're deceiving yourself but not me. You just think you are."

Hands under my head, your warmth against me, I thought back. "About Marvi and me, I don't even know whether we loved each other. She was just infatuated. As for myself, I don't know. I needed her, needed her desperately then. She healed me and gave me back my sleep. We needed each other. Perhaps she needed me even more than I needed her, for her life had reached a crucial point. It could have withered away like a flower without water.

"Both of us needed each other at that particular time, that's why it was easy to believe in fate. Or would I perhaps have devoured someone else who happened to come along? A fiery cloud compels me to it. Afterward I'm stolid and quenched. I submit to the daily grind, to recuperation, to waiting for the next time the spark is ignited. That's the only time I'm happy, when I'm sick or thoroughly immersed in my work. I suppose that's sickness of a sort, too. It takes so much of me—my will, my hopes, my nerves, my strength, until I'm like a wet rag that's been squeezed dry. Only my flaming brain continues grinding away at nothing."

I stared into your eyes with desire and desperation. My very look caused your pupils to dilate. You covered your eyes with your hands and pressed your face against my shoulder.

"Perhaps I'm like that," I continued, thinking aloud. "Perhaps I have to nourish my emptiness with living human flesh, like a vampire. Until you're drained and I take my leave, contented, able to return to my work. I suppose my work means everything to me, even more than you, or anyone. It just grows harder year by year. I've slowed down, but once I get started I frighten even myself. It's as though I were more than myself, more than this miserable body. Of course, that's only my imagination. Self-deception, to make me feel that life is worth while.

"One autumn a little bird persistently escorted me from bush to bush. It had brown arrowheads on its back. The Etruscans prophesied by lightning and birds. Perhaps the augur in me came to life, because since then I've been afraid of birds that spear their victims on hawthorn brambles. It was the dreaded bird of my childhood and it, too, had returned. It was a shrike."

"Darling," you begged, "don't torture yourself. Why do you always torture yourself so?"

"I'm like something that lives and grows in the dark and requires warm blood for nourishment," I went on relentlessly. "Human blood, human life. Perhaps that's why you were sucked into my whirlpool. And I once told you that I never deliberately destroy anyone's life!"

"But you've made me rich," you insisted. "I'm the richest woman in the world when I can be with you. When I can touch you like this. I didn't even know how beautiful life could be before now." That's what you said. Infatuation, lies. Lies, all lies. But you believed them yourself at the time.

"Marvi is dead," I said. "It happened years ago. I was abroad then, and didn't even know about it until I learned it quite by chance. The news stabbed me. Perhaps she still meant a lot to me. But I don't think she hated me. We needed each other so desperately then, for we had to free ourselves of that childhood memory that bound us. She probably believed she loved me, but I didn't want that. That's why I always called her my playmate. My dear playmate. Rubbish!"

"Don't torture yourself," you pleaded again. "You know how I am."

"I didn't mean that. Forgive me. That word 'playmate'—it was supposed to make everything so innocent, so fleeting. But it wasn't a game. Good Lord, how can one play with fire? Perhaps you and I are only children who accidentally have found a box of matches and from sheer curiosity light the first match. Until, sooty and singed, we drag ourselves out of the flames. Or perhaps perish. And irreplaceable values go up in smoke: duty, goodness, self-respect—everything that once seemed worth while. Darling, the bridges are already burning behind us."

"I don't care about anything, if only I can be with you," you declared stubbornly. "At least sometimes, even like this. Nothing else matters. Let them spit in my face. I can wait weeks, even months, if I know that one day the phone will ring and I'll hear your voice. And I'll come flying."

"You're absolutely mad," I said fondly, caressing your hair and forehead.

"We're not disturbing anyone," you continued. "We're not aggravating people. We don't even appear in public together. We're like mice that stay in a hole lest something bad happen."

"It's already happened," I told you. "You. I. Love itself aggravates people because so few know how to love. Because so few dare. In a way it's humiliating to lose one's pride and self-respect. Well, I don't have much to lose that way. Fortunately.

"The bridges are burning," I repeated, "but I know how to swim. I can always swim back. That's why I'm such a terrible person. Everything collapses, and still I always swim back to the familiar and the secure. Knowing what I am, how can you like me?"

"You're you."

"Fire and earth. I've never felt it so strongly as with you. I don't even know whether I'm lying when I say that, because of course it's never the same. But you were born to love. In another country, another time, kingdoms would have slumbered under your belt. Darling, because of you I'd like to believe in immortality. Am I still drunk? The bottle has been empty for a long time."

Again I thought of Marvi. "Snowflakes on her cheeks, the glow of her eyes on dark December mornings. How she thrived on love! And yet it was merely infatuation. She had found herself and been freed. In loving me she freed herself of me. And I still don't know whether I loved her at all, or whether then, too, it was just cold, cruel curiosity."

"Then, too?" you repeated, in your eyes the frightened look that I feared.

"Then, too," I repeated cold-bloodedly. "You know that. That's why I talk so much. I'm practicing, testing words, weighing them. Of course, the greatest art is in speaking between the lines. That's called style. It doesn't matter what is written, only what can be read between the lines. That's real skill, and that's why I keep on talking.

"The best time of all was when I was in the mental institution. But only until I began to improve. Then I wasn't happy there anymore. When I knew that I was well, everything somehow became more difficult. You know me—I'm no good at deceiving. Of course we still met occasionally, Marvi and I, but it wasn't the same. Something between us had fled. Oh, those dreary winter nights, the hard snow, the air-raid sirens, the infrequent cheerless sunlight! I was relieved when she began telling me about another man. I didn't need her any longer. Her presence disturbed me, and it was no longer thrilling to touch her. Only sneaky. It couldn't continue like that.

"Although Marvi thought that she was unhappy about me, actually she had already made her choice. 'Of course get married,' I urged her, 'but we mustn't meet anymore.' She exclaimed, 'Oh, I can't,' but already there was a look in her eye. A home, social status. Certainly being the wife of a company director was better than being an ordinary office worker. 'Is he repugnant to you?' I asked. She considered the matter for a moment and said no. 'Then why are you hesitating?'

" 'You,' she replied. I told her that nothing would come of us anyway, that this was the best way for us to part, when everything was still beautiful. 'Shall I tell him about us?' she asked. I hesitated, then suggested that she at least mention her engagement. If she wanted to mention me, it might be better not to let him know that all this happened recently. It was all over for her, anyway. I assured her that I would never forget her, and so we parted. As I rode back into town in the rumbling streetcar the wheels groaned, 'Marvi, oh Marvi!' But actually I was relieved that I had gotten out of it so easily."

"Didn't you really ever meet again?" you asked in disbelief.

"I'm not quite that reprehensible," I said. "She called me a few days before her wedding to tell me that all was well and that she had become quite fond of the man. He had been unusually understanding when she had told him about her past, and in turn had told her about his own mistakes. Such things occur, although they don't mean anything when two people really love each other. It isn't wise to say too much, however. It hurts, and might fester for years before breaking out. After that I didn't see Marvi for a year and a half."

You raised yourself abruptly on your elbow, the sheet dropping from your breast. "So you did meet again!"

"We separated as friends," I assured you. "Naturally I was curious about her. She had a pile of my books she had borrowed and in moving had come across them. Marvi was very honest. Or perhaps she just used the books as an excuse to see me. I visited her new home. The man had been sent off somewhere. They had managed to put together an attractive home despite wartime restrictions. And don't stare at me like that, darling. Of course we kissed, but only casually. Nothing happened to either of us. And so we sat sedately on opposite sides of the table drinking the coffee Marvi had made. She was prettier than ever. There was something strangely mellow about her, and her eyes glowed with womanly gentleness. But not for me. Not for me any longer. That really hurt. Only then I realized that I was just a milepost in her life. She had continued far along the road that I had opened up for her. After freeing herself of me she had ripened into womanhood. I had meant no more to her than that. We had met only to liberate ourselves from each other."

"Oh, you men, how vain you are!" You sighed and reached for your purse. You examined yourself critically in the mirror. I halted your hand as you were about to put on some more lipstick.

"Not yet," I begged. You smiled, a human smile. Is there anything lovelier?

"Marvi was a stranger whom I no longer recognized," I continued. "I suppose that wounded my pride. She had developed according to her own capabilities and regardless of me. I had merely removed a barrier from the path of her growth. Something like that happened once when ice floes buried a silver birch and I waded out in rubber boots to pry away the ice with an iron bar. The tree was buried in mud, but when the weight was removed it rose by itself, slender and strong. By itself, with no help from me. It was like a miracle, even though I did catch pneumonia. I must have done something like that for Marvi.

"I never met her again after that," I went on. "But as we parted she looked into my eyes and said something that I didn't understand then. 'You taught me what love can be,' she said. 'Beautiful, and not merely selfish. I'll always be grateful to you for that. But now I know what passion is.' It was like a denial of all that had been between us. That's what I thought then. Now I understand what she meant, and I'm glad she said it. Marvi is dead, but because of you, darling, I feel a great tenderness toward her. She granted you to me, so that I might experience the same. Because without me she would never have been free to accept love."

"How did she die?" you asked with a woman's curiosity.

I hadn't thought much about it. Only as I spoke something flashed into my mind like cannon fire. "I don't know. It's such a long time ago. She had weak lungs, but they weren't the cause. It might have been an infection, some internal infection. When

I heard about it I could think only how much she loved life. But—"

"But what?" you asked.

"Nothing," I replied. "Absolutely nothing." I couldn't look you in the eye. "Let's not talk about her anymore."

I took your hand in mine and scrutinized your wrist. The wound had already healed. I kissed the wrist. "How could you do such a thing?" I whispered. "How could you? Such things aren't done."

You withdrew your hand quickly and looked away. "I was just drunk," you said defensively. "I was cruel and disgusting. But we've talked that out already. Let's not continue."

"One doesn't do such things," I repeated, "at least not when other people are present. I'm afraid the scar will remain. It was all just hysteria. Most unpleasant. And you didn't die, just soiled the rug and your dress and made an unfortunate scene."

You squeezed your eyes tight but tears forced their way between your lids. You put your arms around my neck. "I can't live without you," you sobbed.

"Nonsense," I said. "Don't be foolish. Don't ever say such things. We're both adults. We can always live if we must. You without me, I without you. We can live somehow. Don't say that again or I'll leave immediately."

"If we must," you repeated slowly and opened your eyes. There was no passion or gentleness in them now, just mortal terror. "One doesn't have to live. No one has to live if he doesn't want to."

"There you go again," I said. "Why the hell are we spoiling even these few moments? Why the hell do I have to talk so much?"

A strange room. An empty bottle of sherry, dying roses in a vase. A heaping ashtray, a rumpled sheet, a blanket that had covered strange people. Their presence lingered in the room.

No, we didn't talk anymore. It didn't change anything, and who cared what the surroundings were?

A century later we were drinking tea. You sat curled up with your feet in a chair, a lingering glow still in your limbs.

You placed a saucer in front of me, poured the tea and put two lumps into my cup. You were a woman. It broke my heart. As I moved my hand I felt my nerves tensing from shoulder to fingertips, cramping my hand. My body still remembered the warmth of your limbs. I had only to move to feel you. It was frightening but also beautiful. Never before had I experienced anything like it. So I thought.

Even trite phrases can be significant. At that moment, in my infatuation, I thought that I knew how heartbreak felt.

7

It was spring already. We were eating Sunday dinner at home. Everything was as before, on the surface. But everything had been as before on numerous other occasions. And still nothing really was as it was. It never is, for everything changes. There are only good days and bad days, and the only thing to do is to enjoy the good ones without fearing the bad, even though one knows that they'll come again. Otherwise one hasn't the strength to live.

A hyacinth on the table spread its fragrance. Liisa had brought Heikki with her to dinner. We were speaking of the theater, as one does around the dinner table on Sundays. Enthusiastically. Naturally, Liisa had heard some gossip. When the conversation died down after that she glanced at me.

"Well, what have you been doing this spring?" she asked as one does when there is nothing better to say.

"I? Just drinking and whoring, that's all." That was one way of putting it.

It took a moment for Heikki to realize what I had said, then the piece of roast dropped from his mouth.

We laughed, although there really wasn't anything funny about it.

Marvi, I thought. I had to read her letters at long last. I had already talked myself free of her, but I had to read her letters to know what she thought, to know what really happened. I had been thinking of her only as I remembered her, and memory can play tricks.

After the guests had left I sat down at my desk. Outside, windows sparkled in the spring sunshine. On the wall opposite me hung a new painting of shadowy spruces. The evergreen fragrance of my life would end someday. Life comes to its conclusion with a scent of evergreens and a brown pillar of smoke. A copper urn full of oily ashes in a heath amidst copper-brown pines.

That's one way of saying it, a very good way.

No one can ever know, anyway. No one can understand what occurs between two people, not even they themselves. Too much remains between the lines.

I opened the box reluctantly and took out the slim packet of letters. Marvi still lived in her handwriting on the envelopes. Through death I touched her hand in touching her letters. It was unpleasant, and I was afraid. What reluctance kept me from opening the letters, although I had been thinking of her so much?

Finally I tore open the string. It cut my finger, like an omen. I spread the letters on the desk before me and leaned my head on my hand. It was an agonizingly heavy head.

I read:

> As though I were lost in a dark forest. Your hand so kind and secure. So glad if you remember me.

I read more:

> You asked me to write. How could I not write, when I am still so full of you? Perhaps I'm taking advantage of your nervous condition. Perhaps I'm hurting myself, too. It might be better if we didn't meet. Even a wise general retreats in time. But all these years I've unknowingly been searching for something. Now I know: goodness, tenderness, beauty. There were selfish, greedy hands that made me freeze to my depths. How can I explain it? I wouldn't visit you again if I could help it, but I can't. You called me playmate. Dear playmate, did it have to be you?

And again I read:

> You said something that hurt me. But then I tried to imagine how
> it would be without you, and only then realized that I can't go on
> like this. Dreary, gloomy years, nervous, prosaic years. That's not
> life, merely existence from day to day. What good is that kind of a
> life?

On a half-sheet of paper torn from a notebook she had written:

> I can't find any other paper. I worked late but I wanted to say
> good night to you. Tell me, darling, is it Christmas already? There's
> a festive spirit in the air and everybody is good to me and I'd like to
> be good to everybody. Or is this all just a dream from which I'll
> awaken in the morning when the alarm rings? But why should I
> pretend? I'll wake up when you leave the hospital. Even if it is a
> dream, it's the most beautiful dream of my life. Are you asleep
> already, darling? I'll kiss your eyes. There, you didn't wake up.

In another letter she confessed:

> My heart is so full. Please ask your doctor whether a heart can
> burst from joy. Dear playmate, I used to wonder so often what pur-
> pose my life had. Now I know. All these years I've just been waiting
> for you. How fortunate that you didn't come along sooner! I wasn't
> humble before but now I am, now I dare to be. And it's incredible
> to think that you were the first one ever to kiss me, even though I
> didn't understand that I was meant for you.

With a wrench in my heart I read:

> Thank you, thank you for everything wonderful that you have
> given me. Every time we meet I have the feeling that I'm not good
> enough for you. I don't have a will of my own anymore, or a life
> either. Everything is yours, and it makes me so happy. I don't
> understand how I could have lived at all before you came along. If
> you were to leave my life now, I couldn't go on living. Tell me,

darling, what have you done to me? You only have to look at me. What have you done to me?

Three weeks had elapsed to the next letter. I had left the hospital, and everything was becoming difficult. But Marvi wrote:

> I'm afraid that I'll just create problems for you. But I love you so terribly that I could even give you up if it would make you happier. Otherwise I won't let you go, though. All the other people are only shadows with whom I talk. Only you are reality. I can never see enough of you. Thank heaven that you exist and that I was allowed to meet you. What have I done to deserve such happiness?

The same words, still the same words. My fingertips were numb. I spread the last letter before me. She had already had time to think, but still she wrote:

> Actually, I wasn't alive before. Life was like a cold dream, and in that dream I performed the tasks that were allotted to me. But everything was purposeless. Only through you I learned to know myself. How can I repay you for everything you've given me? There has never been anyone but you, not in the past, not now, and never will be. How many years I searched for you! They were agonizing, wretched years, but now I'm grateful even for them. I'll never be alone, I'll never be surrounded by emptiness. Darling, I'm so happy. Surely you'll at least let me see you some day?

That was the last letter. Only a few days later we met. She was very nervous and didn't even look me in the eye. She thought she was hurting me in telling me that she had found another man. She hadn't lied in her letters, it was just that she misinterpreted what had been between us. When she believed herself to be closest to me, actually she was drifting away. Everything happened only for the other man. I believe her marriage was a happy one.

So it was only infatuation. But a drop of Marvi's blood still remained in me. I felt her nearness and the touch of her hand as

I touched her letters. If she hadn't written them, there would have been only my account of the affair. A secret feeling of guilt would have remained in me, a feeling that I had misused another person's life. But with her letters she freed me, even after death. I hadn't hurt her. I had only been good to her. Had I really?

But still, how and why did she die? And she so young and vital. I couldn't understand how it had happened. Then something in me trembled, as the earth trembles under the fire of heavy cannons. The cranberry tree. The will's decay. A crack through which decadence seeps in and destroys the tree. A white scar on a slender wrist. Blood on a rug. Blood on your pretty dress.

Blood on your pretty dress.

In that moment I drew apart from myself. The fragrance of hyacinths, the darkness of spruce trees. A vision appeared before me, and in a dazzling moment I experienced and saw everything that I had pondered, read and planned so agonizingly. Work had nothing to do with me or Marvi. It had developed within me knowingly and unknowingly. The realization swept away everything irrelevant, and I knew that even in my weakness and misery I was strong. I was still able to do something. I was not snuffed out yet. A long road lay before me—a year, perhaps even several years. But at this moment I was thirstless. This moment I was sated, and my emptiness was so filled to overflowing that tears smarted in my eyes.

The intoxicating discovery was followed by a relapse, a blissful relapse. I knew that I couldn't fulfill my vision as I had seen it briefly. I'm only human, after all. And everything human is only an approximation. I would be exasperated, I would flee. But work would compel me to return, the work for which I was born, for which everything else was only preparation and cold research. The fever in my body could never conquer the fever in my brain. I felt my face and it was hot. The spirit burned it, the spirit that was greater than I.

I smiled to myself in the realization that never again would I want to exchange places with anyone. Why couldn't I be satisfied with a calm and modest life? Why couldn't I be content with a safe, workaday happiness that only an external storm could threaten? Why did I myself destroy everything good that I had? My joy, happiness, success, everything—everything I would have to shatter in order to build anew.

My head was burning, and I felt a fiery, nerve-racking cloud spreading invisibly over me. It touched the walls of my study, made the paintings flame in strange colors and gave new life to the old familiar books. My head seemed to fill the entire room.

I knew that I would hopelessly torment those whom I loved, but I also knew that I would carefully put everything that had collapsed together, piece by piece. That had happened before, and each succeeding time it became more difficult. I was wearing out and so were the others. No, security was the thing I could give no one, whatever else I might be able to give.

But in that moment I didn't pity anyone. Pity was small compared to what lived and glowed in me. It was bigger than I, and if I lived on human blood I couldn't help it. The gods demand their sacrifices. Although I was unable to kill even a mouse, I could slowly drain everything good, gentle and beautiful. No, you didn't know me. You still didn't know me.

Miss Dior fragrance. Your eyes widening under my gaze. The warmth of your skin, your beauty.

I grew cold and numb thinking of you. You were only a distraction that prevented my concentrating on work and meditation. I had gotten everything from you that I wanted. I didn't need you anymore.

8

I met you once more. I had to. In a private room of a restaurant and cold sober. The waitress smiled understandingly. I did not; I was annoyed.

"Salmon?" I suggested. "Baked or broiled?" I couldn't meet your eyes.

"I don't know," you said wearily. "Don't ask such difficult questions."

We ate. You looked at me but I avoided your glance. "The trees outside the window are already green," I said. "Old, beautiful trees."

You asked, "Why are you like a stranger? What have I done? Have I hurt you somehow?"

I pushed my plate aside and lighted a cigarette. "That's what the others have said—like a stranger. It must be true, but I can't help it."

You reached across the table. "Please don't," I said, evading your touch.

You stiffened and grew cold. "So," you said.

I thrust my chair back to a more comfortable position. "I read Marvi's letters recently and they taught me a lot. Nothing is new. Everything has been experienced before. Perhaps not in the same way, but almost. Even to using the same words. It's frightening."

You stared at me. Your head was like a flower, a painted flower at the end of a slim, lovely neck. Your eyes were glacial and your pupils contracted.

"I can't talk as well as you," you said.

"In reading the letters I suddenly remembered all the unpleasant things," I explained. "How repulsive her room became, and how I hated the dirty rug and the smell of dust. The sheets weren't clean. As for her landlady, she was coquettish and sly. And Marvi. Once she had a cold, and there was a drop at the tip of her nose when I kissed her. Something like that spells the end of romance. Of course, if I had still loved her, I would have considered it enchanting. And when she undressed I no longer watched her, but her clothes. Her brassiere strap was broken and she had fastened it with a safety pin. The death of romance is terrible. I felt as though there were a coffin in the room when I tried to embrace her. But she didn't notice anything because she was still infatuated. I suppose I hated her already because she disturbed my orderly life."

"Do you hate me already?" you asked. "We said we'd speak only the truth to each other. There would be no sense in our lying."

I looked straight into your eyes and smiled. "How could I

hate you?" I asked politely. "How can you even ask it? I love you."

You stared at me as though seeing me for the first time. "What kind of a monster are you, anyway?" you asked.

"Now don't get tragic," I pleaded. "You should know me by now. The flame ignites, burns brightly and then dies down. It always happens like that. It can't be helped."

You leaned over the table, your pupils again black. You were more sensitive than I had thought. "You don't mean what you're saying," you declared. "You're just lying to yourself. Don't try to make yourself worse than you are. I know you."

You rose from the table. "I know you." You touched my neck with your hand and pressed your cheek against mine. The fragrance of Miss Dior enveloped us. "Why are you torturing yourself again, darling?"

"Be careful, you'll smear me with lipstick," I tried to say harshly, but everything in me melted. I couldn't be cruel, not if I tried.

"Dearest, this is hopeless," I said and put my arm around her waist. "Don't love me. For God's sake don't love me, or something terrible will happen. We can't continue like this, not for your sake or mine. Passion has no place in the world. It brings disaster and death. Don't lead me to the death of my heart, dearest. Don't."

You smiled. "So this is how you are when you're sober. I love you this way, too. You don't know how I love you."

"It means war," I said. "Merciless war. Whoever loves more is always defeated, remember that. Watch out. I have my work and that keeps me going. You can't compete with it."

"You wouldn't be you otherwise," you replied stubbornly. "That's why I love you. Give me just a little hope that I can still see you. Otherwise I have nothing to wait for."

Your nearness, your warmth and touch. The power was stronger than I, stronger than goodness, honor, the world. My own helplessness made me sob. How could I have relinquished you? When we met, when we were alone, everything was so simple, so right.

"Let's drink, then," I suggested. "Bottoms up. Nothing matters anymore."

"Don't drink unless you have to," you advised. "It'll make you feel bad."

"Bad!" I cried. My bitterness tasted acrid in my mouth. "It's bad enough that I'm alive, and that I had to meet you."

"Oh, you!" You sighed. "But I know how to be nice, too."

"Wipe your lipstick off," I ordered. "What the hell are we waiting for. Why the devil are you teasing me?"

You laughed, exquisitely. "Now which of us is teasing?" you asked triumphantly. "Why did you suggest that we meet here? Why so devious? Did you think that you could get rid of me so easily?"

"Then let's see it through," I said grimly. "Let's not drink or waste time. Let's go with clear heads for once. That's how desperate you've made me."

Your touch, your cool skin. You pressed your hands against your breast. "Soon you won't be desperate any longer," you whispered. "You'll be happy. You'll know how to laugh again. Don't drink, darling. We don't have to drink. Don't. It'll only hurt you."

But your eyes closed and I again saw the long lashes, the silvery blue of your lids. How could I ever have given you up?

After an eon I awakened sharply from a deep sleep. At first I didn't know where I was, then imagined that I was safe in my own bed. I fumbled for a cigarette on the night table and only then really awakened.

I recognized the room and the walls. The same transients' room, the same invisible feel of strange steps. Disappointment stabbed through my body like a knife. With the salty taste of despair in my mouth I turned to look at you. You were sleeping soundly beside me in the strange bed. You were sleeping there. You.

Suddenly I remembered the dream from which I had awakened so abruptly. It wasn't an ordinary dream but a real dream, clearer and truer than life itself.

The door had opened without a knock and a woman stepped

in leading a black dog. Her face was covered with a veil that made her a thousand times more fearsome than if her face were bare. The dog's eyes were gleaming, and the veiled woman raised the three-pronged spear in her hand and declared, "Now this room will be emptied."

That's when I had awakened, trembling. I lighted a cigarette and began coldly analyzing the dream. I knew the black dog; he was dead. That meant that nothing could return to what it had been, as though that were possible. Still, everything does return, at least superficially.

The veiled face I also knew, and the three-pronged spear. Amusing. But I didn't smile, because it wasn't a mere dream, it was a vision. And I realized with a feeling of horror that she was Hecate, the goddess of death. The characteristics fitted— the black dog, the trident. My own body was the room that must be emptied.

Was it the piece of marble that I had picked up from Aphrodite's floor on Mount Eryx that haunted me? But Aphrodite had had her time. Now it was Hecate's turn.

Cigarette in my mouth, I propped myself up on one elbow to look at you. Your face was naked and defenseless as you slept. It was a strange, hateful face. Coldly, triumphantly, I noted every line, every sign of wear. I had already worn you out. My passion had worn you out.

I looked at your body and its beauty, and knew that I would conquer you because I was stronger. Always he who loves less is stronger. Suddenly a great tenderness came over me, because you were weaker and I could afford to be generous.

You opened your eyes under my gaze and a frightened expression came into them. It was an expression that I feared.

"Darling, why are you crying?" you asked. You extended your arms and buried my face in your bosom. I felt the lingering glow in my limbs whenever I moved. I was beginning to hate that glow. I hated my own body, the body of death.

"Why are you crying?" you repeated anxiously.

How could I tell you that I was crying because of you, because I knew that it was all over between us and that I must get rid of you.

That's probably why I was crying. I knew that I would have to exhaust you and torment you to the end so that you would flee to the arms of another man. You were ripe for it, just as Marvi had been.

I didn't realize then how easy it would be. Only the look of a wounded animal in your eyes. Only a street, and blood on your pretty dress. Then everything was over.

At that moment I caught the fragrance of a cranberry tree, the acrid smell of its crushed leaf in my fingers.

NEVER A TOMORROW

Translated by Lily Leino

1

EVERYTHING happened very suddenly.

The boy ran toward the automobile on the wrong side of the road at a bend and fell beneath the wheels only a split second after I had slammed on the brakes and gripped the wheel as the swaying car screeched along the surface of the road and came to a stop some ten yards beyond the bend, its every part howling and quivering. Pity the car, for it was like a noble metal beast, taut-nerved and shiny. It was as if the murderous braking at high speed had dealt a mortal blow to its precious vitals. It came to a trembling halt and stood on the side of the road, its patrician hood burrowed in the dry grass of the deep ditch.

The sun still shone hotly in the soft blue sky. The road was deserted. Not a car, not a person was in sight. The speedometer had stuck at forty. We looked at each other once. The glow in my veins from wine and speed congealed into heavy lead.

Abruptly I flung open the side door and ran the ten yards to the figure lying on the road. He was a little boy, perhaps six years old. He lay on his back, his cheek against the rough road, one leg twisted abnormally under the other. There was blood in his nostrils and at the corners of his mouth. His thin limbs were still twitching when I gathered him in my arms. He was very light. I noticed then how the drooping little head had been crushed, like an egg flattened against a table.

I looked around. Still not an automobile or person in sight. No houses glimmered through the trees. Our car was concealed by the cliff at the bend. From there the road stretched ruler-straight across the plain toward the city, disappearing into a line of woods beyond the gray-green fields.

I returned to the car with the boy's limp body in my arms. Still we said nothing. She had stepped from the front seat onto the road and stood looking at me. Then she climbed into the rear seat, spread the expensive car robe over her lap and opened her arms. Carefully I thrust the boy through the wide door to her. She took him, his head leaning against her cool arm and one dirty fist drooping over her knee. I slammed the door, slid quickly behind the wheel, backed the car onto the road and headed straight for the city, all the while looking for a Red Cross signpost. But perhaps it would be better to drive directly to a hospital. The city was barely fifteen miles away.

I drove slowly over the rough surface of the road. I knew very well why I was driving slowly. My entire being was coldly confident as I mentally went over the map of the region and its side roads. I knew every road and its terrain; my hands held the wheel firmly but my veins were thick with gray lead.

I had driven scarcely half a mile when from behind me her voice said flatly, "The boy is dead."

I met her eyes in the rearview mirror. Her fair soft face was bent over the small body lying limply in her lap. I noticed the graceful, expensive lines of her hat, the white ruffle at the neck of her black jacket. Her makeup was flawless but underneath it her skin was very pale. Her eyes looking at me in the mirror were vaguely apprehensive, but she was too proud to say anything more at the moment.

"Obviously it was an accident," I said stubbornly and turned my gaze to the road to avoid hers.

It was, after all, only an accident. A speed of thirty-five miles was not excessive for such a car even on a curve, when the road was a highway and I was on the right side. The boy had run blindly toward the car just at the bend and on the wrong side. In the split second I had even had time to see a smile on his little face. Everything had happened so quickly that he had scarcely realized he was being run over.

True, the wine and speed had intoxicated me; the scenery and the air still full of the freshness of spring. But a bottle of wine and a few drinks of cognac could not so intoxicate me as to cause the accident. The parents were to blame for not teaching their children to avoid automobiles on highways.

It was obviously an accident and I didn't have to fear serious consequences. Besides, I had connections that might help with the matter. The boy came of a poor family; that was apparent from his clothing, his face, his clumsily cut hair, from the bare scratched feet, the dirty little feet lying limp on the limousine's plush seat. One could give some money to the parents. But a police hearing, a newspaper story and a trial still faced me. And the automobile was not mine.

I looked into the rearview mirror again and met her glance. Now her eyes were frankly pleading for help. She shook her head feebly. It was impossible. In any case the boy was dead. I had known it instinctively even as I had lifted him into the car and begun driving to gain time. I had seen many dead people. Merely by touching a hand or cheek I knew when life had fled.

I stopped the car and savagely swung it around to return by the same road. She didn't say a word, nor did my eyes seek hers. An automobile came toward us and roared by; a Helsinki car full of bareheaded people returning from an outing just as we were, clutching chokeberry branches in their sweaty hands. Could any one of them have noticed us, the unusual elegance of the car, its number? Hardly. They were returning from somewhere far off, exhausted by the spring and the sun, their faces burned suddenly red. They had other things to think about.

I took the bend very slowly. The marks of the front tires were visible in the ditch, and close scrutiny might reveal signs of braking, but no one would notice the few already dust-covered dark splotches of blood.

The road was the same, the familiar scenery the same, the sun the same with its hot gleaming rays. But the glow of wine and speed in my veins had congealed to lead, the joy that had flowed through my body in warm waves was still. I was cool, calculating and alert now, weighing every individual factor and considering the various possibilities. I had the same feeling as in skiing through a chain of riflemen in a snowy forest, or in moving around enemy territory dressed as a worker and with forged identification papers in my pocket.

A tired truck came toward us, swaying emptily from one side of the road to the other. The glassy eyes of the driver and his companion told of whisky and a hangover. I wondered how far they would get on their pleasure trip before sliding into a ditch. Not that I had anything against their slipping into a ditch. Every careless crash, every drunken driver, was a fortunate occurrence for me today.

A few miles on I passed a cluster of small prosaic homes. A man on a porch was reading a newspaper in his shirtsleeves. He pushed his eyeglasses up his nose and looked after us through perspiration-blurred eyes. I was driving fairly fast by then, and on the other side of the bridge I turned the car onto a side road. After a while the road led to some woods and narrowed so that alder branches scraped against the car door. The region became a wilderness. The car's frame responded gently and easily to the holes and roughness in the road. There was no sign of habitation anywhere.

In the middle of a thick cluster of young spruce I stopped the car, stepped out and opened the rear door.

"Let me have him," I said with unnecessary harshness.

Still she said nothing, but merely looked at me. I lifted the small body into my lap; it was still warm. One brown hand was clenched into a fist. A curiosity stronger than my will prompted me to pry open the dirty fingers. Two coins which the fist had clutched faithfully even in death fell to the ground.

Now I understood the smile that had illuminated the boy's face for a split second as, blinded by triumph, he ran straight into the car. As we had left the city that morning, many barefooted, poorly clothed boys and girls had lined the road, offering bunches of cowslips and lilies of the valley for sale to the cars speeding by. Seldom did a car stop, but they stood steadfastly in the heat of the day, watching the automobiles with patient eyes until the flowers began to droop and the whiteness of the lilies turned black.

The little boy had clutched a bunch of lilies of the valley and waved it at the cars. When someone at last had stopped and casually dug into a vest pocket for a couple of marks, the boy had gone running home with them. Heedlessly and forgetting all warnings, he had run along the wrong side of the road straight toward gliding, gleaming death.

It was as if an old wound within me had opened and after the piercing pain warm blood had begun to flood my lungs. For a moment I was confused, for a moment my cold confidence failed me. Then I cursed silently and stepped from the road into the woods.

I didn't take him far; only about twenty yards beyond the road. I laid him in a little hollow among some wood anemones in the shadow of some willows and could not resist looking at him. He was a very serious, very quiet little boy now. Next to the childish softness of his cheeks the ragged shirt seemed almost an insult. I made no attempt to cover him in any way. I couldn't. I brushed his soft hair with my hand. The brown, scratched legs lay motionless among the flowers.

Returning from the woods I saw that she had also left the car and was standing beside the open door staring with a preoccupied air at the ground before her. She was very beautiful, very blond and very cold-blooded. She started when I approached but stared stubbornly at the ground. Then she absentmindedly prodded one of the dropped coins with the tip of her shoe.

I reached behind her to the rear seat of the car and picked up the robe. It was stained with blood. I folded it carefully.

"Money," she said as if to herself. "Money." She bent to pick up the coins and as she straightened again, whispered, "Ugh, I've got blood on my hands!"

"We've got to hurry," I said impatiently.

She climbed absently into the rear seat, wiping the bloodstains from her fingers with an absurdly small lace handkerchief. I put the folded robe beside her slender legs. They were sheathed in transparent silk as thin as cobwebs. I took the wheel and began to drive along the bumpy road. After a moment I began whistling to conceal the trembling of my hands. In times of action and danger my nerves never fail, but afterward my body turns wretchedly weak.

"Don't whistle," she said nervously from the back seat. The car climbed a hill and popped from the shelter of the woods like a cork from a bottle. I stopped whistling, stepped on the gas and my hands tightened around the wheel. The speedometer showed forty, then fifty. Houses again, a passing auto, bicyclists with elated faces. Defiantly I allowed the horn to sound its raucous warning. A railroad track flashed by. The paved road swished under the mighty wheels.

Once again the city's gray and brick-colored mass loomed before us under the soft blue sky. Billboards, ramshackle wooden buildings, trash heaps on empty lots. The road became asphalt. A streetcar horn blared. Sullen, happy, stupid, expectant, patient faces.

"This is a boring road," she said from the back seat, merely to be saying something.

I sought her eyes in the rearview mirror. She was sitting stiffly upright on the plush seat. To avoid my gaze she took out a cigarette and lighted it. Her nails were polished. They were like tiny pink oval mirrors.

On the edge of town the road changed into a thoroughfare. Brick buildings, steep and ugly, lined both sides of it. The smell of food swirled from third-class restaurants. Phonographs and radios blared loudly from open windows. A pair of mounted police clattered down the street, their horses' heads drooping.

"Don't you want to take the wheel now?" I asked.

She shook her head sharply. Terror was in her eyes. I drove on aimlessly.

The sea. Factory smokestacks. Metal cranes black against the sky in the harbor. In the rearview mirror I saw her nervously extinguish the cigarette in the ashtray. Its tip was stained red from her lips.

"You must take over now," I insisted.

She said nothing.

I stopped the car at a vacant lot beside a large warehouse. The sea glinted infinitely. Windowpanes shone.

"I must go," I said. "Good-bye."

But I remained standing beside the car and looked at her through the polished glass. Her indecision angered me.

"No, don't leave," she pleaded. "I can't go home." After a moment she said, "I'll go with you. Nothing matters anymore."

I said nothing. The sea shimmered as pellucidly as her eyes had this morning. The sea shimmered blue as eternity. No, nothing mattered anymore, I knew that. I opened the side door and fumbled for a silver flask. Seating myself on the running board, I twisted off the cork and poured some cognac into a silver-rimmed glass.

"Cheers," I said. "Actually, what does anything matter anymore?"

The tire marks had remained in the soft road and would be visible for many days unless it rained. I didn't hope for rain, for it would also wet that serious little face, soft hair and ragged shirt. The tire marks didn't betray much. But at midday any number of people might have noticed us. This kind of car and her kind of face attracted everyone's attention. Oh, everything depended on chance. Quick, unscrupulous action is like sand in the eyes of the world.

"Pour some for me," she asked and leaned closer to the door. Her silk-covered knees were right beside my head. The lead melted to fire in my veins.

And if we should be caught, the charge of manslaughter and the resultant headlines would mean very little to me. For one who has fled barefoot through snow, head bloodied and pistol in hand, mentally reserving the last bullet for his own skull, many things seem trivial even long afterward. Anything but becoming a prisoner. Never a prisoner, not then, not now.

But I knew that we would not be discovered. It would be ridiculous to be caught for an accidental killing and its concealment when one had once shot full-grown men with one's own hand and played with death at the risk of one's own life.

"There's blood on my hands," she said again.

Besides, it was senseless to sit here beside an empty building near the shore road when at any moment someone might drive by and see us. But everything was just as senseless, just as immaterial.

"We couldn't do anything else, could we?" she said. Her face was no longer pale under the rouge. The cognac burned my mouth.

"The most idiotic thing of all would be for you to come with me now," I said. "Someone might see us and then everything would be over anyway."

"Are you afraid?" she asked sarcastically and touched my neck. I shook her hand away.

"Which of us is afraid?" I asked. "For whose sake—" Ashamed, I cut short what I had intended to say. It was all my fault. I had gotten her into danger, because of me she was about to lose all that she dreaded to lose. Few women would risk as much for a man. Nor did I have the right, in this case to criticize if she considered concealment and self-contempt preferable to losing everything. My task was to hide our traces as well as possible.

I drove the car straight across town heedless of witnesses. I did not, however, dare to leave it on the street before my apartment house. Instead we took it to the nearest service station. I promised to come for it later, picked up the folded robe from the car floor and tipped the attendant. He didn't even glance at me but gaped openmouthed at the woman who stood beside me smoking a cigarette near a gasoline pump despite the warning sign.

Very cold-blooded, very blond, very beautiful.

We walked together and climbed the stairs to my apartment. It was not the first time.

2

I had two rooms in the Töölö district in a new building marked by a telephone at the entrance and luxurious bathroom fixtures. I had spent quite a bit on furnishings, overstuffed chairs, a comfortable bed, a few good paintings, but it was as difficult for me to call it home as I would have the rooms of a new hotel or in general any other place on the face of this earth. I had a bar cabinet with all kinds of bottles, as well as books that none of my guests suspected me of having read.

In addition, the management had provided me with a well-equipped kitchenette, and an invisible but undeniably kindly hand placed a bottle of pasteurized milk beside my door every morning. On most mornings I poured it down the washbasin and used a soda siphon instead. Besides, I have for years drunk my coffee black and preferably seasoned with a few drops of rum. That habit dates back twenty years, for near the end of the First World War, more rum was certainly consumed at the front than milk behind the front. But who would still remember that? The habit has merely been retained as habits are, without anyone's remembering their origin.

Well. At any rate we arrived at my apartment, and if it is true, as I have heard, that in the French language there is no word which means home, the French are fortunate people. The word home is annoying to a man who passed forty several years ago and who recognizes no place as home beyond this miserably small world in which several billion people are ruled by hatred, greed and lust for power.

She seated herself on the edge of my bed and lighted a fresh cigarette. Undoubtedly she felt most at ease in that place. She had even lain there. She sat with her knees crossed despite her narrow skirt and watched me. I mixed a drink with my back toward her just to be doing something and to avoid her eyes, which irritated me.

"You smoke too much," I said. "Your fingers will turn yellow."

She put the cigarette aside obediently but without extinguishing it and stared at her fingers. I went to her and put out the cigarette, pressing it so sharply against the ashtray that it crumbled in my fingers and tobacco spilled onto the table. I looked at her hands.

"Give me that rag," I said.

At first she didn't understand, then she followed my glance and quickly took from her purse the absurdly small handkerchief on which the bloodstains had already dried to a dark brown. Her fingers trembled, but her voice was steady.

"Do you want the money, too?" she asked mockingly.

But perhaps there was as much despair as sarcasm in the words. She took the two marks from the open purse and jingled them in her hand.

"Oh, stop it," I said and dropped the handkerchief onto the floor. I loved her, I had for almost a year, and I knew that it couldn't last and that everything else also had to come to an end.

"That certainly won't help," she said when I emptied the glass at a gulp.

"You don't know what poverty means to me," she continued and with a sudden weary movement swept the hat from her head. Her ring was an engraved platinum band and she herself enjoyed drinking. When she was intoxicated she would lean her head on her husband's shoulder, toy with the top button of his vest and tell him all kinds of silly things. She had her own checkbook but still she didn't pay her own bills, requesting that they be sent to her husband at the office. "Otherwise he wouldn't believe that I love him," she would say. "He finds it so refreshing to come home and be able to argue about bills. What else would we talk about?"

Her husband was blind in one eye and collected old Dutch paintings. In addition, he was the managing director of a machine and iron corporation in which he and his family, the Bergases and the Valtimos, owned the controlling stock. Besides, he was my immediate superior in a job that was considered quite demanding, requiring that I travel all over the country and often abroad as well, meeting various kinds of people in various positions. His engineers used slide rules, logarithm tables and graph paper; my tools were business cards, a typewriter, money and alcohol, of which the last-mentioned was the most important.

"You don't know what poverty means to me," she repeated again quite unnecessarily, hugging me and pressing her face against my knees. Perhaps I really didn't know what poverty meant to her. To me it meant sickness, debility, a piece of bread snatched from a dog, lice, an unwashed shirt, an unstamped letter, manhood sold for money.

"It's useless to talk," I said.

"Not a single pretty dress, soiled books from the library, dish-washing in a kitchen on the courtyard side, caring for a neurotic mother, sheltered with pathological strictness, every pleasure denied me to make sure that I remained unsullied, so that the merchandise would retain its value, you understand."

I shrugged my shoulders. What else could I do? I had heard it all too often before. Poverty was her spiritual cancer, the fear that even many years later returned as nightmares. As for me, I forgot to mention that the furniture in my apartment was still unpaid for and that I had many other debts. On my return from South America I had only a suitcase whose lock had been broken going through customs. In it were two shirts and a shaving kit and perhaps as an invisible load a handful of ashes from burned dreams. Why pretend? I had lived like a stray dog, stealing or baring my teeth, until Bergas discovered me and gave me a job at the beginning of the business boom.

The main thing is that by certain old-fashioned concepts, Bergas was my employer and at the same time my benefactor. Since then my policy had been: Anything goes.

I smoothed her hair; she buried her face in my knees and wept into my trouser legs.

"What good . . ." I began. But she rasied her face to mine, her wet eyes, her smeared makeup. I took a handkerchief from my pocket and wiped her eyes roughly.

"Your handkerchief smells good," she said. "I must look terrible. Give me a mirror."

I kissed her. I pressed her to me and kissed her. Actually, what is kissing? Nothing. A parlor game? I don't know. Still I kissed her as a drowning person clutches at an extended oar which slips from his numb fingers.

There on a chair was the car robe on which this morning we had lain by a lake shore far from the city. We shared a bottle of wine. The sun shone warmly in a soft blue sky. The water was still very cold. Her bare arms, her neck, her hair— Why continue? Between us now lay the lifeless body of a small boy, a thin face with blood oozing from mouth and nostrils, soft child's hair and bare scratched feet.

During our retreat in East Karelia long ago my troop was

surprised in the middle of the night and I left my boots behind drying atop a farmhouse oven. I ran barefoot through the snow, and after seeing that the horses were harnessed and the men on skis, I bandaged my feet.

Later, two toes on my left foot had to be amputated. The men who were left behind were bayoneted to death, for the Bolsheviks had to conserve their ammunition. We heard this later.

Had a few drinks gone to my head? Usually those memories haunted me only when I was drunk. I kissed her, but my thoughts were on the little boy who lay among the flowers in the woods.

That was enough. I rose and poured myself still another drink. It was Sunday. The emptiest, dullest moment of a Sunday afternoon before dinner. I was suddenly preternaturally hungry. The sun slanted into the room through the windows. I ate a few crackers from a box and said nothing. What was there to say?

She reclined on my bed, head tilted, and shielding her eyes from the rosy afternoon light with one hand. Her neck had the grace of nobility. Her figure was slim. Only bitter passion bound us. What, in truth, did we have to say to each other?

"His parents must be getting worried," she said. "Especially his mother. Fathers probably aren't so concerned about their children. But I've heard that many mothers love their children madly."

"It was an accident. We couldn't do anything about it," I said stubbornly.

"But if we hadn't been together. If I'd really gone to see my sister."

"Don't say 'if,'" I snapped. "The very word has a bad taste. 'If' is only for the weak." Then I remembered. "Are you sure your sister won't say anything, even accidentally?"

"Don't be afraid. After all, she gets money from me." She spoke the word with the bitter contempt of a person who has sold her own youth and beauty for money and the glittering life. Illogical, perhaps.

"It's idiotic," she said, "to run toward death because of two paltry marks. And now no money can buy back his life. There's nothing worse than restlessness."

She jerked around and looked at me, her eyes two tearless abysses of despair. The wound, the incurable wound somewhere within me, began to throb slowly, in time with my heartbeats, shutting off the blood to my lungs.

"Now don't get hysterical," I warned her, my mouth so dry that I had to dampen my palate with my tongue.

A year ago we had sat together under a cherry tree at a small outdoor café beside an old wooden building in a small town. A warm breeze shook white and pink petals into our chicory-flavored coffee. A pretty gray cat leaped from a windowsill on soft, careful paws toward a buzzing bumblebee. We were together for the first time, still not knowing each other. We had met only at the Bergas home, at restaurants, wherever one talks only for the sake of making conversation. We sat alone for the first time and knew that even that was a crime. But how wonderful it was. The pink lips, the flawless complexion and those eyes, those quizzical, playful, searching eyes, the eyes of a young girl, an experienced woman.

Curiously, as though under the irresistible spell of danger, she looked into the black abyss of my loneliness. And my passion welled up desperately, unquenchably to meet her, like a flame-tipped sprout pushing itself out of the tired earth under an old sky.

I think that she had been absolutely faithful until then. Essentially she is very honest and frank in all her folly. Only then did she begin to waver. And I infected her with my own restlessness and loneliness. Infected her with a whole world's despair: anything goes. It's wonderful to play without looking at the cards and to put everything at stake, fully realizing that one might not even be holding a pair of sixes.

And what joy is there after all when one realizes that time is rolling on irrevocably, when one sees one's temples graying and one's face drooping into folds, and knows that nothing of one will live on. When a world that is scourged by depression and unemployment, eroded by tears and pockmarked by suicides, once again swathes itself in a golden veil of success and glory, and Bergas' factories and foundries run day and night on three shifts and women dress in prewar clothes and the latest color in cars is black and steel-gray. When millions of little people in the gigantic struggle over war, money and power have forgotten everything and learned nothing, angrily rejecting every thought of the future in order once more to eat their morning porridge in peace, to see the latest movies, hear the sports results on the radio and imagine that they are controlling their own destinies.

At such a time what meaning have dishonesty and a little boy who on a Sunday in spring accidentally falls under the wheels of a limousine which crushes his head like an eggshell on a rough road?

If only I were still young. But my temples are gray and my time is rolling on irrevocably. The world is ruled by stone gods and, compared to the death that they sow, reputation is a pallid word.

I remember well the time almost twenty-two years ago when the door of my fraternity house closed behind me for the last time and I stepped into the wintry day in old Helsinki with the fare in my pocket for the Tornio train that night. Hoarfrost was on the streets, and a perfumed Russian officer in a fine long mantle was just stepping into an apothecary shop opposite the fraternity house. Two men wearing caracul caps, their hands thrust into their overcoat pockets, were huddled at the entrance. Their searching glance followed me as I stepped out of the fraternity house. I was very young then, my heart swelled with elation, and in my wildest imagination I could not have guessed what actually was in store for me.

That night I boarded the train for Tornio, and the memory of that day's excitement and rapture will never disappear. It is one of the few memories that I should like to relive on the day I die. I never smile at it. There was something splendid and big about it, even though I was young and stupid and knew little of reality. But it is my fault that I can never again feel the same.

Another memory that will never fade is the outdoor café under flowering cherry trees in a small town.

"Are my eyes clean? Has the mascara smeared?" she asked

with a laugh after fixing her face. Yes she laughed, and she is beautiful on the rare occasions when she does laugh. But the laughter was appallingly mirthless.

"You don't need makeup," I said. "You'll only ruin your complexion."

She stared past me into the distance while closing her purse. Then she asked, "What else is there for me to do?"

A valid enough reason, but she added, "I don't want anyone to see my real face. I'd be ashamed. Streetwalkers paint themselves too."

Her hand was cold and limp. I offered her something to drink but she refused it.

"I'm a fish in a net," she said. "I flounder, I struggle." She thought a moment. "And even if I could free myself, what would I do? I'd just swim in circles until I was exhausted."

I knew that there was nothing in the world that I would not gladly do for her. Why? Who knows. I loved her, even though love is a silly word.

The door closed behind her. She walked over to the elevator and pressed the button. I poured myself a drink. Emptiness welled inside me, such unreasonable emptiness that my hands slackened and pain cramped my stomach.

3

It should be borne in mind that I keep myself physically fit. My body hasn't a single flabby muscle or roll of fat. Slack figures and soft hands repel me. If I drink and stay up late, I make up for it in some way. I want to retain at least a vestige of self-respect. I've taken long hikes with map, compass and knapsack —longer and more dangerous than anyone can perhaps guess. If I ever achieve a feeling of sheer physical joy, it's when I ride along a bridle path or through the park as the leaves are turning and after I've had some black coffee and smoked my first pipeful.

I said physical joy, surely the purest and most enduring joy known to man. The nearness of the woman I love doesn't make me happy, for passion is as much suffering as joy. And I don't care a fig for the soul. There is no more terrifying thought than the prospect of eternal life, if one stops to consider it.

It's appalling to realize how easily a person's spirit can desert him without any warning, like an eggshell crushed against a hard surface. Whereas in other cases the spirit refuses to depart no matter how desperate the plea or prayer. Like Johnny, who was shot in the stomach during that ghastly retreat and whom we carried for days in a sleigh, until his face turned blue and his body twisted in agony like a worm, begging for death. Finally I couldn't stand it any longer and left my pistol beside him. But I have no one who would perform the same act of friendship.

Sometimes I meet old comrades and experience all the degrees of hatred, distrust, discord, envy and disagreement. We are able to have a drink or two together now that I no longer have to borrow money from them merely to exist. Many of them have achieved quite prominent positions. Some have remained in the army and risen in rank or moldered in their places. Others have settled indiscernibly into modest jobs in the provinces. Still others have vanished without a trace into other countries. Years ago, before death and hospitals had decimated our ranks, it seemed that being a Jäger meant little in the opinion of those who mattered. We were an undependable and incalculable element. Or could I have been wrong?

Now we are old; our kind of man ages rapidly and we no longer pose a threat to anyone. We have become settled. Only the more adaptable remain.

But something still lingers in us. I've observed it with some curiosity at drinking sessions, on the street, in warehouses, on trains. Something in the glance, the angle of the head, perhaps the manner of speech. Something in us is still the same. Many of us have a home and children and gray hair, but the something still remains.

What that something actually is, I don't know. I thought of it recently when I heard that K had shot himself. Many consider that a peculiar case. He was a major, he had a fine wife and two children, he was not known to drink excessively, and his debts were not worth mentioning. Not even his wife could think of any reason for the deed. But one night this past spring he had sat reading by an open window. The book had remained open on the floor beside the chair. He had simply taken a pistol from a table drawer and shot himself in the head. In full possession of his senses. Even though everything was apparently going well with him.

Once we dedicated our lives to preserving our country's freedom. What does it matter now, when the world sacrifices everything to the gods of power and fear? But it is as though death had then marked us for its own. We who remained alive seemed to have lost a part of ourselves, something important and irreplaceable, without even being aware of it. For that reason death does not forget us even though we may for a brief moment forget death.

I no longer read the morning newspapers. Of what concern is it to me how much the price of scrap iron has gone up, or what city has most recently been bombed? I read the papers only in my office; all the papers, even the provincial, for it's part of my job. But I read them without any curiosity, merely to earn my salary.

Therefore, the next morning after that Sunday I didn't buy any newspapers before going to the office. But my mind was bleak and below my heart I felt the squeeze of an iron fist when I finally glanced at the news columns of the papers. A truck driven by a drunken driver had landed in a ditch outside Helsinki; an unknown man had knifed a policeman Sunday night; a dangerous criminal had escaped from police headquarters. Nothing else.

Nothing the next day or the day after, either. Bergas summoned me into his private office to explain his latest plan and what I was to do. He wanted me to go to Turku and offered me a cigar. I looked at him. He is blind in one eye and his lower lip is misshapen.

I shrugged and told him that his plan was stupid. He smokes

hand-made Brazilian cigars which the captain of one of the ships he has built brings through customs. They're black and as strong as a charge of blasting powder.

"You're nervous," he said accusingly. "You ought to drink less."

"Find someone who understands this work better," I said. Few men can afford to say that to their employer. I don't know whether I can, but at least Bergas thinks I can. He appreciates men who live recklessly and unscrupulously. I think that in his own hard way he likes me, for he often invites me to his home. Even my position is such that it demands confidence.

I struck his boy once. He has a son by his previous marriage, an eighteen-year-old husky good-for-nothing who inherited all his father's weaknesses and none of the qualities that have made Bergas himself a man. He was beating a dog in their yard as I arrived, whipping the cowering terrier without apparent reason, muttering to himself.

I've seen people suffer; with my own hands I've had to shoot people. Let people be cruel to one another, that's their business, but something in me rebels at senseless cruelty to animals. Perhaps because animals are dumb and can't speak. Man can at least curse. It isn't sentimentality. Rather, it's pride in being a human. At any rate, I snatched the whip from the boy and let him have it around the ears. The little terrier lay quivering on the ground. I looked at it and struck the boy again.

Trembling with rage, his eyes tear-filled, the boy went to tell his father. Bergas demanded, "Didn't you hit back? Didn't you even try to hit back?"

"Oh, hell, what a boy," he said when I came in. Still, in his own way, he's very fond of his child.

I'd struck his own son without his becoming angry. He wasn't angry now, either.

"Then think up a better plan yourself," he said. "And don't get nervous; it'll spoil everything."

His wife sat on the edge of the enormous desk, smoking a cigarette, when I went in that afternoon to explain my own plan of action. A slim, beautiful woman with calculating eyes. Without a word I turned and went back to my office.

A moment later she appeared at the door and looked at me, smiling with her pink lips.

"You're crazy," I said.

Her smile froze. Her face was like a painted mask. She shook her head inquiringly.

"Nothing," I said. "Nothing yet. Don't get excited."

"A day has twenty-four hours," she said. "An hour has sixty minutes. A minute has sixty seconds. And every second concerns me. It's terrible. I never knew that things could be like this."

"You're crazy," I repeated. "Go away from here, go back to Bergas."

"He asked me to come," said Astrid Bergas. "He insisted that you're upset."

I swore.

"Come to our place for the weekend," she pleaded. "I'm going to the country. I can't stand it here any longer. He's flying to Stockholm the end of the week."

"You're stark raving mad," I said again.

"He suggested it. It would cheer me up. He's so afraid that I'll be bored. More than anything else he's afraid that I'll grow weary, because I'm difficult with him then."

"Keep your bedroom to yourself," I said.

She pressed the burning end of her cigarette against the back of my hand. I didn't flinch.

"You're crazy yourself," she said.

The next day it was in all the papers. A ghastly crime. Six-year-old boy found murdered in the woods. Struck in the back of the head with some blunt instrument. Escaped convict seen in the vicinity.

Nothing was said about the tire marks on the road. People are peculiar. The boy had only been missed on Monday. His foster parents had been in the city and one of the boy's playmates had said definitely that he had been sailing toy boats in the river with the boy as recently as Monday morning. Apparently he had felt very important at the police inquiry. "Mikko went home for some bread and butter," was how he had explained the end of their game. One clever reporter even made this remark the subtitle of the gruesome tale.

I admit that I was amazed. I hadn't expected anything so stupid. At least they should have looked for an automobile. The deed was obviously considered the work of the criminal who had escaped on Sunday. He had stolen a coat and a bicycle in the neighborhood, but would be apprehended.

What then? Under the circumstances it was very likely that he would ultimately confess his guilt. You couldn't have guessed, poor fellow, what a predicament you would find yourself in, slipping away from the police station.

Callous? Perhaps. But of what concern was a thrice-convicted criminal to me? Of what concern was the whole matter, now that we apparently had eluded detection for the time being? Yes, for the time being. After all, we weren't afraid of reporting an accident to the police, but of letting Bergas know that we had been together all that morning when his wife had said that she was visiting her sister.

At any rate, now he would never know. The danger was past and I should have been calm. But I wasn't.

Why? I don't know. A little boy whom no one cared about, whose absence was only noticed after twenty-four hours. A little boy who went to get some bread and butter. Had anyone ever really given him a sandwich? He was wearing a ragged shirt cut down from a man's old shirt. His feet were bare and scratched. But his little face was solemn when he lay stretched out, thin and insignificant, on a patch of white anemones under some willows.

If only we hadn't hungered for each other so madly that we had run the risk of discovery to spend a whole morning together. If only she had gone to see her sister.

The word "if" is like a rusty spike thrust slowly into human flesh.

A neglected little boy who, blinded by elation, ran straight into glittering death, clutching two nickel coins in a dirty fist. Rifle bullets also have a gleaming nickel jacket. If one saws off or splits the nose, the bullet leaves a cup-size hole in the body. That, too, was of small concern in those days.

In the evening I was at the club playing poker. I played unusually badly and lost a great deal. "I don't understand what's wrong. It must be nerves. Shall we raise the stakes?" I asked. We did, and I lost even more. A man who had chanced to join our table and then had won the most became generous. He ordered champagne and became boastful. His face burned with greed, he became flushed and sweat rose to his forehead.

He had a slack jaw and soft hands and I didn't pity him. He won a lot of money that night, became drunk and talked big. In his victorious superiority he wanted to make himself important in my eyes. I didn't even have to question him. When I finally escorted him to a taxi and gave the driver his address, he didn't seem surprised that I knew it. He didn't suspect that the money he had won was company money and that I was spared a trip to Turku.

"How much?" asked Bergas the next day. "That's not much," he said with a laugh. "Will you come to the country for the weekend? You'll feel better. There'll be other guests too."

Bergas doesn't consider it wise to have his wife drink during his absence. Bergas himself drinks only rarely. On such occasions he falls into a pathologically drunken condition that lasts for several days. I think he's ashamed of it, and because of this never drinks at home.

"Gladly, if I won't be in the way," I said. "It's almost summer already."

"Bring a tennis racket with you," Bergas urged. "Astrid likes to play, but the youngsters aren't much competition."

He was hesitant, avoiding my glance and shaking the ashes unnecessarily from his cigar. I could see that he wanted to say something more.

"There'll be lots of fresh air and as little alcohol as possible, if I have my way," I said.

He laughed and looked at me guilelessly with his one eye. It was one of Bergas' rare, deceptively artless glances with which he instantly wiped away all disparity in age and social position and somehow made people like him. Perhaps he was sincere then, perhaps it was mere shrewdness on his part. I don't know.

"Bare your teeth if necessary, Wolf Dog," he said and gave me a friendly smile. "Astrid collects all kinds of worthless characters, but what does it matter if it amuses her?"

Bergas didn't willingly display his jealousy. Instead, he gnawed his nails and seethed internally. Everyone noticed it, although he probably didn't suspect that. Even with me he was ashamed to betray his feelings. He was about ten years older than I and had bought himself a beautiful wife. That wasn't easy either, but he trusted me.

"Wolf Dog" was a name that Astrid had once given me and which Bergas considered fitting. It may seem odd for one man to address another by a pet name, but Bergas was an unusual man. I was the wolf dog whom he left to guard his wife during his absence. But wolf dogs are unpredictable. They can bite their keeper's hand, and sometimes lacerate children.

On Friday, Bergas flew to Stockholm. On Saturday, the escaped convict was still at large. On Saturday afternoon I drove along the shore road to the country in a company car.

4

The estate is old. Bergas bought it at the beginning of the depression and renovated it. The two-storied brick main building has twenty rooms, central heating and hot and cold water. On the edge of the old park, on a bluff right on the seashore, he built a summer pavilion with a porch. Below it is a beach on which a shipload of fine sand has been spread. What has this to do with the story? I don't know. It's Astrid's home.

Sharp explosions guided me to the porch of the beach pavilion. The floor was littered with empty bottles.

"Whisky," said one of the youths, tossing an empty bottle over the railing into the sea. Mrs. Bergas raised a rifle and fired. The bottle splintered in the water. Her hand didn't tremble.

"Pommard," said another youth, throwing another empty bottle over the railing. He was Astrid's cousin, a pale, dark young man who imagines himself to be an artist. Perhaps he is. He paints women with broad hips and unnaturally small heads topped by corkscrew curls. "I'll buy them, but they won't hang on my walls," says Bergas, who collects Dutch masters and has a

Cézanne that he bought by mistake. He likes Daumier best of all. "That man at least knew how to draw." He himself would undoubtedly make a fine subject for a cartoonist.

Glass tinkled in the water. The cold water exuded dampness onto her bare back. A third youth loaded the rifle, carelessly pointing the muzzle toward me. I shoved the weapon to one side and said, "You'll chill yourself."

"Curaçao," announced the first youth and flung a bottle over the side. A shot rang sharply. There was a splash in the water.

"What of it?" asked Mrs. Bergas. The dark cousin stroked her bare back amiably. It was a lovely tan after a winter under a sun lamp. The tan covered her fair skin warmly and enticingly. She was wearing slacks but her back was bare. This, after all, was the outdoor life.

"Too many empty bottles," she said. "They'll have to be destroyed so that the servants won't see them."

"It's shocking," said a man sitting cross-legged on the porch floor and keeping careful record of each shot and kind of bottle tossed over the railing. "We've been carrying them out secretly all day and burying them in ditches. We've stuck them through the cellar hatches and dropped them into the neighbors' wells. We've crept as stealthily as murderers, hiding empty bottles in our shirts and avoiding the glance of every passerby, but the bottles never end."

He was a well-known chess player. He drinks a lot of coffee, smokes heavily and plays chess. In addition, it's rumored that he spends his days in some office, but no one really believes it. He himself nods mysteriously and sighs that he even plays chess in his dreams.

"Let's fill the bottom of the sea with glass," suggested the third youth. "Two thousand years from now scientists will find a layer of glass beneath the seaweed and build fantastic theories on those faded, worn pieces. We're making history right now. We'll create one of science's unsolved mysteries. As well as leave something permanent behind when our bones have turned to dust."

He claims to be a poet, although he doesn't write anything worth while. They all try to outdo one another in annoying me by saying whatever comes to mind as plainly and protractedly as possible. They had all been drinking and knew that I can speak only in short sentences. It's some kind of speech impediment. I can utter only a few words before the sentence stumbles to a halt, as though something has contracted in my chest. Then the tension relaxes and I can continue until the next jarring halt. It amuses them and they always do their utmost to get me to say more than usual.

"Say Adrianople," suggested the dark cousin. "Say Onomapotopoulos. Say the Bashkircavalrybattalion'salpinedivision'smilitarymarch. I'd like to paint your portrait as you say that."

"Clever," I praised him. "Intelligent. Brains where they ought to be. Bravo."

It's only in a group that they dared pounce on me. I'm much older than they and united, they're firmly convinced that it's something quite amusing. But when I meet them individually they become embarrassed, carefully ask my opinion about various matters and even timidly seek my advice, for their actual knowledge of life and people is appallingly small. All that they know they have learned from their own kind or from books so that they parrot themselves and others. I almost believe that they vaguely respect me for all that I've experienced, but when they're a group it irritates them no end.

"Put your coat on," I said. "You'll get a chill."

She thrust the rifle into the hand of the nearest boy and faced me. It was growing dark, the sea was turning pale blue and far off on its surface some dark red spots were swimming as though they were on the Arctic or the Atlantic. Spring. The sea was exuding cold from the base of the bluff but it was as though someone were intermittently pouring warm water on my neck. On the bluish, hazy surface of the sea the dark red spots swam distantly. Everyone was suddenly quiet; there was no more laughter. Darkness fell, the flame of a match became visible and faces grew white.

"I suppose you've read the paper?" I asked.

"I don't know what's wrong with me," she said. "I wash my hands constantly. Every five minutes I simply have to wash my hands. See, the nail polish is wearing off and the skin is chapping."

"It's over. We've nothing to fear," I said.

"Do you think so?" She laughed briefly. She was further sunk in despair than I. Women undoubtedly possess some vague instinct unknown to us men.

"The devil take you!" the chess player said. "How you laugh. I've got gooseflesh on my back. What are you two talking about?"

"A blond angel was cast in chains, she was pricked with scissors and fed castor oil, but she laughed a heavenly laugh," said the youth who fancied himself a poet. He was revolting.

"I'd like to paint . . ." began the dark cousin but stopped in mid-sentence, looked at us and whistled. "A secret tragedy," he suggested. "Bills unpaid. Bobi fallen into a sewer."

Bobi is Mrs. Astrid Bergas' famous platinum fox which actually has been lost innumerable times in restaurant foyers and powder rooms, on the street and in service stations. It has always returned and for some reason it is called Bobi. Why? I don't know. What else should it be called?

"You may stay on the beach to play, children," Mrs. Bergas said. "I can't watch you anymore."

"At last," I said happily. "Is there anything more nauseating in this world than the people with whom you surround yourself?"

She rested a weary hand on my shoulder. "But they're really quite harmless," she said. "Sometimes they make me laugh. All of them have to die soon, when everything comes to an end. Why shouldn't I be nice to them? I'm tired of concerts and fashion shows. What else is there for me to do?"

The sea remained behind us, its pale blue dappled with the purple of sunset. Gold and purple, two hackneyed words. Her hair and the dark red dots swimming in the sea. The rooms in the pavilion were dim. Her hand still rested on my shoulder.

"Look at me," I pleaded and seized her wrist.

"I can see very well," she said. "You want a drink."

"Look at me," I pleaded again.

"No," she said. "No, no, no."

Bergas' son came into the pavilion on soundless, rubber-soled feet. He looked at us with an eighteen-year-old's greedy eyes.

"Well, Mother," he said mockingly. He had noticed that Astrid Bergas couldn't stand his calling her Mother, and since then had systematically addressed his stepmother as "Mother." He could say it gently, caressingly, in wonderment and surprise. I sensed that he himself enjoyed using the word, that it was to him like a physical contact, the touch of a hand on bare flesh. Astrid slowly withdrew her hand from my shoulder.

The boy only glanced arrogantly at me from beneath raised black brows. He always remembered that I had once whipped him. Nowhere is it more difficult to meet alone than in a big house in the country.

"The bell's ringing," he said. "Come to dinner. Can't you hear?"

The sound of the bell was in truth quivering almost inaudibly through the pavilion. I sighed. An iron fist squeezed relentlessly at my heart.

In the center of the dinner table was a silver bowl full of flowers.

"Prussic acid kills in a fraction of a second," the chess player was saying. "It affects the respiratory organs or something like that. I've just read a wonderful detective story. The murderer cracks a nut, scrapes the shell thin, fills it with prussic acid and seals the nut with wax. Only one person in the group has the habit of cracking nuts with his teeth. He even keeps nuts on his night table."

"Nobody keeps nuts on his night table," declared the dark cousin. "Ridiculous. Why should anyone keep nuts on a night table?"

"It would be exciting if one of us would suddenly collapse in his chair and fall lifeless to the floor," said the boy who considered himself a poet. "Nobody could touch anything, we'd all be fingerprinted and gradually a shocking skein of passion and crime would be unraveled—the secret of the Bergas family. What a story that would make!"

He wanted to be different and so had asked for raw ground

beef with onion. Tears rolled from his eyes. He gulped drink after drink to force the meat down his throat.

"I wonder if any of us could crack a nut with his teeth?" asked Bergas' son. "Mother, why haven't we any nuts?"

The third youth, who had loaded the rifle and had hardly spoken, suddenly collapsed in his chair and slid slowly to the floor. I gave him a kick and he rose with a yelp.

"The floor under the table hasn't been dusted," he said accusingly, brushing the seat of his pants. He had on a mud-colored tie and his vest was old and double-breasted, but he was very wealthy. He often visits a club just to make a nuisance of himself. His guardian has bought him a car probably in the hope that he'll break his neck. He won't come into his inheritance until he's thirty. His parents had some sense, after all.

Astrid Bergas suddenly rose from the table and left the room.

"Nerves," observed the dark cousin. "A long season, too late hours, too much alcohol. Too many dresses and hats. Too much Helsinki."

"There aren't more than three places in Helsinki where one can go," complained the third youth, who had never been thrashed as a child and suffered accordingly.

"You mentioned nerves," I said. "What are the symptoms? Facial twitching? A disturbance in the lower part of the body?"

The dark cousin was momentarily confused. He paints broad-hipped women with disproportionately small heads, and one doesn't need Freud to explain that. One look into his eyes is enough.

"I just went to wash my hands," said Mrs. Bergas and returned to the table. "I don't understand what's wrong with my hands. I seem to be washing them constantly."

A bowl of fruit was placed on the table. The boys devoured it like pigs.

"Inhibitions," said the young poet. Pear juice trickled from the corners of his mouth. He thought he was being witty.

I stood in the yard. The sky was pale and soft, and in the dusk there was something very helpless about the bare tree branches. The house glittered behind me like a Christmas tree. Every window on both floors was lighted. Bergas had the habit of going from room to room, switching off lights that weren't needed. He had no scruples about important things, but such little habits revealed why he had become wealthy. Now he was away, and the youths were enjoying themselves hugely. When he was present, they felt constrained, fingering their ties and whispering together like schoolgirls.

In a way I understood Astrid. She was a mature woman who had never been able to enjoy a carefree childhood. Her father had been a missionary, her mother a neurotic. Now she was groping for something she feared was lost forever. Jewels, furs, a limousine—they were the toys that she had never had as a child. The companionship of immature youths amused her because as a child playmates had been denied her as setting a bad example.

At first she had been amazed to discover tentatively that she could defy everyone and everything. Now she recklessly squandered herself and Bergas' money, ruling him like an elephant whose mahout pricks it with a spike behind the ears and at the bend of the forelegs. Bergas had his weaknesses, for passion is a weakness. Having discovered that, Astrid used him like a toy, crushing then healing him with the slightest caress, like a child fascinated by her own skill in handling a complicated mechanical toy.

The big house shone behind me like a Christmas tree. The bare branches of the trees were helpless against the pale sky. The bare legs of a boy on moss amidst white anemones. Never, never would that sight fade from my mind.

She was not happy even then. She had a vague feeling of having been cheated. Perhaps all this wasn't real life after all. She became restless. Grew nervous. Cried without cause. Became argumentative. No, no, no children. On that point Bergas was in agreement. He already had a son from his first marriage. Mrs. Bergas took care of herself, cultivated her eyelashes and had massage treatments.

It's useless to reflect on it. Nothing explains anything anyway.

We became acquainted and the bottom fell out from under her. She was cold blooded, untouchable. She was like a salty spring which never slakes one's thirst but only makes it more burning. I drank a treacherous tankard without realizing what I had done. When do we really know what it is we're doing?

I had been accustomed to taking what was offered to me. I've often caught myself feeling as though I were only on leave behind the front, or that I've received orders to start off on skis tomorrow with my patrol, rucksack heavy with explosives, to cut a railroad line. Something like that isn't easy to forget once it's been experienced. It makes a man accept what is offered him, with no thought of tomorrow.

During the first months I worked at the office and earned a far handsomer salary than I ever had before, I sometimes had a vague dream about tomorrow. A house somewhere far off in a forest where there was still game and bear, trees so dense that cutting them would provide me with income for life, and undisturbed solitude in the quiet snowy woods. Childish, perhaps, but as a matter of fact I managed to repay a part of my debts and to save some money. I even had a bank account, laughable as that may seem.

Then I saw her and knew that it is useless for a person to flee his fate. For me there would be no tomorrow. That can happen even though I had never thought that I would be broken by a woman. True, I can't claim that all that was particularly profound; stealing is not a profound activity. But then came something small, very small and insignificant: a child's dirty fist clutching two coins.

How can something like that happen? How could it have happened? I gripped a bare branch and looked at the sky. Everything within me was shattered, I knew that. Never again would I be the same as before.

The ground under my feet became indistinct. Darkness fell. The lighted house shone behind me. Once again I stood on the iron deck of a grimy freighter in the middle of a dark ocean and past us, quite close, glided a giant liner, a lighted city whose radiance rose to the sky above it. Music carried to my ears above the throb of its engines, and the ship glided past as hundreds of blobs of light, to disappear in the distance into darkness. I was on my way to South America then and didn't know what lay ahead of me. I thought that nowhere else could one feel the emptiness of the universe so penetratingly as in the middle of a black ocean.

She came to the front of the house. Her neck was white in the darkness.

"Come inside," she called. "Come join us; we're playing hide-and-seek."

5

They were indeed playing hide-and-seek, running from room to room in the lighted house, stumbling over thresholds, their faces flushed with pleasure and alcohol. I had time to see the chess player crawl under the large rug in the living room and glide like a seal toward the table.

"Come quickly. Run!" She pulled me upstairs by the hand, although I shook my head.

We hid on the attic stairs. It was the only dark place in the whole house. Swiftly she pressed a kiss on my mouth with burning lips.

"You've caught a chill anyway," I said. "You're feverish."

Her hair fell softly against my cheek. Somewhere from deep within her rose a silent sob, a racking sob.

The bell sounded hollowly downstairs. The seeker was on his way.

"I can't stand it," she moaned. "It's the only thing I think about. I can't sleep, I can't breathe. His blood spilled on my hands, you know."

"You're hysterical," I said, trying to make my voice as sarcastic as possible.

"How does it feel to kill people?" she asked helplessly. "Why do I feel so terrible?"

"It was an accident," I said stubbornly. "Anyone can have an accident. It can't be helped."

From downstairs came a burst of laughter, loud talk and accusations. The seeker ostensibly had started his search too soon.

Now there were two. They climbed the stairs, whispering to each other.

"Once I had to execute two men with my own hands," I said. "No one volunteered. I was the leader. I had to do it myself, to set an example."

"To set an example," she repeated. We sat on the dark attic stairs and a black dread chilled me.

"Their hands were bound behind their backs with rifle straps," I explained unnecessarily. "It didn't surprise them. They were used to such things. They themselves would have done something even worse."

"Would you die if you jumped from the sixth floor?" she asked. Her hand was hot and dry.

"Don't talk nonsense," I snapped.

The eighteen-year-old and the dark cousin came to the foot of the stairs. They looked upward from the light to the darkness, to us.

"Is anybody there?" called the Bergas youth. The painter giggled and covered his mouth with his hands.

"What are you doing in the dark?" asked the Bergas boy and ascended the stairs with outstretched, fumbling hands. I sat motionless. "Well, Mother," he said and felt Astrid Bergas' knees. "So I've found you." He pretended to stumble and pressed Astrid by the shoulders to the steps.

Astrid cried out and thrust the boy from her angrily. "Don't touch me," she said. The boy stumbled a few steps downward and laughed nervously. "Captain?" he said questioningly but didn't extend a hand toward me. He was careful; his breath came in short spurts.

"A stupid game," Astrid said and walked down the stairs to the light, her hands clasped to her breast. I followed her, filling my pipe. The dark cousin looked at us and again giggled behind his hand. There was an ominous gleam in the black eyes of the Bergas boy.

"Your father's forbidden you to drink," Astrid reminded the boy.

He looked at her legs and said nothing.

"Two of them still haven't been found," said the dark cousin. "Come on, let's all look for them together."

I hauled the chess player from under the big rug by one leg. His face was dark red and he coughed dust.

"That was a heavy rug," he said. "I thought I'd choke there. I'm thirsty."

Astrid promised the boys champagne. After all, Bergas was away. They tried to slip pieces of ice down one another's necks. They had fun. The chess player's nose turned yellowish and he hurried outside.

"Mother, where's the robe that belongs in the limousine?" the Bergas boy asked suddenly. "The chauffeur said it's missing."

It came too suddenly. I didn't flinch, but a cold lead weight plummeted through my body to my feet. Astrid's eyes flew open in terror; she began to stammer.

"What's wrong with you?" asked the dark cousin. "What robe?"

"I'm frightened," declared Astrid. "Someone looked in through the window. Someone's outside."

Everybody looked out the window. The dark cousin became even paler than usual. I went to the window and opened it. There was no one outside. The trees were bare against the sky, the air was damp from the sea. Bergas' son said nothing; he wasn't stupid. An iron fist clutched at my heart.

"The robe?" asked Astrid. "How should I know? Someone's left it somewhere. Or the chauffeur has lost it. Perhaps it's been stolen."

She spoke too fast and said too much. I looked unblinkingly at the Bergas boy but he wasn't interested in me. He was concentrating, his forehead furrowed, his eyes fixed uncertainly on Astrid, not knowing himself what doubts he harbored in his mind.

"What's one robe?" asked the young poet in surprise. "What will one robe mean a thousand years from now? I feel like crying. Champagne always makes me cry. It's such a waste of money. I'd like to go out and pluck some stars."

"I'll help you to the bathroom," offered the dark cousin helpfully.

"A lot," said the Bergas boy, looking at his stepmother with a reddish glow in his eyes. "One robe can sometimes mean a lot. To me it means a great deal. I'm going to find out where that robe is."

"A robe is better than a pelt," I said. "Pelts always get vermin. I've slept in snow wrapped in a heavy blanket. If you burrow deep into the snow you don't feel cold at all. Lots of dogs sleep in snow."

It would have been better had I said nothing.

"Ahaa!" cried the Bergas boy in sudden discovery and looked at me. He was almost handsome with the glow of triumph lighting his face. My wrists went limp as they always do in moments of stress when one can do nothing but wait. It's a terrifying feeling to sit in a dugout listening to the howling approach of a shell the size of a suitcase. A second seems interminable then.

Astrid looked at me, pale and motionless. Again her eyes were black windows staring into despair. What did anything matter anymore, when the crock was broken and the wine already on the ground?

"Are you crazy, the three of you?" demanded the dark cousin. "Arguing about a robe. What would we do with a robe? We don't need a robe when we have champagne."

Suddenly I began to laugh. Probably even a rat laughs when he hears a snap and sees that the trap has closed.

"What an unpleasant laugh," muttered the drunken boy. "It gives me gooseflesh. I've never heard a hyena laugh. In fact, I thought hyenas laughed only in English novels. Certainly the hyena at the zoo doesn't laugh. Or do they even have one there? But that man's laughing. Make him stop."

"You'd better go to bed," Astrid said. "You've had too much to drink although I told you not to."

"Which of us will go to bed?" asked the Bergas boy. "Try to guess. Heads or tails?"

He tossed a mark into the air, caught it and extended it between his palms toward his stepmother. A coincidence? I've seen stranger ones. But Astrid didn't cry out. She rose, her gaze became glassy, she craned her neck as though under a ghastly compulsion.

"Heads," she whispered hoarsely, one hand clutching her

throat. The boy opened his palms and revealed the money. "Tails," he said triumphantly. Astrid extended her hand mechanically and took the coin from his hand. She turned it around in her fingers, staring at it.

"Are you playing?" asked the dark cousin. "Never mind coins. Next to the last number even or odd?" He took a bill from his vest pocket, crumpled it in his fist and extended his hand expectantly. "Next to the last number even or odd?" he repeated but no one took him up on the offer.

"A mark for your thoughts, Mother," the Bergas boy said. "Two marks." He suddenly stiffened, his eyes became expressionless, he wiped his forehead. "What did I say?" he asked with a start. It was as though a strange being had briefly taken possession of him, then tossed him aside. Astrid dropped the coin on the floor, drew a tiny handkerchief from her sleeve and wiped her fingers.

"Cognac," I demanded. "Bring some quickly."

"What's wrong?" asked the dark cousin in amazement. The Bergas boy brought a cognac bottle from the cupboard and poured a drink. He extended the glass with concern, but Astrid shook her head sharply and pushed it away. She tried to say something but no sound came from her throat.

"Drink it," I said. "Drink. It'll help you. You're not feeling well."

"Pat her on the back," suggested the cousin helpfully.

The chess player appeared and leaned against the door. "Who wants a fish?" he asked mysteriously. "I've got a fish." He produced a large red fish from behind his back. It was a child's toy he had found in the bathroom.

"With tear-filled eyes he gazed at the red fish," said the drunken poet. "A fish is the symbol of hope, the symbol of immortality. The walls of the catacombs have pictures of fish. Do any of you believe in the immortality of the soul?"

"Turn on the phonograph," suggested Astrid Bergas. "Play the Caruso records. You can break them if you want to; I don't care anymore."

The cognac had brought the color back into her cheeks, but her dull eyes wandered uncertainly around the room.

A dead man's magnificent voice filled the room. Perhaps there is no death. Involuntarily everyone turned to listen. Perhaps, after all, there was something in the boys that responded to the call of the immortal voice. The Bergas boy listened too, but his thoughts were elsewhere. I could see from his face how intensely he was pondering something that annoyingly eluded him.

A little boy's smile again shone before me momentarily as the sun's hot rays glinted off the proud hood of the car under the soft blue sky. I had driven on the right, I'm sure of it; there could be no mistake. I wasn't even drunk. And he died so suddenly that he probably didn't even realize that he had been run over.

Like an eggshell crushed against a hard surface. Thin legs in the shadow of the willows. Then the rain wet his face. And yet I had lived through the war. Were my nerves really beginning to fail me? But my hands didn't even tremble or my face twitch. No one could see through my face.

"You have a fever," I said. "Your back was bare. You've caught a chill."

Astrid moved her head from side to side. The glorious voice of the dead man filled the room, filled the entire house which shone, its windows lighted, in the darkness.

"Mrs. Bergas is ill," I announced. No one moved. "Have you a sedative in the house? Bromide? Luminol?" I asked impatiently.

"There's probably some Medinol in the night table," the Bergas youth said reluctantly. "Do you want me to show you?"

Astrid looked at me and preceded me into the hall. The others remained. The dark cousin began to giggle behind his hand. "Turn off the phonograph and go to bed," I ordered. No one moved. Bergas' son didn't avoid my eyes as he usually did but looked at me with open hostility. I no longer had a hold over him, and he knew it. Finally he had realized it.

We climbed the stairs. "I'm not sick," Astrid declared. We walked across the floor. "Good night," I said.

We stood facing each other before the closed door. "Take some Medinol, sleep, and it'll pass," I said.

"Can you really leave me alone?" she asked. She looked at me, her hands clasped over her breast, her blond head strained be-seechingly toward me, her lips parted.

"Good night," I repeated. She looked at me as if she was seeing me for the first time and was wondering who I really was.

"For your own sake try to calm down," I urged her. I opened the door for her and pushed her by the shoulder, but she didn't move. Her shoulder was soft under my hand. Black dread again filled me.

"The robe," she whispered. "The two marks. How was it possible? Did he know? The boy clutched them in his fist; they were still damp and warm when I took them in my hand."

"Imagination," I said roughly to help her. "Go to bed. Read something. Polish your nails. Good night."

I switched the light on for her and closed the door after her, but she remained standing with her hands against the door. I knew her as a cold-blooded, pleasure-seeking, cruel child. Now all that had dropped from her. Now she was alone and fright-ened of the unknown that moved within her. I couldn't help her. Everyone has to bear his loneliness once.

I went downstairs with weary steps. They were sitting with their heads together, all four of them, whispering and giggling like girls. They started when I stared at them over the rim of my glass.

"Did you undress her?" the Bergas boy asked in an insinuating tone. "Did you cover her well? Did you have fun?"

They all looked at me insolently, curiously, as though eager to see how far I could be pushed. Four uncivilized boys prod-ding a caged beast, watching as he turns his head frantically, unable to escape.

I left my brandy unfinished and went outside. Bergas was away. Clouds had gathered in the sky, a single star twinkled artificially on the horizon, the sea spread a cold dampness over the park. I walked slowly down the driveway. I was alone; no one missed me. The earth was bare and despairing around me. I went to the garage and opened the doors wide. The company car was there, like a toy beside the limousine. I had arrived in it. In the dark I slid behind the wheel and fumbled for the head-light switch. But I didn't press it.

I sat in the dark surrounded by the smell of gasoline and oily metal. Through the broad doors the black trees were visible, and at their feet the paler band of the driveway. If I left now, no void would remain. Is it easier to exist knowing that one bears the knowledge of a crime alone? It was as though something within me had burned to ashes, leaving only the charred edges.

I was a human being. Did that, after all, mean more than I had thought? What kind of man is it who throws away his weapon and flees, leaving a wounded companion behind to the mercy of the enemy? The bullets pierce both of them anyway. Bullets don't hurt; only with words do people wound one another.

I sat long in the dark. Darkness is kind. Lights went out somewhere. The yard grew darker before me. I once saw a skilled diver lose his footing on the board. He prepared for a graceful dive but hit the water with his stomach. It was excruciatingly painful. Perhaps the same thing had happened to me. Perhaps I too had lost my footing. I got out of the car, slammed the door and returned to the house.

The upstairs windows stared blackly into the darkness. Only the living room and the hall were still lighted. I went inside quietly. The youths were playing cards at the card table. There was money on its green felt surface. They didn't look up at me. I meant nothing whatsoever to them.

I went upstairs and into my room without turning on the light. I locked the door and undressed in the dark. What did anything matter anymore? I felt my way across the room to the bed and my hand touched a cool shoulder. She was waiting for me in my bed.

"I'm cold," she whispered from the dark.

I wasn't surprised. I had known that she would be there.

Exhaustion swept over me. A feeling of futility. In the dark my hand touched her hair, her cold face. I lay on my back in the too soft bed. I thought of those who already had died, those who would never have to be born into a hopeless old world when a new one was just in the making.

"I'm cold," she whispered in the dark. Her cold finger traced the outline of my lips.

6

"I'm cold," she repeated passionately. "Be good to me." The bed groaned. She pressed against me, burying her face in the hollow of my neck. I lay motionless.

"You're crazy," I said. I loved her. I loved her more than anything else in the world. There was nothing I wouldn't have done for her.

"You're crazy," I repeated. She began to cry. She sobbed and dampened my neck and the collar of my pajamas with her tears.

"It's better that I leave and never come back," I said with my hand on her head. "It would have been better if I had never come in the first place. You were happy before that. You had everything a person could ask for."

"I can't live without you," she whispered. Her lips were wet and despairing against my neck.

"That's an old story," I said. "Foolish. You'll forget soon. All women do. Women have no memory."

I thought of Bergas. Bergas had bought her fair and square. Bergas believed in the inviolability of contracts. He had only one eye, but he was a man and he trusted me. To him the matter presented no problem. He would merely have raised his eyebrows and wondered. The merchandise was his. See, here were the papers, with everything in order.

The merchandise was his and he had the right to do with it as he pleased. Love? Only a word used in books. Attachment, sympathy—that exists. Comradeship too. Love? Bergas lifts his brows and smiles. "Of course, my child, of course." Children must have words with which to play. Bergas doesn't need them. Bergas builds his own heaven according to his own specifications.

"The boy was a foster child," she whispered against my neck. "He didn't have real parents. He was probably beaten. He was in the way. No one even noticed that he was missing."

I had a youthful romance. Once upon a time, before I left, she too wept against my cheek. I was only a callow youth then and hadn't touched her. It was very romantic. I spoke to her mysteriously about my trip. She was entranced, she promised to wait for me her entire life if necessary. She gave me her photograph and a lock of her hair to keep in my watch. She insisted upon accompanying me to the train.

The engine swirled steam in the frosty night, ugly boards covered the station under construction. The overcoats of the Russian soldiers stank in the musty waiting room of the old station. She remained standing on the platform, her hands tucked into a black muff, her nose red and her eyes tear-filled. It was very beautiful, the sky was full of tiny frost-stars, the windows of the train were covered with frost.

Then no one yet knew that the world would come apart at the seams and that thereafter nothing could be the same as before. At any rate, she was undoubtedly very sincere, ecstatic and infatuated in promising to wait for me.

I grew to manhood in a few years. It was a trying time. Now in retrospect it's not shameful to admit it. Comradeship strengthened by war, mutual will and perseverance can be beautiful, but one can tire even of that when one is young. My body hardened to a man's, my mind preserved under its sternness and coarseness a picture of that black muff, red nose and tear-filled eyes.

We were so abjectly alone in distant Germany, we Jägers. The mind was quick to leap at every compensating thought. In my imagination we had our own home and lived together for many years. I looked at her picture until it cracked and turned yellow. I sniffed the lock of hair in my watch and seemed to catch the childish fragrance of her hair.

She was in Helsinki, behind the front, while we were doing the job we had come to do. Already in Vaasa, as we were approaching home, I learned that she was married and even had a child. Of course it was all imagination, a dream that I had spun for myself in the log camp under the sod or while plucking lice from my shirt in the sunshine of a Sunday. Even so, I felt that I had been betrayed, that people were not what I had imagined them to be.

"You're a hero," she said when we met in Helsinki and with sparkling eyes introduced me to her husband. She was proud of me and wanted to walk beside me on the street. Her husband had soft hands and a helpless look; I felt ashamed for him.

I scratched my armpit and complained, "I have lice." It wasn't true anymore, but I felt that the remark was appropriate.

"Oh!" she screamed, "What are you saying?" I could see that my prestige had suffered. Later she was said to have expressed the opinion that I had become uncouth and peculiar while away. "Barbaric" I believe was the word she used. Her husband felt the same way. Many others shared that opinion of us.

I lay motionless on my back in bed and Astrid Bergas breathed against my cheek.

"I can't sleep," she whispered in the darkness. "I'm cold." She began to cry again. I didn't pity her; it was good for her. Tears bring relief. It would be wonderful to be able to wash all the evil out of one with tears, but men don't cry. It's unpleasant to see a man cry. One turns one's head away and fights a desire to kick him.

Why did I love her? It's dangerous for a man to love when his temples are already gray and he thinks that he has experienced everything the world offers and has burned his last ships behind him. It's like insanity. Everything is empty and insignificant when she isn't with me. I've seen her glance melt and her eyes hide in the shadow of her lids. Her body has awakened to my touch.

At first I thought that that was all there was. Until then everything had been so easy. It always is. But then comes something that strikes through one like lightning and awakens one to the realization that there is more to life than one has imagined and that nothing is what it seemed to be.

"Come away with me," I suggested. "The world has many countries and living is cheap. . . . Come away with me," I said again and held her tightly. "Come away." I caressed her hair and her face in the dark.

"Where could we go?" she asked. Her arms tightened around my neck. "What would come of it? I don't know how to do anything. For us two there is no place in the world. You know it. Why do you torment me?"

Yes, I knew it only too well. I caressed her shoulders. My arms were weak. I kissed her.

"I love you," she said. "I love you; I can't live without you, you know that."

In Argentina I met a touring couple. The man shot feather balls off his wife's head with a pistol. The mestizos howled on the benches. The Indians sat quietly and watched attentively. The troupe had toured all over the world, bribing police and soldiers, drinking sour wine and again harnessing their colorful wagons. The man shot feather balls off his wife's head with a pistol; then the woman danced. Her body was aging but she had done her best to paint her face.

The foreman gave the husband some money and took the wife to his tin shack for the night. Fireflies buzzed in the air. The man spoke a little German and we shared a mugful of locally distilled whisky. He was a Czech who had fought in Siberia. His wife was the widow of a Russian officer. They loved each other and wandered homeless from country to country. That, too, can happen.

In the morning the woman came into the circus wagon with matted hair and dull eyes. The man angrily demanded whether she had gotten more money. Then they harnessed their horses. I drove with them for two weeks from village to village, singing Finnish songs and playing the accordion. It was obvious that they really loved each other, but there was no place for them in the world. That's the way it is.

Once I had tried in vain to build myself a future in a new country. Then I had been alone and younger. Then I still had faith. Now my time was past and my nerves were beginning to fail me. Bergas might use me a few years more but he was the only one. He liked me. I had experienced poverty; hunger, too. I knew what it was. And Astrid Bergas could no longer do without French bath salts. A dress that she had worn twice was old. I should have laughed, but I couldn't. My throat was tight.

"I'll go away," I said, "then everything will be all right again."

"You don't know what poverty means to me," she said as she always did. "I'd like to be poor with you but I can't. I only know that I love you. Isn't that enough?"

"What about the robe?" I asked. She flinched and pressed her palm against my mouth.

"You mustn't," she said in a quivering voice, "it doesn't mean anything. The boy will forget it by tomorrow. He was drunk."

"He's not a boy. He's eighteen years old." I squeezed her wrist too tightly. She moaned.

Clatter and footsteps sounded on the stairs. We both stiffened. Someone drunkenly tried to whistle an aria from *Rigoletto*. Someone stumbled and fell on the steps. He wailed that his leg was broken. The dark cousin's voice expressed the wish that his tongue likewise were broken. "Then it would be easier to live," he said.

We lay motionless. Doors slammed. It was quiet again. The room had become very dark. I could only distinguish the window and the cloudy sky. The star had disappeared from the horizon.

"If I go away, everything will be all right," I said stubbornly. "You'll forget. No one will ever remind you of it. Now you remember it every time you see my face. Whenever I touch you, you remember it. You can't help it."

"The boy's blood spilled onto my hands," she said accusingly. "It was terrible."

"He died suddenly, without even knowing he was dying. He'll never have to cry again. He'll never have to work hard, never have to humble himself to get bread. He's better off."

It was ghastly to feel another person beside one, hear her voice and know that she was forever unattainable. Her body would die, her voice would die, her spirit would depart and there would be nothing. A small body lay between us and I knew that never again would I touch her as before.

"If this is living," she said, "I wish that I had never been born. Before you came I didn't know what life was. I hate you, I hate every word that I say to you. I hate the air you breathe. I hate your hands, I hate your eyes, I hate you so that I want to stamp on your face."

And then, "No, no!" she cried. "It isn't true. Forget what I said. Darling, forget what I said. It isn't true. I only hate myself. I hate my body because it's beautiful. I hate my face and eyes, my lying mouth. If I weren't beautiful, no one would have bought me. Would you love me if I were ugly? Would you love me if I were old and quarrelsome and fat? Why does life have to be like this? It can't be true."

I pressed my hand against her mouth. She bit my palm. Her body shook. She sank her nails into my wrist. The room was very dark. Through the window the cloudy night sky of spring was visible.

"There is nothing that a person can't stand," I said. "They'll realize it when the sky is red from burning buildings and the antiaircraft guns bark neverendingly. There's nothing a person can't stand. He can endure air raids, hunger and fear. He can endure pestilence, and the tears of children and women. They'll realize it. Man is as tough as a bedbug. Man is a parasite on the face of the earth."

Her head dropped onto my shoulder. I held her wrist and my arm grew numb under her neck, but I didn't move. I've lain awake many nights. Many nights under a frosty sky and many nights in illuminated, smoke-filled rooms. Nights are long and time passes slowly. Then the sky lightened to pearl gray and the objects in the room were etched into view. I looked at her tangled hair, her bluish eyelids. The weight of her head felt good on my shoulder. Her arm was bare and lovely. Her body was beautiful clay, but death has no pity for beautiful clay.

Her face was small and delicate in the faint light of early morning, when the gray sky changes to a white glow. In dreams I was gentle; I was her father and her mother, as fathers and mothers are in fantasy. My shoulder was her little home in a beautiful, beautiful world. My eyes grew moist; the light stung them. Light hurts eyes accustomed to the dark. Time spares no one.

I, a man, knew that night why man craves immortality and dips insatiably into the well of dreams. It is beautiful but bitter. Neither shame nor grief can keep one from it; not even self-contempt. Her wrist was thin in my hand, her head rested sleepily against my shoulder and the pink child's mouth breathed softly, knowing nothing of want or death. The scratched, tanned child's legs were warm under the merciful silken quilt. Her soul would awaken to a beautiful morning, to the glory of spring under flowering cherry trees.

The sky began to redden. Somewhere in the distance a ship let out a long blast. She started from her sleep, her mouth twisting in the disappointment of awakening.

"It wasn't real after all," she said wearily. "It was just a dream." She rubbed her eyes with her fists and stretched. Her feet were icy under the soft quilt.

"I suppose I must go," she said. "I'm sure I look terrible. Forgive me. It's over now."

The morning was still long. I immediately fell into a dreamless sleep.

7

"Forty—advantage!" I called. "Serve!"

The cable on the net twanged. I hit again. She lowered her racket briefly.

"Play," I urged. "Play."

"Game," she said and dropped her racket.

"The score's only five-four," I said. "Play."

A million chips of broken mirror sparkled in the sea. The sandy court responded resiliently to every step and the service lines were freshly chalked. The ball whistled over the net, the strings of the racket twanged, perspiration prickled the skin.

"You're playing poorly today, Mother," the Bergas boy observed critically.

Finally the ball landed weakly in the net.

"Game," I said. "Six-four. Too bad. What's wrong with you?"

"I took some sleeping pills. My body's still numb," she said defensively, as though reciting a lesson.

"I don't see how you have the strength to play," groaned the

boy who considered himself a poet. He was hunched on the back
of a garden bench like a crow, the better to see. "I shouldn't
drink, it only makes me sick. Don't you have any bicarbonate?
I don't think I'll ever take another drink again."

"A little drink with a drop of Angostura," suggested the
dark cousin hopefully. "After all, this is Sunday. I'm perspiring
just from watching you."

The beach exuded the fragrance of seaweed and invigorating
salt water. A million chips of broken mirror sparkled in the sea.
Sunshine bathed the skin in waves. Faces grew flushed. Summer
was at hand.

"Who wants to go for a drive?" asked Astrid without looking
at me. "We'll go to the ridge to pick flowers. Heath anemones
grow there."

"Who'll drive?" asked the Bergas boy reluctantly. "I certainly won't."

"Why go for a drive?" I asked.

She avoided my eyes. She had not even put on lipstick and
her face was tired and somber.

"It's Sunday again," she replied. "What else would we do?"

She herself drove. At first she drove carefully. The big car
glided along the dry road almost soundlessly. The dark cousin
sat beside her, chattering constantly. He talked about the pic-
turesqueness and colors of the landscape, about the new waitress
at the club bar, and about the art society's spring exhibition, in
which all forty still lifes still consisted of a bottle and three
fruits, with the single exception of one which had the surprising
addition of a dead fish.

The car's speed increased imperceptibly. It was a big car
which easily exceeded sixty and which was difficult to drive under fifty on a good road. The scenery changed. The chess player
slept beside me on the rear seat with his mouth open. The
wealthy youth and the young poet sat in front of me on the extra seats and were angry because the car's silver flask was empty.
The Bergas boy stared at me absently from beside the chess
player. He was thinking. He was an eighteen-year-old.

"You've passed the ridge," I said. The sky was clear and the
hood of the car shone handsomely against the pale road.

"Heath anemones," she whispered. "You can't pick them. Didn't you know?" Her gloved hands gripped the steering wheel tightly; she stared stubbornly ahead.

The city flashed into view beyond a bend and across the bay, the city with its reddish factory smokestacks, window-dotted gray buildings and black piles of coal. The new bridge was graceful above the sparkling sea.

"A little drink with a drop of Angostura in it," the dark cousin said again hopefully. The car turned down the wrong road. It didn't lead to the city, it didn't lead to Sunday peace and satiety at a hotel, it didn't lead to the familiar and the safe.

The road led away from the city, our generous, gleaming home. It led away from the city and joined the highway to the north. Shiny cars rolled alongside us and dropped behind, cyclists pedaled along the asphalt as if for their lives with flushed, perspiring faces.

Then I knew.

"You're insane," I muttered. It wasn't the first time. I had repeated it to the point of exhaustion. The close game, physical exhaustion, a million mirror chips twinkling in the sea, had not helped her. Bitterness gnawed at my heart like a bold, insatiable rat. Wasn't it enough that I myself was sick with worry, despair and failure? Why did two have to suffer when one sufficed?

The Bergas boy looked at me oddly. The dark cousin shrugged his shoulders resignedly, leaned back against the seat and fell silent. The limousine whizzed down the hard road; a thin little girl with pleading eyes extended a bunch of withered lilies of the valley toward the car window, but the car didn't stop.

Cleared woods with newly built small homes flashed by. Before us the road stretched across the plain, straight as a ruler. Suddenly the speed slackened. Madness.

"Drive," I urged under my breath. "Drive."

The cliffs that rose sharply on either side of the road suddenly amplified the car's low hum manyfold. We reached the bend. No people, no houses. The dry grass filled a deep ditch on either side of the road. The sun beat down on us hotly, the hood twinkled haughtily. Icicles trickled down my back, my face became hard, my eyes stared stiffly down the road.

The bend was behind us. The speed accelerated. "What's wrong, Captain?" inquired the Bergas boy superciliously. "Don't you feel well?"

I said nothing. The slim neck in the front seat was bowed, the eyes were glued to the hard road, the gloved hands clutched the wheel. There were houses on both sides of the road now. A bald man on a porch was reading a newspaper. He raised his glasses and glanced at us in annoyance. A yellow-green robe hung over the birch tree in the yard.

A bridge above slow flowing moss-green water. At the entrance to a side road there was a cluster of new, shiny cars. Sunday drivers. A blond young man, one foot on a running board, was pointing up the side road and saying something through the window eagerly. The limousine slowed down, hesitated.

"Drive on!" I almost shrieked. "Drive!"

The big car hesitated, pulled over to the side of the road and stopped. The unnaturally pale face turned from the wheel to stammer, "What's happened? Why are people so excited?"

"A murder," I said. "A little boy was murdered here last week. His body was found in the woods up the side road. Drive on."

A leather-jacketed man came down the road from the woods. He was explaining something to the woman beside him. A gloved hand rolled open one of the side windows.

"Dreadful," said the woman on the side road, her face flushed in excitement. "Inhuman. Shocking."

"How thrilling!" exclaimed the dark cousin, opening a door. "Who wants to go for a walk?" he asked and stepped out.

"Drive on," I said weakly. "Drive on."

"An escaped prisoner," recalled the poetic youth. "A milk can, a stolen bicycle—I remember reading about it in the paper. He struck the boy on the head with a shovel, wasn't that it? A good idea for a story. I must remember it."

"Drive on," I said sharply. "Drive on." Everything in me was coming apart.

"You're nervous, Captain," taunted the Bergas boy and reached over to open the other door. "A walk will do you good." He thrust the wealthy youth before him onto the road.

"I'll stay here," I said and stepped down last. They started off down the side road. I looked after them.

"This is daily fare for you, of course, Captain," observed the wealthy youth. "You're experienced, but I've never seen the site of a murder. Is it far?"

"You can't drive there in a new car," warned the blond man. "The road's too narrow. The sides will get scratched."

"The road's wet," I said, stepping beside her. "Your shoes will be ruined."

She just looked at me, and her eyes were those of a stranger. Bluish shadows surrounded them, and she was very pale. She had no makeup on at all. Her face was that of a stranger.

"I'd like to sketch—" began the dark cousin, then suddenly cut short the sentence. An elderly man in a black coat jumped across the ditch from the woods onto the road and extended a hand to help his wife. It was an entire family: an elderly man, his wife and three grown children. The woman's hair was gray under her hat.

"Terrible," she said. "Simply terrible." She leaped across the ditch like a duck. "Shall we eat our sandwiches? I'm famished."

This was the place. The road was wet and covered with footprints. Paper bags and eggshells littered the ditch.

"A new hiking trail," observed the cousin. "Invigorating exercise in the fresh air, a stretch of rugged terrain and then lunch. I'm getting hungry myself."

Astrid Bergas looked at me. Then she slowly drew off her gloves. The rich youth perspired and wiped his forehead with a soiled handkerchief. We all leaped the ditch in turn and stepped into the woods. One couldn't mistake the way, for a wide path had already been beaten through the trees. We arrived at the hollow. Some people were there, staring at a spot on the ground. We joined them.

"This is where he was," explained an enterprising little boy with freckles on his nose. Energetically he pointed a dirty finger at the depression under the willow bush. The white anemones had been trampled.

"This is how he looked," continued the boy, dropping suddenly to the ground on his back, closing his eyes and bending one arm limply over his stomach. He was perhaps twelve, his face was thin and lively. He rose quickly.

"That's how it was," he said, looking down and rubbing one foot with the other. His legs were bare and scratched. The ground was cold and wet. Someone gave him some money. He thanked the person and tipped his cap jauntily. Someone else gave him some money. He repeated his thanks and tipped his cap just as jauntily. His eyes were shining.

"I'd like to sketch him," said the dark cousin and stared in fascination at the boy.

"A childish game," announced the chess player. "An insignificant pawn sacrificed. The queen gambit would be something else again."

I looked at him. He became flustered. "I mean the escaped prisoner," he amended quickly. "I didn't mean anything. Of course reverence, a dead boy and so on. Beastly."

The white anemones were flattened to the ground and smudged. Bright streaks of sunlight shone into the woods. Everybody was staring at the spot at the foot of the leafless willow bush where the grass was crushed. Voices sounded from the road, and laughter and exclamations. New arrivals were coming. Astrid Bergas stared at the ground, clutching her purse with both hands. Her nails were colorless. Their white half-moons rose ghostlike from under the cuticles.

"Modern times," observed the young poet.

"Come on. I'm perspiring," pleaded the rich youth.

We returned to the road. The ground was wet, and our shoes were muddy.

"A little drink with a drop of Angostura in it," the dark cousin reminded us hopefully. The sky was blue above the woods and the sun shone.

"Go to hell!" I snapped. The youths laughed.

"Who'll drive?" asked Astrid. "I feel dizzy. I'd land us in a ditch."

"Who'll drive? Not I," said the Bergas boy and he looked demandingly at me.

I drove. Mrs. Bergas sat in the back seat and smoked a flattened cigarette. I met her glance in the rearview mirror. We drove to the city and went to the club to eat. The doorman smiled and shook his head on seeing Mrs. Bergas with us. Women were not allowed in the club. I gave him some money and he shrugged. The dining room was empty, and we went into a side room. The chess player shot a few balls at the billiard table. The youngsters had a drink. They were enjoying themselves, talking enthusiastically.

"Say something. You're dull," remarked Mrs. Bergas. But she didn't drink. The glass remained untouched before her. "I'm cold," she said. "Shall we go?"

"Art is only surplus," the chess player was explaining. "Culture too is surplus. We're all surplus."

"Surrealism means the same in art as parapsychology in psychology," the dark cousin insisted. "If something doesn't exist, then one must be able to paint something that one doesn't see. Who can deny that?"

"A poem is more than a human being," said the poet dreamily. "A poem is blood and earth. A poet must be more than he actually is. That's why I must die young."

"A poem is surplus too," the chess player insisted. "So it's better to do what one can to die young. All surplus is unnecessary. It doesn't correspond to the mathematical ideal. The whole universe strives for the mathematical ideal even though it will never achieve it. A microcosm and macrocosm are only based on the theory of probability. The whole universe is a mistake, because it can never achieve its ideal."

"I don't believe in love," said the Bergas youth, and his face flushed slowly as he watched his father's wife. "There's only lust, and it's terrible. It can make one lie in bed listening to every sound. Since I was twelve years old I've been lying awake in bed and listening to every sound."

"Complexes," observed the dark cousin. He actually believed himself to be witty.

"I don't believe in love," the Bergas boy repeated stubbornly, his face red. He was eighteen. "But I've had enough. I'm tired of it, do you hear—tired of it!" He flung his glass against the wall with all his might, and the splinters tinkled along the floor. A black-clothed waiter immediately appeared at the door, quietly, tactfully.

"You rang?" he asked without the flicker of an expression. "I'll bring the bill right away." He was accustomed to being tactful; it was his job.

"I know," said the Bergas boy and rose, gripping the edge of the table. "I know. You can't hide anything from me. Where for example is the car robe? One can lie on it in the woods. I know that."

"How do you know it?" asked the chess player. He couldn't resist the temptation to be witty.

"He's drunk again," the young poet said contemptuously and wiped the pallid tip of his nose with his hand. He couldn't stand alcohol.

"I'm tired of watching and listening to everything," the Bergas boy shouted. "I can't stand it anymore!" Eighteen is a difficult age.

"Let's go," I said. The waiter extended the folded bill on a small shiny tray. He looked at the floor where the splinters of glass crunched underfoot and coughed. He bowed courteously and said, "Welcome again, Captain."

"Let's go," I said and allowed Mrs. Bergas to precede me.

"There's some seltzer in the men's room," the dark cousin said soothingly to the Bergas boy. "Take some."

"We're staying here," the chess player and the rich youth said simultaneously. The poet hesitated at the door and looked at them. "Do you have money?" he asked in astonishment. "Who'll lend me some?" The three of them remained there. We left.

8

"Why do I have to learn to draw when there are compasses and rulers?" asked the dark cousin in candid bewilderment. He was sitting on the balcony of the beach pavilion, looking at the sea as distastefully as though it were a too well done steak. He had a pile of crayons, some drawing paper and a large glass of whisky before him on the table.

"For an artist, drawing means—" I began, then stopped short. "Where's Mrs. Bergas?" I inquired sharply. My back stiffened into an iron bar.

"You're antiquated, Captain," the dark cousin explained. "You don't understand the basis of modern art. Whatever exceeds conventional realism also exceeds your limited comprehension. You're the personification of the critical public, but unfortunately, new art isn't born of criticism but of faith. You lack faith, so have a brandy instead."

The dusk reddened and purple streaks again swam on the pale blue surface of the sea.

"Where's Mrs. Bergas?" I asked again, my voice tightening. Night was approaching, the pavilion behind me was shadowy, but the park was ablaze with crimson light.

"You have no sense of humor," the dark cousin lamented, but stopped jesting when he saw my face. "How should I know?" he demanded peevishly. "I'm working, can't you see? On the beach, in the tower room perhaps, how should I know?"

I climbed up to the tower room, ascending the stairs with the silent tread of a hunter. I was in a hurry. A small vein throbbed at my temple, my breath came quickly. A few flights and I knew that I was old. The door to the tower room was open. Sunset stained the shadowy hallway crimson. I heard the floor squeak.

"What's going on?" I demanded from the doorway, my heart suddenly chilling.

The Bergas boy turned toward me. His face was red with

anger and passion. An angry glow flickered in his eyes, his neck was hunched.

"Nothing at all," said Astrid Bergas and moved away from the boy, trembling.

I stepped slowly toward the boy.

"It doesn't mean anything!" cried Astrid, raising her hand in protest. "Don't."

The boy retreated before me to the wall, his eyes blazing. Suddenly he thrust his hand into a side pocket, pulled out a gun and pointed it at me.

"I'll shoot you if you touch me," he said tensely. "Go away."

I glanced at the blue mouth of the revolver, looked sharply at him and stepped forward. The tower room was bright with the light of sunset and through its windows the sea stretched infinitely.

"I'll shoot," the boy stammered. In a second his face turned pale. He pressed against the wall. I took the gun from his hand and boxed his ears.

"Don't be an idiot," I said. "A big boy like you."

Suddenly he burst into racking sobs and covered his eyes with his arm to keep me from seeing his face. He was only eighteen years old and still was able to cry, lucky boy.

Astrid was still trembling, but she laid her hand gently on the boy's shoulder. He looked at me, his face contorted like a small child whose toy has been stolen.

"Why is she so beautiful?" he moaned. "I dream about her; she comes to me in my dreams, and when I awaken I want to die."

"You imagine too much," I said. "You're still a child. Only children have dreams."

"Don't cry," pleaded Astrid, her hand still on the boy's shoulder. "I'm not angry with you; you couldn't help it. I like you very much." She patted the boy's shoulder.

"You'll forget soon," I said calmly. "You're young. Your future is still ahead of you. Someday you'll laugh at all this."

The youth looked at me, his face pale and drawn. "Never," he whispered. "Never. You can't forget something like that." He was very young and I pitied him.

Astrid Bergas smoothed the boy's wet cheek. She wasn't trembling anymore. The boy suddenly kissed her hand fiercely, passionately, full of youth's limitless yearning for tenderness.

"Isn't it true, after all?" he asked, sniffling and looking beseechingly at me. "Have I just imagined it?"

The red glow died from the room. The sea suddenly paled and the sky was translucent above it. Darkness was approaching somewhere in the distance, drowning everything, rolling in from afar in an immense wave.

"You've been reading trashy books," I said harshly, my face expressionless. After all, he had his life ahead of him. "If you had more sense you'd realize how childish you are. You know Astrid. And you know me. You know how your father relies on me. Surely you can't believe me to be such a scoundrel. You've been reading too many trashy books."

He devoured my every word, and his unhappy eyes brightened. He believed because he wanted to believe, now that his boyish defiance had dissolved into tears of relief. I looked at him and felt worthless.

"Come," I said and put a friendly arm around his shoulder. "Let's go turn on the lights. It'll be dark soon. We're all a little upset, but it will pass. Everything passes. Life is like that."

I talked more than usual. One always does when lying. One tries to convince oneself that the lie is perhaps the truth after all. The boy looked at me and smiled, a pathetic boy's smile.

"Captain, you're a fine man," he said, touching my sleeve timidly.

Astrid looked at me. I looked at her. We descended the stairs in silence to the lower floor. There was a puzzled look on Astrid's face as though she were searching her memory for something long forgotten. The boy's eyes were bright. He was eighteen years old and I think that he had just made up his mind to be like me someday. A man. So he thought.

Dinner was over. Only we four around the big table as the crystal and silver gleamed in the light of the chandelier. Astrid Bergas was very beautiful. I looked at her as a drowning person looks at land for the last time. I looked at her to impress eternally on my memory every line of her face, her hands, her shoulders. The glow in her eyes, the red of her lips, etched themselves in me like burning acid, dissolving my will. The sheen of her hair was mine. No one could wrest that from me. Eternity is a long, a terrifyingly long time.

The dark cousin was drawing meaningless doodles with his crayons. He was bored; he yawned may times.

"If only the future were behind instead of still ahead, it would be easier to live," he said. "The future is an awful word nowadays. There shouldn't be such a thing."

The Bergas youth said good night and went to his room. He wanted to be alone. Astrid Bergas and I remained in the big room. The floor was too large around us, the walls too far from one another, the rug too thick and expensive, the old Dutch paintings in their darkened frames too valuable.

"You know that we can't go on like this," I said.

"I love you," she replied hollowly. Her will had weakened, her strength failed. I knew that if I were to touch her now and take her away, nothing could separate us. She would be mine for a week, a month, two months. After that only gaping emptiness.

But before me she had been happy, she had gotten all she had asked for and hadn't wished for more. Man should never eat of the tree of evil knowledge. No, never.

I thrust my hands deep into my pockets and didn't touch her. We were together in too large a room, too far from each other. Only a week ago we had been content cold-bloodedly to steal whatever we thought would gratify us. Now too much had happened to us. I had believed myself to be ruthless, hard and selfish. But I had awakened and was now paying a bitter price for it.

"Do you think there could be a God after all?" Astrid Bergas asked and thrust away the horrifying thought. I looked at her sharply. The corners of her mouth were twitching; she was like a spoiled child who has suddenly struck her head on something hard and is trying to decide whether to cry.

"Don't be absurd," I said for the millionth time. Wasn't it enough that one person suffered?

"I can never be the same as before," she moaned. "But I do love you," she repeated stubbornly, like a child.

"Nothing lasts forever," I said bluntly. "There is no truer saying."

"At home we had some red plush furniture," she reminisced, staring somewhere far away. "It was always dusty and the backs of the chairs were scratched and dirty. We had some inherited silverware that was polished every Saturday. I rubbed it with an old piece of chamois, and the spoons and heavy silver handles of the knives were worn. There were photographs in black frames on the walls; the men had uniforms and mustaches and the women narrow noses. But Father was a missionary and Mother never forgave him that. At the time I thought that no one could have such an unhappy, empty childhood as I, but now I'd like to be home again."

The room was too large, the walls too far from one another. They moved even farther away, they moved ceaselessly. We stood together in the middle of the empty night and life was in our hands like a fruit from which a merciless hand has squeezed all the juice.

I looked at her and said quickly, "I must go. Tomorrow is a long day."

She hesitated, her head tilted as though she had forgotten something crucial at the last moment and was trying desperately to recall it.

"Remember, nothing lasts forever," I repeated. "Good night."

The old Dutch paintings, their colors darkened, looked down at me from the walls in the artificial light. The thick rug muffled the sound of footsteps. I kept my hands tightly in my pockets and still didn't look at her. After all, I loved her.

"Good night," she replied, all the color, all the warmth gone from her voice. "Good night," she repeated and reached her hand toward me but I didn't turn back. I clutched the door-jamb but it didn't crumble under my touch. I went through the door and it didn't splinter. I stepped out through the high white door guarded by lions with curled tongues and tails and didn't look back again.

Outside, the night was blue. The big house loomed motionless behind me with a few lighted windows. The trees were black, the driveway a lighter streak under my feet. Somewhere a gigantic pile driver was pounding piles into thick clay. The night around me trembled from the weight of the blows. I stopped to listen for the source of the sound and only then realized that it was my own heart.

I went into the garage and turned on all the lights. The company car stood by the wall like a toy beside the limousine. I stepped in, the headlights flashed on, the car slid onto the driveway. The first moth of the summer strayed into the headlights' enchanted circle and was unable to break through the wall of darkness again. I closed the wide doors carefully behind me. The stench of gasoline and oily metal was left behind. The black trees in the park glided past. The night around me was blue. I drove away from the Bergas house and turned the car onto the highway.

Far ahead of me through the blue night the lights of the city were reflected in the heavens. A passenger plane roared over me, its lights shining like a row of fireflies. I was alert and alone, gliding with the car toward the approaching night. This was best. This was, after all, best. Before I came she had been happy, even though she had stretched her empty hand after me. But nothing lasts forever. There is no truer saying.

Cars streaked toward me with fiery eyes. Cars passed me from the rear on the dark road and their red rear lights disappeared like glowing dots into the night. I drove slowly and steadily, I drove at a slow, uncompromising speed along the dark road. This was best, after all.

Eons later the city lights dotted the darkness beyond the bay. Rows of streetlights beside coal heaps reflected unwaveringly in the water. Directly and unrelentingly the illuminated steel span of the new bridge led across the dark bay to the city. The steel hummed around me as I drove into the city over the lighted bridge.

9

Monday afternoon Bergas returned from Stockholm. He went directly from the airport to his office to empty his locked brief-case. Innumerable papers awaited his attention, the telephones rang ceaselessly, his single eye shone in boyish glee after the successful trip. He was only a few years past fifty.

I waited my turn in his outer office. People came and went. A typewriter hammered out a letter. The director of the experimental plant was also waiting his turn. He was very worried and constantly rubbed his small plump hands together. He wanted more funds for his laboratory, which devoured money the way a beggar devours butter. He revered Bergas above any other man in the world. He was very short and rose on tiptoe from sheer respect when talking about Bergas. Bergas was his benefactor, Bergas gave him the opportunity to do scientific work although it wasn't productive to the firm. Bergas had fore-sight.

"What do we actually know about metals yet?" he asked me nervously. "Nothing. Our knowledge ends when we have com-bined a mere three or four metals. And we know nothing about the theory of alloys, although in practice we can make deduc-tions on the basis of friction and durability tests."

The laboratory's original purpose was to serve as the corpora-tion's testing plant. The scientist had made something entirely different out of it. The engineers and sales chiefs cursed him bitterly. Bergas merely smiled and spent hours with him while he propounded his theories concerning the true nature of metals, even though they had no practical value to the company as yet. Bergas himself was an engineer, although he had transferred from the technical branch to become head of sales and then had risen to the position of managing director. Even the skilled and self-assured metal workers indicated their esteem of the scientist whenever they came in, sooty and dirty-handed, to deliver some test pieces. They considered him slightly mad and listened respectfully while he spoke to them of electrons and ions.

"If only I had a microspectroscope," he said to me wistfully, peering at me nearsightedly and rubbing his hands in anticipation of disappointment. "You know, when atoms are smashed, there are protons and neutrons."

"You're forgetting man himself," I remarked brusquely. "Doesn't man mean anything?"

The little scientist looked at me with perplexity. He didn't understand what I meant. He was happy so long as there was enough money for the laboratory. Perhaps some day his name would echo throughout the scientific world and the company would be bombarded with letters and telegrams. He himself didn't even think of, much less know how to adapt to use, anything that brought something new into the world. But that's why there were engineers whose task was precisely that. Some day the corporation might earn a fantastic interest on the money it invested in the little scientist. Some fragment, some fact from his fevered brain might swirl into millions and raise new factories from the ground. Bergas knew it well. It was his kind of game; he was playing for high stakes.

"Don't you sometimes suffer when a man like you has to stand at the door of the wealthy like a beggar, asking for assistance?" I asked. "Doesn't your self-respect suffer? Aren't you ever bitter?"

"But I do get money, an outrageous lot of money for new equipment," he replied in amazement. He hadn't the faintest idea what I meant. "Bergas is a great man. Sometimes I rub my eyes for fear that it's all a dream and that I'm still at the university."

His spirit bubbled inside a tensile metal ball. Nothing could scratch its surface. We had no point of contact. He was a happy man.

"You go first," he said timidly. "Then tell me if he's in a good mood today so that I dare bother him." He rose on tiptoe and looked pleadingly at me with his nearsighted pale blue eyes. He was like a little porcelain dog.

I pitied him. A complicated new apparatus loomed before him like a wonderful dream. He couldn't believe that he would actually have one for his own use. I felt a need to be kind.

"No, you go first," I urged him. "You'll get your microspectroscope or whatever it is. When I come out of his office he won't be in a good mood any longer. And then he'll leave on a trip. Now, if ever, is your chance. Seize it with both hands."

He clutched the doorjamb with both hands and rose on tiptoe, his head quivering with excitement. Then he went inside. Once again I stood alone in Bergas' outer office looking out the window. Summer was at hand; there had already been some fine days such as this one. Enormous heaps of coal rose in the distance beside the harbor, shimmering blackly on the swashing surface of the sea. Ocean liners stood beside large docks, and cranes sketched the harbor with giant metal fingers. On the factory's red and still-clean wall were a hundred wide windows. The door of the first floor opened and closed, flashing a crackling, blue-white glow into the yard.

I tried vainly to whip up bitterness toward Bergas but I couldn't feel any hatred. I was a different person from the man I had been a week before. He was implacable toward his opponents but good to his friends. He was unscrupulous in business and contemptuous of old moral standards, but what did that mean when the cold gods of the times had already unhesitatingly accepted expediency and provocation as the Great Powers' way of life.

He had bought me into his service and paid a good price for me, but he also liked and trusted me. The work that I did wasn't clean and above reproach by the old standards, but it was necessary, a requisite of the times. In the company books my salary was carried under advertising expenses. I had been formally hired as market observer.

Bergas was ruthless, he drank, and unpleasant things were said of him in that connection, although the same is true of almost anyone. But he was good to his friends, and in my mind's eye I could see him at home in a worn smoking jacket and old slippers among his books and paintings. He dressed carelessly at home, and for the first time I began to look upon him as a very lonely man. He waged a huge battle single-handedly. He was a strong man, an unusual man, and with the prerogative of the strong he also took beauty unto himself. Only when surrounded by beauty does strength come into its own.

The little scientist stepped through the door, walking on tiptoe as in a dream, his pale blue eyes glowing. He was completely happy. I went inside. The enormous desk was overflowing with papers, the telephones rang. Bergas sat in his shirtsleeves and his one eye sparkled with joy. I was a wretch.

"I got on the trail of something big in Stockholm," he began. "I'm glad you came in. Have a cigar."

"Bergas," I said, studying the greenish-black Brazilian cigar in my hand, "when did you last have a vacation?"

He started and a sudden hard look came into his eye. Strong men are always hit when everything is going well with them and the sky is cloudless. They are also hit where they least expect it.

"What do you mean?" he asked and looked at me. But I studied the black cigar thoughtfully, turning it in my fingers.

"Take a vacation, Bergas," I suggested. "Last year you expanded the factory and didn't take one. The year before you spent three weeks abroad but had a meeting every night."

"What do you mean?" he repeated, a hard glint in his eyes. He was already hesitant, fearful. Even the strongest men can be afraid. It's nothing to be ashamed of.

"Take a vacation, Bergas," I said and my voice broke. "Travel abroad, take your wife with you. She's nervous and ill; she needs you. You deserve her love."

"Wolf Dog," he muttered abruptly and looked at me with great and bitter distrust.

"You know yourself that she's in bad company," I said quickly. "She's unhappy. You're neglecting her. Go abroad with her. Visit the Mediterranean. The chestnut trees are still blooming in Paris. Leave tomorrow. There's still time."

"My work," he reminded me. "The factories won't get along without me. The stockholders. But perhaps in late summer."

"The corporation is you," I said calmly. "You know that. No one is indispensable; that you know too. If you became ill, if you died, the factories would get along without you. Try it."

"It's an idea," he admitted, staring at his desk and not looking at me anymore. His thoughts wavered, doubted, sought everything that he didn't want to or couldn't ask me. He was a proud man. He was a man.

"In late summer you'll have just as much work as now," I said. "You know that yourself. And at the end of the week you'll have as much work as now. So go immediately. Leave tomorrow."

"A million-mark loss," he said. "A step backward. I can't. Surely you're exaggerating. You're nervous."

"Don't evaluate everything in money, Bergas," I pleaded. "There are things that can't be evaluated monetarily, you know that."

I looked at him expressionlessly. The cigar was as powerful as blasting powder. Beyond the window was the yard and beyond that the huge factory. But right behind the window grew a lone tree which, sooty though it was, dug its roots deep into the earth and with its branches sought summer's first green from the air and light.

"I assume that you have your reasons for talking like this," he said wryly without looking at me. "I won't ask what they are. I trust you. But first I want to see Astrid."

"She's exhausted," I said quickly. "She sleeps only with the aid of sleeping pills. Something has shocked her. She must be gotten away from here to completely different surroundings, so that she'll have something new to think about."

Bergas scrutinized me carefully. The hand that held the cigar twitched as a thought occurred to him. "Her mother was a neurotic."

"Her father was a missionary," I said with equal gravity. "Perhaps that was even harder to bear." But Bergas believed me. Still it didn't amuse me. These are modern times. Rarely have I felt their senselessness as bitterly as in that comical moment by Bergas' huge desk. Strong men have their weak spots.

"Good," he said and rose. "We'll let the Stockholm matter go for now. Thank you." He hesitated, then extended his hand to me. I clasped it. He thanked me. He actually thanked me.

I went to my office. The sun was shining. I went through a pile of newspapers, turning the pages and seeing nothing. I drew a black notebook from a locked drawer and made notations about my coming tasks without knowing what I wrote. I sent some money to a man who had asked for it over the telephone. I wrote two letters and put them in plain envelopes.

The office staff considered me a parasite who somehow, through previous service or friendship, had managed to get a nominal position with the corporation. That's been known to happen. But I had my own room and two telephones and nobody disturbed me. I was a market observer, was well paid for the job and wasn't ashamed of it.

One winter I spoke to a group of somber peasants in a farmhouse living room. Normally they were garrulous men who chattered with me in their strange dialect with childlike curiosity. But on that occasion they said nothing, merely looked at me skeptically as I sat there with a fur cap on my head and a rifle awkwardly between my knees. They were ready to sacrifice their homes and buildings, their families and cattle because of a vague dream that not all of them even fully understood.

There were gray-bearded old men and bashful boys with clear foreheads and the bright eyes of youth. They all looked at me and no longer talked or asked anything. I was wearing a Jäger's green uniform with its insignia. They wanted desperately to believe, and I lied to them that all was well, that relief forces, ammunition and food were on the way from across the border. They had only to stick it out, to try one more time. I spoke to them that way although I knew the staff officers were already busy packing papers, typewriters and telephones into the sleighs. Although I knew that all was lost and a retreat under way. I had to. Someone had to protect the flight during the last wretched days.

Then I was ashamed. When I went out of the farmhouse into the wintry day and saw the frosty woods and the unfamiliar cluster of buildings, I felt the weight of the pistol at my hip and was tempted to raise the barrel to my temple and pull the trigger, because everything was futile.

I was no longer ashamed of it. It was the exigency of war. Now I had something else of which to be ashamed.

Shame pierced me so agonizingly that I couldn't even think of food, for my body would not have accepted it. I went directly to my apartment. People's faces on the street were animated and happy; display windows exhibited bathing suits and sporting goods; the sun shone on the roofs of the high buildings between which radio antennas swung shiningly. I lay stretched out on my bed, with corroding shame as my only companion.

Some time that evening the telephone rang. I rose quickly, cold hail trickling down my back. My wrists went suddenly limp and I knew that my face was no longer impassive. But that didn't matter, for I was alone. Somehow I had to control my voice. Only one task remained—the only task in many years for which I could respect myself. But honor is merely a word and doesn't glow for me.

She was on the telephone. Her voice was with me, as near as if she herself were in the room. That made it difficult.

"I can't," she said. "I can't go on. Bergas came home today; he was very cheerful; he's leaving for Paris and wants to take me along. What shall I do? I don't understand anything, I'm empty and desperate."

"Excuse me," I said. "Who is speaking?"

She was shocked. She was so near that I seemed to see her face in the dusk.

"What? What did you say?" she whispered as though disbelieving her own ears, disbelieving the receiver in her hand. "Don't you remember my voice anymore?" she demanded as though drawing back from the edge of an abyss.

"Excuse me," I said in an impersonal voice. "Do forgive me. I must be drunk."

"I must see you," she said intensely, pausing between words as though to listen to my breathing. "I can't go without seeing you. I don't know what to do. I'm alone now. I'll take a taxi and come over. Shall I?"

"I'm very sorry," I stammered in confusion, "but unfortunately I have a guest just now, a lady."

She was speechless again. Then her breath quickened. My wrists were so weak that I had to lean my elbow on a table in order to hold the receiver. I was old already; there was a lot of gray at my temples.

"It isn't true!" she cried. "It can't be true."

"I'm sorry," I said and pretended to put my hand over the mouthpiece while saying to an empty room, "Just a moment. This won't take long."

She sighed. With immense disappointment in her voice she said, "I've been thinking that I wouldn't even be afraid of poverty. I wouldn't be afraid of anything. I can't stand it any longer—that boy—"

"I'm sorry," I repeated, "but I really must be a little drunk. I don't hear well."

She was silent for a moment. Then she whispered softly, "I hate you!"

"Come, now," I said as though soothing a cranky child.

"I hate you more than anything else in the world!" she cried, her voice breaking.

"Well, that can't be helped now," I said dully and hated myself. "Nothing lasts forever."

"I'll be leaving the day after tomorrow," she said stiffly as though to a stranger.

"Have a good trip," I wished her. She hung up.

I was alone in the unlighted room; its windows were covered with drapes. No one saw my face. Not even I myself. So greatly did I love her.

After a long while I snapped on the light and looked around me. This was my apartment in a new building, in a meaningless world, and soon I would leave it. But I wouldn't miss it, because I had never felt it to be my home. For me there was no home; I was alone and unneeded. Slowly I went to the bar and poured myself a drink. But I didn't touch the glass. I remained staring at the wall. Gray lead seeped into my veins.

The dead boy was before me with his thin, serious face. He was clutching two still-warm coins in his tanned fist and his legs were bare and scratched. But he no longer had to live in a strange world, he didn't have to fear beatings and angry words, he didn't have to ask vainly for bread or do manual labor with the future a dim uncertainty before him. It was the only thing that made me happy.

10

"You were right," said Bergas. "We leave tomorrow. Something has shaken her; she isn't the same as before."

"Perhaps she's becoming a human being," I surmised. "It could happen. Sometimes it does, although it's difficult to believe."

"You look tired," observed Bergas, his one good eye studying me searchingly. "What's wrong with you?" Actually, he was very cheerful and expansive, and there was a boyish smile on his face. It seemed an amusing prank to leave the factories without a director for a while. How the engineers would swear, how the department heads would scratch their heads in learning to assume responsibility. It would develop initiative; it would do them good.

"What should be wrong with me?" I asked stiffly. "I happened to have had too much to drink last night."

"You really shouldn't drink so much," Bergas scolded me amiably. "It's debilitating, believe me."

"I take care of my work," I said loftily. "Or do you have a complaint?"

"No, no," Bergas replied quickly. "I didn't mean that." He fell silent and his ruthless face became tender. "Oh, Wolf Dog," he exclaimed, "it's wonderful to get away for once. If I actually should die, actually become ill. She is beautiful, my life is rich, why shouldn't I rejoice? Tomorrow morning we'll step into an airplane at seven and we'll have plenty of time to dress for dinner in Paris. I've wired for tickets to the Menuhin concert. I intend to buy some new paintings. It's wonderful."

"Modern times," I observed. "Once again Europe is enjoying golden years as it did before the First World War. Why indeed should you always think of tomorrow? No one thinks of tomorrow anymore. And it's right, for no one can stop tomorrow."

"That's true," he admitted and became serious. "It's coming, but we'll be strong then. You know that we'll be strong then. Until we die. Why shouldn't we be happy while we can, for when it comes, no one will be happy."

"Happiness," I said, "that's a strange word coming from your lips. Bergas, you have the soul of a schoolgirl."

"Soul," he repeated musingly, looking out the window. The sooty tree gleamed pale green outside the window. He was intoxicated with joy and anticipation. Perhaps something new was about to open up for him, something for which he had not even dared hope. He was only a few years past fifty. "Soul," he repeated. "Perhaps we do have some sort of soul after all. I wouldn't be surprised."

"Bergas," I chided him, "you've been drinking. You, in the morning, before noon. You should be ashamed of yourself."

He laid his hand on my shoulder and looked at me. We were very close. I turned my head away, for I felt my face quiver.

"Oh, Wolf Dog!" he exclaimed. It was childish, but perhaps it was also touching.

And again it was night and I knew that there would be many more nights after this one; desolate, endless nights in a lonely burrow with memories as the only companion. But why should two suffer when one could carry the burden? And the fault was mine. Mine must also be the atonement.

There was a letter at my apartment but I didn't even open it. Slowly I tore it into small pieces, merely to be doing something. The hours passed; darkness came, the relentless clock measured the time with luminous hands. It measured the time that she would still be near me, in the same city, under the same sky.

The telephone rang. I didn't answer. It rang ceaselessly. I buried my head in a cushion. I was nervous, ill. That can happen. The body can't last forever. Only the spirit endures.

The relentless clock measured the time with luminous hands

as I tore up papers and made preparations for my departure. The hours of the night passed. A faint pearly glow spread over the sky, the lovely dawn of an early summer day.

Slowly, with physical weariness, came peace, the peace of defeat. I had felt it before.

I felt it when somewhere behind me rose the black smoke of a burning village, when the crackle of rifle fire began to die down and finally dwindled to single, sporadic shots in the frosty wilderness. All was lost, our deeds had been in vain and we left behind only misery, tears and death. The lines of sleighs progressed slowly through the deep snow, flanked by exhausted, cursing men on skis. But in the middle of the wintry forest my disappointment and despair were blanketed by the peace of defeat, peace such as I had never before experienced.

Similarly, on returning from South America and stepping from a freighter in the gray rain once again onto my native land bearing only a broken suitcase and the ashes of burned dreams, I experienced the peace of defeat. It is a peculiar feeling, as though one could never again lose anything because everything is already lost. It is also a treacherous feeling, because even then there is still much to be lost. Never in his lifetime is a person so destitute that he has not something more to lose.

But nothing lasts forever. There is no truer saying. It brings the salty taste of blood to the mouth, but I bless that saying.

The pearly glow in the sky changed to gold and blue. The metal hands of the clock lost their color. The day began. The first automobile swished through the empty streets of the city. Time began to run out. I washed my face with cold water. It was an aging, wrinkled face, an expressionless face, and there was much gray at the temples. But no one could see through that face and that was good, for somewhere within me there was still a vestige of pride.

As the clock approached seven, I was riding a wise and handsome horse at a walk along the bridle path at the edge of the city. I knew that it was the last time for many years, and I enjoy riding. It was the first morning of summer. The trees had burst into shimmering greenery within a few days. The earth was full of morning freshness. After a sleepless night, when all has been lost, it feels good to ride in the morning light on the back of a handsome and wise horse.

I looked at my watch. Now the chauffeur was unloading the suitcases in front of the airport terminal. Now they were having their passports stamped and the silver-gray wings were rolling to the edge of the field. I thought of the cherry blossoms in the small town and of the gray cat that carefully extended a paw toward the bee in the berry bush. I thought of the thrill of speed and wine that was forever gone. I thought too of the little boy with pleading eyes who offered a faded bunch of lilies of the valley to the shiny cars on the new highway. Astrid Bergas stood on the narrow forest road beside the limousine and wiped her fingers on the absurdly small handkerchief. Her nails were like tiny mirrors and her eyes looked darkly into mine. I thought of the cherry blossoms that dropped on her neck once upon a time in the old yard of a small town.

The hands of the watch indicated seven. My horse laid back his dainty ears and began to trot. He didn't need spurs; a word would have sufficed. And so he was deeply hurt and tossed his head as he trotted gracefully along the path between the green trees. Somewhere far away, giant silver-gray wings were gliding slowly to the end of the runway, the wheels were turning, the morning light was shining brightly through the cabin windows and the hum of the motors drowned out all words. The plane glided ahead, the hum swelled to a great roar, the plane's speed accelerated, it rose gradually and soared into the air. It soared into the air in a shallow arc, rose still higher, and then the blinding light-rings of the propellers turned westward under the blue sky.

Everything was over.

I bent to pat my horse's neck apologetically. His reddish nostrils flared and his ears pricked up daintily. He slowed to a dignified trot, a handsome horse on a bright morning.

Just then, for some reason, I remembered a place by a shimmering forest lake a few years ago as I was leaving on a long mission in shabby clothes and with a map and compass hidden in my knapsack. Then I had been searching for the past, but the roads had changed and the burned villages had either been rebuilt or left as grass-covered wastelands, and the people whom I dared question looked at me with distressed eyes, fearing that I would sow even more suffering than they had experienced years before. I couldn't find even the graves, for they were already covered with earth and their Lutheran crosses destroyed.

A dull hum sounded high in the air, and against the summer sky the passenger plane, a dreamlike shadow, faded toward the west, toward Europe, destined soon to mangle itself again after the frivolous, golden years.

I rode back to the stable and for the last time left the horse with the groom, who tipped his cap to me. Once again I went to the apartment that was called a home. Carelessly, as though in fun, I opened a drawer and glanced at my pistol. I looked at it and laughed. Then I closed the drawer again, for voluntary death is not atonement for a man who has experienced all that I have had to go through.

I cast one final glance around me and saw that everything was ready. I walked downtown. I didn't walk fast; I was in no hurry.

The chief of police was a personal friend of mine and because of that I reported to him at police headquarters. It made the matter easier, although I wasn't looking for alleviation when I started on the path toward retribution for a little boy's death.

I felt relaxed and relieved as one sometimes does in finally falling asleep after a sleepless night. In the long, echoing corridor the bitter peace of atonement seeped into my mind. Then the iron door clanged shut behind me.

FINE VAN BROOKLYN

Translated by Alan Beesley

1

I HAD arrived in Paris in October, 1927, and studied diligently throughout the long winter and spring semesters. The language created some problems at first, even though I had prepared myself carefully for the journey. True, I could read even difficult French texts with comparative ease, and I still feel that the French language has the capacity to mirror even cumbersome thoughts effortlessly—so effortlessly, in fact, that it sometimes disturbs and confuses the serious student. I mean specifically the annoying habit that even famous men have of introducing some bon mot or pun wherever possible in their writings, even into the most demanding thought process which is hard enough for the reader to grasp as it is. For me it always evokes the picture of a solemn professor suddenly in the middle of a lecture doing a handstand on his desk to demonstrate his agility, and then casually sitting down again to continue the lesson without batting an eye.

I admit that my Nordic mentality is comparatively slow and ponderous, and I could somehow accept some frivolity in serious work as a manifestation of an unfamiliar national character. But because such flippancy usually conceals an incredibly callous and coarse cynicism with a disarming and sunny smile, I cannot help feeling a certain antipathy.

These thoughts, which spring unbidden to my mind in recalling that distant winter as a student, will undoubtedly surprise the reader in connection with the events from which I now wish to free myself by setting them down and thereby exorcising the last vestige of restlessness from my mind. But although I am about to describe a moral lapse, I must emphasize that there were no serious consequences. And it is possible that at some later date I shall look at these notes with the same feelings as a woman who has smeared a valuable book by pressing a flower between its leaves and then years later looks at the withered and stale blossom without at all remembering why she had once sought to preserve it.

You see, the thing that happened to me was in no way extraordinary. It was not even important in my life. Today I regard it as something quite apart from the purposeful development of my life and work. Let me give you an analogy: The human body isolates a bullet that cannot be extricated by depositing a protective layer of calcium, so that it is no longer a strange, disturbing particle in the body but is simply forgotten beneath the protecting layers. The human soul works in the same way: it slowly grows the protecting folds of forgetfulness around our mistakes, our sorrows and disappointments, thus isolating them from the deeds and thoughts of our daily lives.

I said that at first the language gave me difficulty. My inability to speak it well, or rather my phlegmatic nature, kept me from seeking the company of others during my first months in Paris. I cannot say that I suffered especially, because my spiritual makeup, my entire nature, has always tended toward solitude. I cannot recall having had a single really close companion even during my schooldays.

Those to whom society and friendship mean a lot, who cannot live without continually explaining and expounding their ideas and opinions, must surely pity me and think that I am an unhappy individual. But in truth this view is quite incorrect. Loneliness has its own attractions. A lonely person is never vanquished in an argument. A stranger's irony cannot bruise his feelings, nor does he encounter misunderstanding glances or impatient suggestions. Perhaps some hereditary herd instinct breaks out with atavistic force in many people, so that they suffer an immediate spiritual agony if they cannot proclaim their news and views to others. I have not experienced this. A secret enjoyment, a secret delight of discovery, has always given me greater satisfaction than a shared pleasure. I have also been able to bury my sorrows alone and have not needed the cold sympathy or the affectedly warm handclasp of others.

The result is that people think me sullen and unfriendly. It is said that in company I am sour and boring. I do admit that I become irritated when I hear people talking self-satisfiedly and cheerfully of some trifling, pointless matter as if it were profound and fascinating.

I was not like this that winter in Paris. I was not sufficiently self-reliant to criticize others, nor had I yet achieved the recognition that is the prerequisite of unfaltering confidence. My adolescence had come late and apathetically. My schooldays had been marred by economic difficulties and the conflicts to which they gave rise, and for a number of years I had had a position as a substitute teacher in the country, so as to be able to pay my debts and save a little money for my studies and research. I had become used to a life of saving and skimping, of eating poorly cooked food and of getting along without friends. So the enforced poverty in the Latin Quarter did not bother me at all. In fact I was happy all day, now that for the first time, shyly and inexperiencedly, I began to adapt myself to my surroundings. Joy was a rarely experienced emotion after my wearisome years of study and my prolonged sojourn in the wilds of the country. Living among a foreign people awoke a strange, almost wild, feeling of freedom in me. The historic buildings and streets and the countless, forgotten monuments of Paris—not to mention the National Library with its enormous, inexhaustible catalogues —aroused a delight and a feeling of strength in me that made my work easy and my ideas surprisingly quick and sharp. As my work progressed I began for the first time to think of myself as intelligent and the pleasure this feeling gave me is beyond description. I created my first treatise in the depths of that winter and it is still my most cherished work, despite its clumsiness, its faith in the impeccability of its sources and its naïve honoring of the mistakes of my predecessors. Now I would not be so considerate, but then I could not yet realize that the world of science is, if possible, even more unscrupulous and treacherous than, for example, the world of finance.

As I write now the evening is still. I get up from the table and walk over to my books—out of the bright circle of lamplight. My eyes feel strained, and as I rest them, memories of that winter fill my mnd, memories surprising in their freshness. I am a poor observer and can seldom consciously detach an incident from its surroundings. Thus I feel helpless when I try to visualize the small details that then comprised the atmosphere and emotions that surrounded me. But I can still taste the hot milk in the coffee on a cold morning, when the trees in the park were frosted with snow, and in the glass terraces of the cafés the stoves glowed bright—which did not happen in my hotel room. I used to write in my diary in the little café near the hotel, which I reached by walking down a narrow alley, taking care not to slip on the garbage. I remember vividly the odor of decaying lettuce and the smell of roasted chestnuts that wafted from the doors of the big cafés along the boulevards. Usually I ate only one meal a day, stuffing myself with as much free bread as I could each time. I also used to buy French fried potatoes which I would eat from their newspaper wrapping as I walked.

Thinking of this now, it all seems to reek of poverty, but I can assure you that at the time it never entered my head that I lacked anything. On the contrary, I was happy during those first months, and as I have said, a delightful sense of freedom marked my life. No one kept track of my steps or meals or bedtimes, as they had done earlier, first in my strict home, and later when I lived in a boardinghouse. I do not mean that I had any desire to use my freedom wrongly in any way, but I appreciated it more now that I could eat where I wanted, and come and go without explaining to anyone where I was going. I could not conceive that such freedom could be in any way morally dangerous.

My days were long yet they flew past as if on wings, until I saw with a shock of surprise that spring had arrived. I was concerned, because the time for which I still had sufficient money seemed very short. I did not want to leave my studies unfinished, so I concentrated even more on my daily program. At first glance, it seems that during spring there was room for nothing except a superhuman amount of work—my notes alone

had used up a tremendous amount of paper—but now I realize that those studious days, spent in the same rooms, always at
the same silent desks, fled past and left no memories, while a
short walk or half an hour spent in a café late at night sum-
mons up a whole boisterous crowd of exciting memories.

So I shall never forget that rare morning when, as I walked
quickly along some riverside street, I realized that I was staring
so hard that I had to stop. The plane trees had burst forth in a
green which seemed almost yellow against the rugged black
trunks. And after the cold winter, how delicious the warm sun
was upon the back of my black jacket.

Despite all the work I did, carefree those college days were.
Spring made me frivolous. It squeezed words from me that I
had no cause to utter. It brought me chance acquaintances,
whom I could greet in the cafés. For I had begun to take a glass
of beer every evening in one of the cafés along the Boulevard
(without at all considering the debilitating effects upon my
character of this seemingly innocent drink). As I returned home
the shadows were softly dark, the sky was strangely blue above
the streetlamps, and several times a woman waiting at a street
corner touched me on the arm or looked at me with shining eyes
beneath her black eyelashes and spoke to me seductively. My
heart began to pound in panic and I could not always control
my voice as I tried to explain that I was in a hurry. In my
embarrassment I often had to fall back on the excuse of "another time."

I am ashamed to realize with what amusement I recall those
meetings, the impropriety of which is undeniable. But although
they signified adventure to me, I never felt the least tempted by
such company. And this was only partly because they were not
altogether young.

Family groups were walking along the sandy paths in the
park, and the children's clothes were bright and gay. Vendors
set up their stalls in the streets and the heat of summer fanned
across Paris, so that I kept my window open from morning until
night, and stopped wearing my woolen socks. Sometimes late of
an evening, as I walked down the stinking alley to the dark
steps of my hotel, I had the feeling that my chest was con-

stricted and an unseen hand was squeezing my throat. I would
spend the long hours of night sitting before the open window
listening to all the sounds, the laughter, the whispered voices
and the music from the dance hall. In my heart I felt faint and
my knees trembled so that I thought I had eaten some bad food
or drunk impure water.

My mental restlessness must have shown itself in my letters
for in June, quite to my surprise, I received a registered letter
from a friend of my dead father's, a man who had often helped
me and whom I was under the obligation to keep supplied with
news as to the progress of my studies and the state of my health.
Now he wrote that I had probably been overdoing things and
that the best thing I could do would be to take a holiday. And
so he enclosed a check and told me to consider it as a present, so
that it would not weigh upon my overconscientious mind. He
pointed out that the healthiest thing for me to do would be to
go to Montparnasse and drink myself stupid. However, he imagined that I would prefer to take a couple of weeks' rest somewhere in the country.

Of course there were books that I would have liked to buy,
and the temptation of planning a further month's study was
most attractive of all, but I saw it was my duty to use the
money conscientiously in the manner he had intended. I refer
not to his unsuccessful joke about Montparnasse, but to a holiday trip to the country. So it was with a great feeling of relief
that I felt the decision had been made for me. I began to laugh
to myself and I slammed my books and diary on the table—so
fervently in fact that the table leg, which had wobbled precar-
iously through the whole winter, now finally came loose and
crashed to the floor.

It was the hottest part of summer and the motionless, stinking air in the alleys in the old part of the town was suffocating.
In the Latin Quarter it was a dull time of year, for all who
could had left the city. An Albanian medical student, whom I
had met in a café one evening and with whom I had exchanged
a few words, had gone off without saying good-bye. The proprie-
tor of the bar where I had my morning coffee told me that he
had sent his children to Brittany where, he said, one could spend

a cheap holiday. My landlady said the same thing, though she regretted that the table in my room was broken. It had survived throughout her time and she could still remember how cheaply she had bought it in the Flea Market. It was an old-fashioned well-made piece and she doubted if a carpenter would be able to restore it to its former splendor. I had no feeling of guilt, but following my landlady's advice I hurried to the Quai d'Orsay, bought a ticket to Lorient and inquired as to what time the night train left.

On the dingy wall of the waiting room a number of posters advertised Brittany and after buying my ticket I strolled over to look at them. Among the rocky mountains, the sea views and pleasant sandy beaches, I noticed a strange picture, in which endless rows of rough stones rose above a flat landscape. The picture bore the name of Carnac and it at once summoned to my mind thoughts of Egypt and the mummified enchantment of a long dead civilization. No doubt my natural love of the past singled out that one picture from all the others which advertised ways to spend an idle summer. You see, I did not then know that Carnac in Brittany was a famed megalithic site—one, in fact, that was only surpassed by Stonehenge in England.

For several months I had been taking French lessons from a deaf old lady who charged only a few francs a lesson and on the most enervatingly hot days made me read aloud from a newspaper in order to correct my pronunciation. She would listen to me with her eyes closed, now and again saying something or other and asking me to repeat. I suspect she used these respites for a welcome nap, for she had been giving lessons like this twelve hours a day for thirty-eight years, and I am certain she was able to make any necessary comments in her sleep. When I went for my last lesson I bought her a half-franc bag of caramels and asked her to tell me about Carnac and its rows of stones. She told me a good deal about the monoliths but the clarity of her speech was impeded by the caramels on which she sucked, having no teeth. And my attention wandered as I thought of my impending journey to the sea, so that as I listened I was considering how little luggage I could get along on for two weeks. The less I took the freer I would be to move about, for I had decided to view all the attractions that the Lorient area offered. My interest was aroused for the first time when the old lady brought out a worn map of France and showed me how I could, en route to Lorient, get out at a stop on the way and make my way to Carnac along a branch line. I decided to remember this.

It was in this way that one chance mingled with another, and the decision that I had made to mingle a search for knowledge with my own pleasure deeply affected my peace of mind. Later that evening, carrying only the smallest of suitcases, I boarded the train at the Quai d'Orsay. The porter cried out the numbers on the platforms, as only the French can shout, until the train began to glide forward past the rows of lamps, and with a light heart I leaned back in my seat. I had a pipe and some black tobacco with me. I had learned this habit in France (together with other frivolous ones) and I had chosen a pipe because it was cheaper.

The train departed . . . but I never got to Lorient.

2

Having written these pages, I read them through slowly and carefully and was overcome by a sense of shock. From between those lines a stranger peered out at me, a stranger with a white student's cap upon his head, a serious, earnest face and quiet eyes. I dislike him, for he seems somehow better and happier than my present self. What reluctant envy and misguided sense of superiority has guided my pen as I have described that supposedly wretched creature.

From whence has this sense of hypocrisy and pretense drifted into my story? Still, longing has prompted these lines, longing for my former self who stepped into the bustle of the streets with all his senses attuned to and assimilating everything that he considered beautiful. He perished beneath piles of books, perished that undetected day when I began to be more considerate of myself than of others and was no longer ashamed of it. Should I really envy him?

Having read, I respected writers the more for their fruitless pains. At the same time I wondered at their ability, for normally they are quite satisfied with the result of their work. When I try to describe that period, I feel as if I were ladling water with a net into a bottomless jug. I can read myself between the lines, but it is obviously impossible for a stranger to form a picture of that reality which glittered in my memories, avoiding the irritating yet alluring words. It is a blow to the self-esteem of a distinguished man when he has to admit his inability to describe so simple a thing as ordinary life.

And I stop once more. Again I rise from my books and walk out of the bright circle of lamplight and am astonished at the conflicting feelings that swirl in my mind.

For I am afraid. Of course it pains when the enveloped bullet is suddenly extracted from the organism. Yet this pain is annoyingly sweet to me, for it recalls all those things of which I have been ashamed, but without making me feel like a hollow, worm-eaten trunk, or a grave with yellowed bones. The pain is sweet for I have lived only once and had a brief youth, and even this came too late. And the fact that I have gained a solid reputation among the men of my profession, that I have achieved financial independence and established an agreeable routine for my life, all these have not overcome the blind irresponsibility of youth—although for my own peace of mind I may try to convince myself that they have. Yet I look at the past as at a dangerous abyss, and my mind is filled with the terrible thought—how different things might have been: and I feel a warm contentment that I was able to slip away from retribution for my lapse of willpower, as a fox to its hole. How illogical are a man's thoughts—a man considered wise by others —when they descend from the well-marked highway to the vague and muddy realms of the emotions.

I can still remember vividly that mild, starlit late summer night when the train sped through the warm, breathing countryside. Beside and opposite me sat a middle-class family. They had come well prepared for the journey with pillows and lunch baskets and did not mind partly undressing when the heat of the carriage became suffocating. I particularly remember the old grandmother, who had decked herself out in black lace frills and a cameo brooch and who ate ravenously with her bony fingers all throughout the journey, even while the others slept. She was eating as I put my head against my raincoat and shut my eyes in exhausted sleep amid the lulling roar of the train wheels. She was eating when the engine screeched harshly and I half opened my eyes. And she was eating when the white morning mist curtained the valleys between the low French hills and the train rushed along a high embankment at breakneck speed, as if fleeing the sunrise, and on toward the Atlantic. Her hollow cheeks champed steadily, her colorless lips chewed, her hair hung in grayish-yellow uncombed tresses upon her forehead. She ate and her stomach, beneath her black dress, was an unnaturally swollen dome. The red wine that she drank in careful little sips brought a faint flush to her cheeks with the morning. But even stronger is the recollection of the overpowering smell of garlic which arose from the broad, red-faced, bemustached father of the family as he snored.

I was too delighted at being on my way to allow any discomfort or trivial irritation to spoil things. On the contrary, even my unknown traveling companions aroused a special sense of enjoyment in me as I observed their sleeping faces—faces in which material satisfaction was reflected undisturbed by the least concern for the continuity and value of existence itself. Sleep revealed their mental defenselessness with pitiful clarity and the only thing that disturbed my benign superiority was that eternal grandmother, aged, bony and yellow yet indefatigably tough, who continued to enjoy the good things of life, sucking away at a cold chicken wing. Around her I weaved sleepy reveries concerning the links between the spiritual and the material, until, after I had fallen into a restless sleep, she merged in my dreams with some horrible ghoul who crunched lost souls in the pale twilight of the underworld. Even when I had descended from the carriage I thought of her with mingled terror and respect.

But before that there lingers among my memories one picture whose cold fresh charm still makes me smile. It was very early in the morning, and most of us in the carriage were asleep when the train stopped at a small station that was just waking to the bustle of morning. For the life of me I can't remember its name but it had a bright red-brown roof and its walls were covered with creepers whose leaves already foreshadowed the colors of autumn. A window upstairs was open and from it a brown-eyed French girl looked out sleepily, her elbows resting on the sill. Her cheeks were round and there was a lovely softness to her brown skin. She was young. She had just awakened and she regarded the early-morning train with curious inquiry, while unconscious allure and a wordless joy of living shone in her eyes. I could not help thinking that she looked directly at me and when the train moved off and she waved a brown arm to me, I was limp with delight. Youth had greeted me in the French morning—me, who had never experienced youth—and recovering from my first surprise, my mind occupied itself with wild hopes of adventure which made me strong enough to laugh off all warnings, and even rendered those notebooks (which I had so industriously filled and now had left, to await my return, in a plywood box in a stair cupboard of my hotel), it even reduced those to the status of so much blank paper.

Just as most men who work with their minds must concentrate constantly, so that even when eating they seem to be impatiently working at some mental puzzle, so did I know little of the small material pleasures that life could offer. When I sawed away absentmindedly at a half-raw cutlet, or in the hot summer sniffed suspiciously at a meatball that the menu heralded by the proud name of "*croquet de porc,*" usually I was untroubled by any suspicion that things could be otherwise, nor did I envy the wealthy who could enjoy a dinner which cost as much as twelve francs (and included wine).

So when I stepped from the train and daylight made the light morning mist golden in the hollows and valleys, I was surprised to realize how indescribably delicious was the steaming coffee and hot milk and the piece of coarse gray bread that went with it at the railway station. A pat of cold butter spoke to me of meadows and fields ripening in the sun and I realized that the proud and saltless butter of the city was quite artificial and lifeless. After the restless night my limbs, which had grown stiff on the uncomfortable wooden seat, relaxed, regained their full capacity—or better, a greater strength that I had not felt in the city. It was as if this country butter and bread had given me a store of energy that I had not before guessed existed.

My spirits fell a little as I stepped into the half-empty local train in which I was to travel to Carnac. In the small compartment a few farmers' wives squatted forlornly in their faded skirts. They spoke a language of which, to my astonishment, I understood not a single word. Their mouths were as tightly shut as a money-box and their eyes were the same impersonal color as the rugged gray rocks past which the train now labored. They carried baskets of vegetables which they guarded jealously beneath the protection of their striped skirts, and one of them had bound a bunch of chickens by their feet and hung them from a clothes peg beside her head.

From the dust-smeared window I looked out upon a curiously brooding landscape. The sun beat upon it fiercely from a sky that was wide and blue. But this landscape with its white hills and rugged slopes and its tiny, insignificant plots of land was, despite the light and sunshine, filled with a strange melancholy and secret grief. The white plaster houses were small, and the men who paused before them in their dented slouch hats and earth-gray clothes regarded the train without stirring, and remained unmoving long after the train had passed. Even then there seemed something strange about those motionless figures, but it was only later that I noticed that there were only old people and children around these small farms, and it was this that caused their helpless sadness and silent waiting. The sea had taken the young men, and pasted on the station walls were splendid posters recruiting regulars for the French colonial army from this poor land with promises of lavish enlistment bonuses.

A smothered cackle from the window startled me and I turned around. Only then did I notice that the chickens which hung from a clothes peg, their legs bound together and their heads dangling lifelessly, were in fact alive. A couple of loose feathers floated down onto the bench. Then the chickens flopped down again and their eyelids hooded-over their red-rimmed eyes. No one else looked at them—only I, the foreigner—separated from the others by a silent and suspicious hostility. The peasant women continued their low chattering in their forgotten tongue. The hardness of their mouths and their smooth, unlined, thin faces made me think of the harsh, broken mountains from which their eyes had got their color.

They continued their journey by the little train, on to the tip of Cape Quiberon which pushed its way out from the shore, and I forgot the chickens as I stepped from the train onto the platform of the tiny station of Carnac. I walked along the unpaved road with my case in my hand and my raincoat over my arm. I passed some newly built houses which rose detached amidst their spacious, as yet uncultivated gardens. I passed a service station and I stood in the tiny marketplace of the little town, which was fringed around with buildings blackened by age and clustered tightly together. I asked the way and walked uphill to a little tavern which looked out from beneath its inn sign like a spider from its black lair, a tobacconist's shop that possessed a door, and behind it, between two houses, a filled hole. Suddenly I was on a raised bank and far off on the outskirts of the town, I could see the ocean, dimly—like a blue cloud. I looked at the Atlantic for the first time in my life and took a deep breath. Behind the gently sloping valley lay a grove of low pine trees and beyond these rose the giant mound—Mont St. Michel, the ancient tomb. A small chapel stood on its summit, its melancholy silhouette standing out clearly against the background of sky and distant sea. Far off, standing apart from the rest, rose a great hotel which had been built for rich tourists who came to see Carnac and its relics.

It was, therefore, not for me and soon I was standing in front of the hotel where I was to stay—a hotel which, according to the advertisements, combined excellent cooking, spacious rooms and comfortable beds with reasonable prices. I had already been attracted in advance by these promises and I walked quickly through the angrily creaking gate.

The steps leading upstairs almost filled the hall, which was drably furnished with a brown wooden chair and bare table, with a timetable of the local buses and trains stuck to the wall with pins. There were also two postcards. One of them displayed a blue-striped cat, the other a dog of a violent red color. Looking through the open side door I formed an impression of the spaciousness of the public dining room, and the courage that had sustained me until now sagged a little.

The tall woman who welcomed me combined a motherly friendliness with a sureness of bearing and a firmness that impressed me deeply. When she noticed my shy enthusiasm she promised me the most comfortable and peaceful of her rooms, *petit déjeuner* and two meals a day, all at the very reasonable rate of twenty-five francs a day. (This was apart from attentive service, which would be assessed separately and for which a small sum would be added to the bill.) She crushed the last shred of my hesitation like rubbish beneath her heel and firmly pushed a registration slip and a bottle of coagulated ink toward me. I took the pen and with some difficulty (for the nib was rusty), I wrote down my birth date, the fact that I was single, my profession, religion, and nationality.

After this she led me in her motherly fashion to my room. It was well lit and the window was protected by a screen. The wooden floor was unpainted and polished and the bed was raised a step higher than the rest of the room, and this immediately made me feel both sleepy and at home. The rough sheets and soft eiderdown soothed my travel-fretted body. Above, on the wall, there was a colored lithograph in a thin gilt frame—a picture of the Virgin Mary and the Child. I remember vaguely, as I sank into sleep with the sound of bells tolling in my ears, trying to think what could possibly have made the printer choose purple for the Child's body. The color worried me until I realized that no doubt the pious painter had thought that the Child was cold in the straw of its crib that Christmas night, and so I fell peacefully asleep.

Around about lunchtime I was awakened by a pale-faced, dark-eyed girl who knocked upon my door. Her hands were rough, her body like an ironing board covered with clothes. When she had set a jug of water on the floor, she stopped to ask me in her strange dialect if there was anything else I needed. I could see her in the mirror smiling curiously at my back and I lost all the confidence with which I had tried so hard to cloak myself. I attempted to smile and replied that I was perfectly satisfied.

The dining room was swarming with a crowd of noisy people, all of them French, all of rather sturdy build and with cheerful red faces, and of course with countless children. Their noses were all peeling as a result of too much sun, and they were all screaming loudly. Fortunately Madame took me under her wing and steered me to the head of the quietest table, from where my eyes occasionally caught the dewy glance of some healthy mother. Sitting opposite me was a gentleman with a gray mustache and a watch chain from which dangled a fine collection of implements, ranging from a small compass to a pocket knife and a toothpick. He offered me some bread from the wicker basket that lay between us and remarked politely that it was beautiful weather and that the water was warm. At dessert he leaned confidentially toward me and told me that he had already been swimming, although the best time to go was between two and four o'clock in the afternoon when the tide was in.

The food was plentiful and good. With reckless courage I took a handful of mussels from the bottom of the pot. Their shells had opened invitingly in the cooking and the insides had shrunk. They had in them the salty taste of the sea and were extremely good.

Why do I linger over such insignificant trifles? Why do I see them so clearly? Why do I smile at them, although then I did not see anything in them at which to smile? Why does tenderness lap like warm water upon my mind? Perhaps it is because I can no longer sit in a gloomy dining room, with perfect strangers for neighbors, without becoming irritated. My stomach would find fault with the food and I should want to strike the ill-mannered children. The eiderdown upon my bed would suffocate me and I should distrustfully examine each bill to see just how badly they were trying to cheat me.

Oh! youth (even a late one), in all your goodness, in all your gullibility! You were always pleased that they waited on you solicitously at the table and that the cider bottle beside your plate was never empty. You thought you read sympathy in the searching looks cast upon you, though it was but pity, for you were only a fool of a foreigner who came to look at the gray ruins on the dry moors and agreed unprotestingly to pay ten francs more than the regulars for your board and lodging. Only later can you perceive the whispering and headshaking that then you could not understand as you walked along so carefree. But let this be your solace—that you came from afar and that you were happy. They came from just around the corner, quarreled more often than they laughed, grieved over every centime lost and were so certain that they were shrewder than you. In this they were of course quite correct.

3

Now that for the first time I was eating in a strange place, I felt at once shy and daring and I boldly swallowed the yellowish cider, a full bottle of which had been put before me. The taste of this cheap wine still reminds me of those fine days, for, not wanting to waste anything, I conscientiously drained my bottle and, when the meal was finished, strode out with a tinkling of little silver bells in my ears, while my feet wondered why the steady floorboards should be swaying quietly, and my mind became obsessed with a longing to jog my elbow into the stomach of the fat man who stood cleaning his mustache with a napkin. I was so unused to wine that I only realized that the cider was to blame for my condition when the sun outside fastened its fierce rays upon me and my clothes began to weigh unpleasantly upon my hot body. But in no way discouraged, I lit my pipe and slowly inhaling the smoke of the black tobacco began to walk along the dusty road toward Carnac and its rows of monoliths. My neighbor with the gray mustache, the decorations on his watch chain jingling, hurried after me to inform me in agitated tones that I had taken the wrong road. The beach was a mile off in the opposite direction. I told him that I was going to see the monoliths at Carnac for which purpose I had undertaken my long and difficult journey here. He remained standing on the path, staring after me and shaking his head in amazement. Various other guests who had finished their meal came to the hotel door to have a look at me as I strode off along the hot road, the smoke of my black tobacco trailing behind me. They gazed after me and spread their hands helplessly as if to disclaim all responsibility, and to assure the heavens that in no way did they aim to be their brother's keeper. But the moment was a decisive one, for after that I most definitely occupied a category all my own. I had a stripe to my coat like a jungle tiger, and on the beach, mothers promptly removed their children when I appeared.

It was the hottest time of the day. The low hills, upon whose slopes the parched grass and moss had been bleached by fierce sun, spread out on both sides of the road. On my right was a large ancient mound topped by a small chapel. I passed a couple of tiny narrow houses that lay silent in the heat of the day. I stopped to examine a large ancient grave that stood in the middle of a sloping field. A broken circle of gray, upright stones surrounded a flat boulder that lay upon a stone support. It was like a sturdy stone table which some unconventional nature lover might place in the coffee nook of his garden to the annoyance of his wife and the discomfort of his friends. My cider-clouded brain found it impossible to conceive that this was the tomb of some long-dead, illustrious ancient whose resting place lay by the mighty royal grave of Mont. St. Michel. There were scores of graves in the vicinity and each year still more were discovered as these barren slopes came under the plow. Slabs from them were bricked into the walls of the houses or used as cornerstones for steps, and broken bits of dishes as well as carefully fashioned weapons had also been found.

I continued my journey, and gradually the sweat began to trickle down my forehead and drenched my shirt, although I had taken off my jacket and carried it over my arm. The country with its low hills gradually induced in my mind a melancholy whose origin I was unable to comprehend—as if the burning sun was something inessential and ephemeral; as if it had become bored with the sky that arched above and had been reduced to sulking angrily by itself. I longed for the song of a bird, for some sign of life, for a burst of sound, but I was the only living creature upon the dusty road and when the effect of the cider had worn off, I began to be aware of this well-trodden ground which, for reasons unknown to us, had been holy so many centuries ago. One could imagine pilgrims wandering to this place in the dawn of history to perform forgotten rites.

Near the crossroads, where the road and a few gray buildings cut across the gray rows of monoliths, a group of tousled-haired and untidy children came toward me, staring at me with watchful and suspicious eyes. As they approached, they stopped in a half-circle around me and began to sing a flat, wordless, forbidding song in an incomprehensible language. All the time they were singing they stared at me from unblinking eyes set in reticent faces. When the song was over, their leader, a girl in a brown skirt, picked a white flower from the roadside and handed it to me with her dirty hand. It was a flower from whose thin stalk protruded burs that became enmeshed in the skin, a parasite that lived by twining itself around other plants and strangling them. Later I learned that it was considered to bring disaster and I no longer wondered why it had been so generously handed to me, the stranger from a distant country. I gave the girl a franc from my pocket, not knowing that this was a large sum for these poor regions where children were accustomed to worn and defaced copper coins and their thrifty parents used ancient sulphur matches whose heads crackled evilly when lit and burned with a blue flame, infecting the tobacco with a hellish smell. Unsmilingly, silently, they suddenly turned and ran off together to wherever they had come from, as though fleeing some unseen danger. I put the flower in my buttonhole and walked toward the monoliths.

They reared up from the sunburned landscape, unreal, unbelievable, row upon row, swelling upward and again sinking down with the rise and fall of the ground. Each consisted of one single upright stone slab. These were of all heights, from as low as two feet to gigantic blocks many feet tall. In their straight, regular lines they were like a field of giants or a file of threatening stone watchmen guarding the holy place.

I left the road and began to follow the line of stones whose gray sides had become warm in the sunshine. No breath of air

stirred, save for ripples caused by the heat, as I climbed along
the sloping ridge beside the giant stones. My shoes crunched
upon the moss that crackled with dryness, and thorny plants
from the barren moor stuck to me. I left the low pinewood with
its crested treetops and knobbly trunks behind as I walked at
ever-increasing speed until I was panting and hurrying past the
gray, motionless stones which lined both sides of my path. I no
longer counted them. The back of my shirt was sopping wet
before I at last reached the end of the row and found the main
road once again. Ahead in the distance across the road I could
see a park with luxuriant trees, a garden and the roof of a large
farmhouse.

I paused to catch my breath, and a crow flew cawing from
the top of a pine tree. Its cry and the sure movement of its wings
were like the greeting of a friend upon a dark road. For blackness was in my eyes and it was as if some indefinable unknown
terror rose from the bowels of the earth. Those stone slabs,
erected by the hand of man so long ago for unknown reasons and
with such enormous difficulty, were too tremendous, too incomprehensible. The glaring sunshine must have been too much for
me after my heavy meal, for the sight of this timeless stone
landscape so overwhelmed me that I felt exhausted.

As I rested I tried vainly to dispel that strange depression and
the sense of insignificance this spectacle had created in my
mind. The sun shone fiercely and a bitter scent rose from the
thorny herbs on the moor. The flower in my buttonhole had
already wilted, so I threw it away and, resolving not to let a
desire that I identified as mere laziness get the better of me,
decided not to return to the hotel but to continue my journey
to Lorient as I had planned. I began to walk on, following my
map, and after a half mile discovered the beginning of another
row of stones.

As I walked I began to feel better—so much so that I began
to whistle, although I have no ear for music. The landscape
with its thorny plants, its red-tinged moor, pinewoods and low
hills remained the same, maintaining a monotonous aspect that
was depressing, poor and melancholy despite the brightness and
warmth of the day. When once one had viewed it one felt that

one had always known it, but at the same time it was a landscape that one could never forget. Even today I occasionally awake at night with the agonizing feeling of having strayed in my sleep onto the endless sun-baked moors of Brittany.

There was not a soul to be seen. All was stillness around me save for the whir of insects in the sere yellow grass which somehow gave me a sense of safety. Soon I found another monolith zone. Its stones were not so big as the first one's and only here and there did a boulder rise so high above my head as to impress me with its enormity. Generally their tops came only to my chest, and as I walked between them I looked for the blue of the sea to refresh myself. My view of the sea was, however, blocked in all directions and becoming tired of walking, I began to feel dull and apathetic.

I stopped suddenly and breathed deeply and my heart skipped a beat before beginning to hammer frighteningly. For the sight that greeted my blurred eyes was as unreal in this sun-blasted landscape as were those endless rows of monoliths. On the top of a hill, just a few yards away from me, a girl was lying on a blanket which she had spread out on the ground. She was obviously sunbathing, for she wore only a faded light blue swimming suit and she lay on her back with her eyes closed and her hands clasped beneath her head. Her gracefully rounded limbs were a warm, evenly tanned brown. She had pinned a reddish piece of gauze over her hair and her swimming suit was open at the top. In the flash of an eyelid I had turned my stupefied gaze away as the blood rushed to my face. I was so embarrassed that I stood as if petrified, unable to take a step, and although I looked away, that lightning snapshot against the brown landscape still burned before my eyes. Out of the corner of one eye I saw the girl still lying motionless, her eyes shut. I made up my mind quickly and turned so as to pass without disturbing her. At the same moment she sat up, pulled up her costume and remained embarrassedly clutching it in both hands against her breasts. Her eyes—as blue as the sea—flashed open and from her mouth came a scream of fright.

"Oh!" she cried. "Daddy! Daddy!"

Then I broke blindly into a run, my face blazing with shame, and my forehead crashed against the hard, rough side of one of the stones. Lightning flashed before my eyes and the skin was scraped from my palms. Desperately striving to retain consciousness, I fell into a clump of heather.

The girl cried out once more but I heard her only as if from behind a thick wall. When I opened my smarting eyes an elderly man with a shapeless cloth hat upon his head was walking toward me. Despite the heat he was impeccably dressed. In his hands he had a number of maps and diagrams and his expression was one of annoyance. But when he saw my wretched state and the blood trickling from a scratch on my forehead and falling onto the bridge of my nose, he exhibited some slight sympathy.

"Are you hurt, sir?" he asked in a comparatively friendly tone and with a poor French accent that made me think he must be German. "My daughter gave you a start. She is a naughty child. She saw you all the while."

The girl had risen and stood by her father's side, obviously fully aware of the charming picture she created. For a second she spoke sharply in a language that was familiar, although I could not understand it. Later I learned that it was Dutch. Then she fell on her knees beside me and took my head in her hands.

"Don't believe Father," she protested, "I wasn't looking at you, as he claims. I had fallen asleep and was frightened when I saw you."

She seemed flushed and looked away, but instinctively I knew that in spite of all this she was looking at my face and maliciously enjoying my embarrassment. My head was still throbbing and with trembling hands I took a handkerchief from my pocket to wipe the blood off my face. My hands smarted as if on fire, but I could not resist looking at the tanned neck and lovely face before me. Her hands still held my head and the touch of a strange female creature was such an undreamed of surprise to my senses that my memories of this first meeting remain incoherent and confused.

Her father said something to her in a scolding tone. The girl tossed her head rebelliously, so that the scarf wound around her head blurred my eyes against the background of brown moor and gray stones. She looked at me through half-open eyes that hinted at some sort of secret, shared understanding. The most attractive wrinkles appeared at the corners of her eyes when she smiled—she was up to tricks of this sort—and these emphasized the youthful charm and softness of her face. Dutifully she took the handkerchief from my hand and began to wipe my forehead with it and in doing so, caused me more pain than I wanted. She bent over me and the warm, brown skin of her neck was level with my eyes, so that by moving slightly I could have touched it with my lips. She smelled of lotion and sunshine. Of course, sunshine has no smell, but when it shines on plants or when it melts the snow, even the untrained nose can easily distinguish an extraordinary scent, at once disembodied and earthy. And it is this scent that I have always connected with a beautiful girl's skin.

Although she was needlessly heavy-handed, the pain her fingers caused on my forehead was bearable because of her nearness. At last she released me and carelessly handed me back my bloody handkerchief. She rose and stood nonchalantly with her hand at her side and a vacant expression of indifference on her face. Her father swallowed nervously and, rustling the papers in his hands, turned toward me:

"My daughter is a child," he said. "I apologize for her poor behavior."

He turned and said something sharply to the girl in his own language. She stepped haughtily to one side so that I had the opportunity of viewing her back. It was bare to the waist. She stooped behind a high stone boulder to pick up her brightly colored robe and draped it casually over one shoulder, as if she had not the heart to hide both shoulders from the sun's rays.

The old gentleman had tipped his canvas hat back so as to see me better. Beneath his tufted eyebrows his eyes were hidden by a pair of yellow-tinted spectacles. Deep lines that spoke of dissatisfaction and ill-temper marred his face, and his thin lips stretched over protruding teeth, giving his mouth a tight, hard look. His skin was yellowish and dry and his general bearing gave no hint of any softness. It was as if his body were impervious to heat or cold. He had a stubborn idealist's face and a thin body upon which hung a badly wrinkled sun jacket. When he rolled up his papers I saw that they were covered with drawings of the stone statues and a host of numerals. Presumably he was an archaeologist in quest of knowledge, and his daughter was making use of the hottest part of the day to sunbathe in a place that drew no visitors.

In any case, he fired a series of profound questions at me, without bothering to wait for my answers to any of them. Was I a foreigner? From what country? Was this my first visit to Carnac? Just passing through? Was I an archaeologist? Had I any theory about the stones?

This last question was fatal, for in trying to prolong the conversation (quite contrary to my usual habit), I chanced to mention the solar theory I had come across while glancing through some reference book. The divergent rows of stones were observation lines by means of which ancient man determined, from the position of the sun, the proper times for the sowing and harvesting, as well as the summer and winter solstices. I had not tried to digest this theory properly, still less to consider its veracity: but like a parrot I babbled forth such bits as I could recall, and in doing so must have put my foot in it, for the old man did not allow me to finish.

"Rubbish, nonsense," he burst out. His face flushed and from behind his yellow-tinted glasses his eyes glared at me. Then he turned on his heel, pointed commandingly to his daughter and said over his shoulder: "Good day to you, sir."

With quick strides he set off among the stones in the direction from which he had come. His daughter followed him, glancing mockingly at me as she went. I gloomily raised my cap and half bowed in farewell, but the girl tilted her chin haughtily and did not even bother to nod good-bye. The abrupt end to the conversation surprised me nearly as much as the meeting which had led to it and I stood there, my cap in my hand, feeling painfully helpless.

When I had recovered my aplomb, I resolved to do the only thing possible in such circumstances. I bit my teeth upon the thought that I had no reason to worry myself as to what people thought of me, especially as I should probably never encounter

them again. Some distance off the silent rows of stones ended
and I saw houses once more. The country grew more luxuriant,
and the smell of the sea was wafted to my nostrils as I followed
my map and discovered a third row of stones. When this too
came to an end I was very close to the sea and after a mile or so,
I came upon numerous houses and reached the lovely seaside
town where the Atlantic's dark waves broke with a roar at my
feet upon the rocky cliff.

And still I pressed on along the shore road past the quiet
green shuttered houses. Soon I spotted a giant monolith, bits of
which lay shattered at the brink of the precipice. Once, in ancient times, it had been more than twenty-five feet high, rival-
ing the obelisks of Egypt and I could only imagine how difficult
it had been to erect it with the primitive tools that the men of
the Stone Age possessed. Gray and immovable, it had stood for a
thousand or two years upon its lonely precipice, guarding the
desolate shores of Brittany. The ocean was calm beneath a cloudless blue sky, but in spite of this the unseen waves broke with a
roar upon the precipitous dark cliff wall, dashing foam many
feet in the air. The wind from the sea was cool upon my face,
for the walk had made me warm. The sea fused with the endless
sky, so that there was no precise horizon. Two black fishing
boats with muddy-red sails hovered close to the shore. This was
the first time I had seen the ocean from so close and the first
time I had seen red sails on the sea, and the experience was so
moving that I felt I had to press my hands against my chest,
and I forgot the painful interlude on the moor.

For it had remained irritatingly in my memory all during my
walk, no matter how I had tried to think of other things, and
my brain had already composed various word-spells and jovial
remarks with which I could have saved the situation. Now I
forgot all else and when I saw the red sails, the ocean, the fallen
monolith, I understood the wordless melancholy reflected in the
lonely song the children had sung in an unknown language by
the roadside. The red sails of the fishing boats seemed to capture
the joy that dwelled in the rays of the warm sun, my palms still
smarted, and it was as if this first, thrilling sight had instantly
drained me of all receptibility so that I was inert and without a

will of my own. So as I walked back along the cliff road, I looked only distractedly at the great lobsters that crawled among the flat rocks and seaweed at the foot of the sloping precipice. By the side of the neatly paved road that led to Carnac I saw an age-darkened inn sign. I was extremely thirsty after my walk and I stepped inside.

Rough sleeves had leaned upon the wooden counter for a score of years, leaving it worn and polished. Behind it presided an emaciated woman whose sole glory seemed to be the golden earrings that pierced her ears. Without fuss she poured some cold white wine into a large glass and advised me to dilute it with seltzer from the syphon. I humbly followed her advice. The tasteless effervescent water mingled with the fresh taste of the white wine, and the resultant drink seemed so excellent to my parched throat that I asked for another glass. Slightly giddy, I then left the cool room for the hot sunbaked road. After less than an hour's hard walk I arrived back in Carnac, the sweat running from my face in great drops and my knees trembling.

4

At dinner, the man with the gray mustache peered at me furtively and embarrassedly fingered the mother-of-pearl penknife that dangled from his watch chain before braving the remark that it was still a fine day and would probably be no worse tomorrow. He was obviously greatly relieved when I consented to agree with him and, feeling better, he dipped his bean pods in the melted butter and shoveled them under his mustache with his fingers.

After dinner I walked down to the low pine trees and the tiny villas that bordered the road by the shore. The beach was already cool and deserted. Some bathing huts stood on the sand. Toward evening the sun setting on the horizon created an impression of loneliness, so that I no longer wanted to swim. The sea was too immense and my own shadow fell too tall and frightening beside me on the cold sand. Great purple patches floated across the surface of the sea, and I understood why the people who lived on this shore were so silent and still believed in a great profusion of magicians and witches and vanishing islands.

It was growing dark as I returned home. The pine wood and the needle-sharp sea grass that grew in the sand smelled warm and the ancient tomb of Mont St. Michel rose darkly toward the sky before me. On its summit the raised chapel seemed pathetically small against the shining gold and ever-changing sky. I sat on a stone and time passed. I could hardly distinguish the path beneath my feet when I climbed to the ancient tomb on the hill and watched dusk fall over the landscape. To one side were the roofs and light walls of the little town. The darkling sea jointly ruled the landscape with the sky. Far off the pinpoint of Quiberon lighthouse could be seen upon the tip of the rocky cape. The stars shone above my head, somewhere a dog howled, I was alone; beneath my feet lay the royal grave of some primitive people, and suddenly a causeless, violent excitement seized my mind, so that I wanted to throw myself upon the still-warm grass or shout aloud with all the strength of my lungs. Why was the world so big, time so endless, man so small? The fires had died, the pots broken, the campsite and the chips of clay buried beneath the earth, and indifferent peasants had raised the cover stones of the graves as cornerpieces for their poor houses.

When I had calmed myself, I became ashamed and regretted surrendering to this rash agitation. I had already firmed my understanding of life and men, and I had no doubt that as far as their own feelings were concerned, people were able to create proven, eternal norms as a basis for their actions. This, however, presupposed a peace of mind and a dispassionate calm which, as regards myself, I felt to be on a very shaky basis. Let joy and peaceful exaltation be granted to the wise also, but blind rejoicing and wild dissatisfaction were precarious and dangerous when noticed in oneself. Who was I to beat my fists upon these stone-statutes, demanding that they spring to life and reveal their wisdom? And all because of a momentary whim.

Instead I would remain here for some days to discover something about Carnac and familiarize myself with the different theories about the origin of the stones. The folklore of Brittany could provide much that was interesting and even a slight acquaintance with archaeology would strengthen my general education. It is the noble privilege of a thinking man, indeed it is a duty, to aspire to continually increase his knowledge and his recognition of the living connection between the new and the old. It is true that I was on holiday, that there was a fine beach here, that I had already been delighted with the food and the bed, and moreover that the price suited my pocket.

Besides, if I remained here it was possible that I might again meet the girl I had encountered that day by the stones, and would thus be able to dispel the poor impression that she must have acquired of me. The information that I intended to gather about Carnac would make easier an association with her father, who, as an investigator, could surely throw considerable light upon the riddle of the stones.

While I had been lost in my thoughts, I had also descended the hill. I walked in the starlight along a road that was only a bit lighter than the surrounding darkness and got back to the town. As I approached a little pond, the thought suddenly struck me like a punch below the heart that I had succeeded in erecting a formidable, indeed outwardly perfect, thought barrier—just to hide from myself the fact that the only thing that kept me here was my desire to meet the pretty scatterbrain I had chanced to see lying half-naked in the sunshine and who had caused me to take leave of my senses in the most ridiculous fashion and to such an extent that I had dashed my head against a stone and scraped the skin off my palms. I stopped suddenly. My breath caught in my throat and as the sound of my footsteps died away, I heard the croaking of frogs from the pond by the roadside. It was so loud and clear that I was quite startled before I realized what it was.

My frivolity, my foolishness in seeking to disguise the ridiculous impulse, was revealed in me. My face grew hot, but as I stood in the darkness, I imagined the girl's brown fingers pressing on my forehead. How beautiful she had been as she lay upon the moor, her eyes shut, the sun's rays caressing her warm brown skin, the faded blue swimming costume, the red scarf—a bright splash of color in the barrenness of this sterile land.

I was surprised to find myself enjoying frankly erotic thoughts. In the evening stillness the amorous croaking of the frogs resounded in my ears, and I angrily picked a stone from the ground and hurled it into the pool. The splash was echoed by a hundred gentle splashes. The croaking stopped abruptly and after a moment the last offended ripple died away. I needed quiet, for I had to settle accounts with myself.

But I felt as if what had happened had shaken some strange creature loose inside me. It was quite sullen, sulky and arbitrary as it thwarted all attempts at reproof and intelligent reasoning. It stubbornly assured me that I had found a fine place for my holiday; and as tediously as a politician seeking election, it repeated this argument despite whatever objections I sought to manufacture. With unbearable self-assurance it pointed out that I was after all my own master and that my ticket, which gave me the right to travel to Lorient, was only a rectangular piece of cardboard that did not imply a binding obligation. I was a stranger in a strange land with no one to question or criticize my actions should an innocent desire for company move me to make the acquaintance of new people.

Depressed and confused, I returned to the hotel and as I undressed it seemed that the purple Child in His mother's arms regarded me most scornfully from His place on the wall. I cursed my puritanical self, threw myself into bed, wrapped the eiderdown over my ears, and openly acknowledged my defeat. Having got to this point, the girl now proceeded to enter my dreams tantalizingly and saucily. I chased her from one stone statue to another with surprising agility, until at last I was swimming in the wonderfully warm sea, noticing through the indecently translucent water that her only covering was the reddish wisp of scarf she employed to keep her hair in place.

I awoke to a bright morning, my heart as light as a cloud floating in the sky. My hands no longer hurt and when I examined the scratch that still showed on my forehead in the mirror, I noticed that after one day's holiday my face was already burned red. No doubt both my flaming face and the restlessness which had afflicted me the previous evening were due to my lack of experience with the effects of the sun.

I had good luck in my archaeological research, for it turned out that there was a special local museum in Carnac—the new, white plaster building that I had mistaken for a dairy the day before. Inside its white rooms large collections of stone weapons, fragments of pottery, and small pieces of wood and bone sculpture were displayed in glass cases. There was an ox no bigger than my thumb, and women but inches tall with children in their arms. All were crudely sculpted, as if the primitive artist had tried to capture some vision he had seen but had realized his own lack of ability. Flint, stone and obsidian had been used for the finest and smoothest of knives and other pointed weapons. I spent (with a sigh) a whole forty-five francs of my precious holiday money on pamphlets about Carnac, and the porter began to look at me with a new and surprised respect. He even opened the door for me when I left and followed me with his eyes for quite a while, so I assumed that he must get a percentage on the book sales.

I chose a peaceful spot on the bank in the shade of the hotel wall, opened the paperbacked books and began to thumb through their pages. The green and white covers were dusty and bleached from years of sunshine. It was clear that a fantastic number of theories existed as to the meaning of the stones of Carnac and that these in turn had led to an equal number of violent scientific arguments. Historians, astronomers, geologists, agronomists, sailors, military men and men of religion had all wasted thousands of pages over the last decades attempting to prove their own theories. The religious historians read magical symbols in the stone rows. Astronomers and mathematicians convincingly argued the validity of the solar theory. Some sports enthusiast had developed the idea that they formed a sports track for prehistoric annual games. In short, I had in no time again entered the stimulating world of scientific thought.

I awoke with a guilty start to the sound of a gong, which rippling hollowly, summoned the guests to lunch. After the meal I walked lazily toward the beach with a book beneath my arm, attaching myself to the crowd of people moving in the same direction. The children's screams beat in my ears, as did their fathers' belabored puffing as they stopped every now and then to wipe the sweat from their hot faces and necks. The only bathing kit I had brought with me on my journey was a swimming suit, but as a bathrobe and beach shoes seemed a basic necessity of French social life, I had spent some of my francs (again with a sigh) upon a rough, white robe and a pair of straw-soled sandals.

The sand burned my feet. The sun beat down from a cloudless sky and the breeze from the dark green, heaving sea was cool upon the bare skin. The small beach was crowded with too tight swimming suits, swollen stomachs, solid arms, rubber swimming shoes, needlework, half-grown boys and drooping mustaches. But the children who played at the water's edge were the only ones who really went into the water, although occasionally a solid-thighed mother might carry her child down to the water's edge and, her eyes bright as pearls, might then splash her own arms and breasts with water and run, screaming at her daring, to the protecting sand. So when I stepped straight from my bathing hut into the water and began to swim, I aroused consternation. Glancing back, I saw the anxious watchers on the beach standing up to look at me. My gray-whiskered table companion shouted something after me. In a swimming suit and without his watch chain he was scraggy and not at all imposing.

I swam peacefully out to sea, my body rising and falling with the slow rhythm of the waves. The salt water tasted stronger, more bitter than I had remembered, and a joy of living and a carefree confidence filled my being. I swam long and far without considering the depth of the water below me, and my body become increasingly light as it floated easily upon the surface. A little out of breath, I returned at last to the shore. As I stepped out of the water I felt giddy and had the dreamy feeling that the whole beach was looking at me with eyes as big as saucers. Uncertainly I tried to keep my balance, found my bathrobe and stretched myself full length in the sunshine. Then the whole beach slipped back to rest and sighed with relief.

I had a book with me but the sun shone too brightly upon its pages and I could not concentrate. When I looked around furtively, I saw to my disappointment that she whom I sought was not to be seen. I had the feeling that I had been snubbed again and soon I imagined that the sun was too hot and since I did not want to get scorched, I went sadly into the hut to dress. My thoughts returned to my Lorient trip and in spite of all this dulling of my senses, I still had the gnawing feeling that I was being cheated.

As I walked miserably home, my pipe unlit in my mouth, considering how useless was the bathrobe under my arm, I saw the girl coming toward me. She came from a dilapidated villa beside the road which was surrounded by a broken-down nettle-covered fence. She was walking as if deep in thought and looking at the sky. She wore a short white skirt, her brown legs were bare and around her head was the reddish scarf, now tied on her forehead in an attractive bow. As she approached, I said hello and essayed a smile—a somewhat crooked one I fear, for my heart was pounding mercilessly. With a start she awoke from her reverie and looked at me with dark blue surprised eyes which reflected such a complete lack of recognition and such hurt indignation that it was like a slap in the face to me.

"I don't know you. What do you want?" she said and my cap slipped from my hands in astonishment and fell to the road. My face reddening, I stooped to pick it up from the ground, wiped the dust from it with my sleeve and could not for the life of me think of a thing to say. All the French I knew had suddenly blown away before that icy, dark blue glance.

"Susan, Susan," shouted the girl in an alarmingly loud voice to the old woman who appeared with a kitchen basket in her arms and a blue apron around her waist. "This man . . ." she continued accusingly, only to glance at me more closely and stop in the middle of the sentence. Suddenly a look of recognition and a surprised smile came over her face, which became bright as a mirror so that the stupidest person would have understood its words. "Oh, I'm so sorry," she said. "I didn't recognize you at first"; and turning toward the old woman in the blue apron she explained, "Susan, this is that foolish foreigner who banged his head on a stone as soon as he saw me yesterday. Is your forehead better?"

I stammered that there was nothing the matter with me and that I was sorry for what had happened yesterday. The girl was so obviously enjoying my embarrassment that I had the ominous feeling she had been making a fool of me the whole time. My amazement grew when with shy temerity she put her hand on my arm and said, "Susan, this is Mr.—Mr.—there now, I don't even remember your name. How forgetful I am."

She looked at me inquiringly, and almost beside myself, I stuttered my name. The girl repeated it critically and observed that it was not surprising that she had not remembered it.

"They have such strange names in his country, Susan," she said. "He lives far off in the North. They've got polar bears there—that's why he's so white, just like a polar bear."

For the life of me I could not comprehend this remark, for at the most she could only mean that I was not yet sufficiently sunburned, and she could only know this if she had seen me on the beach, and in that case why had she gone home and . . . ? My suspicious glance fell upon her white pleated skirt and then rose to her eyes. She bit her lip as if realizing that she had said something stupid, turned her eyes away from me and absentmindedly kicked at a fir cone that had fallen on the road. A guilty flush spread across her neck to her face and this too seemed to annoy her. I was able to read her expression as clearly as a mirror and my surprise grew.

In any case she had introduced me to her companion, and I quickly held out my hand to the blue-aproned Susan who stared and stared at her hand in surprise before taking mine. I shook it hastily. It was as hard as a board, and I released it as speedily as I had taken it. The girl laughed, her head tilted to one side.

"Susan is our housekeeper," she explained. "She came with us from Holland, but she doesn't like the French. Do you?"

To answer such a question demanded deliberation and concentration, so that I remained fumbling hopelessly for words, staring into the housekeeper's evil eyes, which peered suspiciously at the girl and myself in turn.

"You see, I don't like the French," said the girl volubly, trying to talk her way around the rebuke the housekeeper was obviously preparing to deliver. "At least not the French men. They're too small and dark, so oily, and they laugh too much."

While the girl was speaking, she looked at me appraisingly and seemed to become more and more surprised. She began to splutter and interrupted her explanation. "I'm sorry," she said, her eyes wide and filled with respectful astonishment. "I didn't mean it at all. I really am embarrassed."

At the same moment Susan burst into a shrill and rapid flow of words in which I could distinguish both Dutch and French. "What foolishness!" she seemed to be saying, while hinting at the imminent return of the girl's father and the punishment that would accompany it.

"Quite, Susan, you may go," said the girl. "I'll go and meet Father. Perhaps you would be kind enough to accompany me some of the way."

So saying, she tucked her hand boldly in my arm and began to walk me toward the town, waving good-bye with her other hand. The housekeeper growled, shook the vegetable basket on her arm in despair, and then went through the squeaking gate and along the gravel path to the villa. As soon as she had vanished from sight the girl pulled her hand from my arm as if it burned her and displayed an expression of cold distaste.

"Susan is unbearable," she said. "She watches over me like a child. I only introduced you to her so as to get rid of her. I'm fed up with this miserable place. I'm going to meet my father—that's why I asked you to come with me."

I took my courage in my hands and asked her if she had been in Carnac long. Generously she informed me that she had been here since the beginning of May. Her father had taken the villa so that he could carry out his research in peace. It was prostratingly dull here—as I had no doubt already noticed. She could not understand how anyone could stay here unless he had to. In Quiberon at least there was a restaurant where one could dance in the evening. Here there was nothing. Perhaps I was leaving soon, too?

As she said this, she fluttered her eyelids at me and her lips parted slightly so that I could see her small, sharp teeth. I told her that actually I was on my way to Lorient, but that I was enjoying my stay here and might not bother to go there at all. I ventured to ask whether her father was an archaeologist.

"He thinks he is," his daughter said scornfully. "He's a silly old man. He hasn't any academic qualifications at all. He used to have a big store near the Hague. But he doesn't look after the shop anymore. All he wants to do is investigate these stones and write a book about them. Our name's van Brooklyn—because my grandfather made a fortune in America. Mine's Josephine van Brooklyn, but Father calls me Fine. It sounds like a cognac, doesn't it?"

I said it sounded most attractive. Absentmindedly she put her hand on my arm again and led me down a side path through the pinewood which was filled with the warm scent of pine branches and of the sea. The air was clean to breathe and my feet moved as if I were sleepwalking.

"Anyway it tastes like cognac," insisted the girl and looked at me wide-eyed. "At least all the men who have loved me," she continued, lowering her eyelids yet watching my expression from beneath her brown eyelashes, "say it reminds them of the taste of cognac."

Again I had the feeling that someone had struck me in the stomach. "All the men who have l-l-loved you," I stammered. She snatched her arm away again, flushed, and stamped her foot.

"Oh!" she said. "Do you think I'm a child? Why wasn't I born in America? I shall be an actress, even though my father won't let me. He's a filthy Calvinist. It's only a question of time before I run away to the theater. Or I'll find him a guardian, because before long he'll be quite mad if he keeps on with his silly stones."

"I'm sorry," I stammered. "I'm sorry. I didn't realize, I mean, I didn't guess . . ."

How deceptive a face can be. At the most I would have put her age at eighteen, but when she looked at me now her eyes were bold and experienced, as if they were already a little weary of regarding men's weaknesses and passion's whims. Only her body was childlike, that and her round cheeks and soft skin.

"Do I really look like a child?" she demanded. "Do I really look like a child?"

The way she stood, the way she held her head, imitated adult worldliness and only the briefness of her skirt and her bare legs marred the effect. She laughed at my thunderstruck expression and again tucked her hand in my arm. "You must think me very bad," she said laughing, and for the first time I realized where I had heard that voice before, had watched those postures and expressions. In countless bad films.

"You deserve a spanking," I said without thinking. But my eyes still closely fixed on her face, her eyes and her bare arms, were so misty that every now and then I stumbled as I walked. Her expression changed again. She raised her thin eyebrows in inquiry and asked in mild wonder:

"I'm sorry, what did you say? I didn't understand. I don't know French that well."

"Nothing," I said quickly, "nothing at all." At the same instant her eyes swerved and fixed upon the foot of a pine tree; she shrieked in fright and instinctively fell into my arms, wrapping her arms around me and burying her face in my shoulder. I jumped too, but couldn't see anything beside the path except the needle-sharp dried grass and the distorted, reddish-yellow pine trunks.

When I asked what had frightened her, she raised her face but remained tightly against my body so that I had plenty of time to feel her tantalizing nearness. Shyly, her eyes still afraid, she looked to the sides of the road, slowly loosened her hands and leisurely released herself. But her face she kept turned away from me as if in shame.

"I was afraid," she said in a trembling voice. "I thought I saw something among the trees, something black that moved. But it was nothing. . . . I'm sorry."

I could not imagine what black and terrible thing she could possibly have imagined in these peaceful woods, where the sunlight cast shadows upon the sand and all that the listening ear could hear was the melancholy swish of the dying waves upon the seashore.

Sensing my suspicion, she turned quickly and said, "You still don't understand. Carnac is a terrible place. Even in broad daylight I'm afraid of those stones when Father goes to sketch them. It's as if the earth were alive and all sorts of evil powers lay hidden beneath." Something came into her mind and, becoming more cheerful, she asked, "Have you been to the tomb yet?"

I looked at her inquiringly and she explained that inside Mont St. Michel there were corridors and cells which one could visit any day for a small charge. A nun let the tourists in and collected the money for the chapel on the hilltop. At the same time she clasped my hand in her warm fingers and led me forward along the path at a run. Unresistingly, I followed her until I saw the giant tomb rising sheer ahead of us, sun-blackened and silent against the sky at the edge of the wood.

"But don't you have to meet your father?" I said, panting. "Perhaps he'll be angry. Will he be coming this way?"

"Oh," she replied carelessly, "he's not coming for a long time. He even forgets the time as soon as he's on the moor. Come on!"

In the side of the hill facing the sea there was a dark opening, as tiny as a mole's hole, which led to the tomb. A crude plank door was open and beside it a nun, in a broad black and white hood, sat with her needlework in her hands. The girl saluted her with an innocent curtsy, her eyes childishly wide, and I could not understand the suspicious, malevolent look on the nun's face as she examined first the girl and then myself. I examined myself cursorily, fearing there was something wrong with my clothes. The nun gave a sigh and crossed herself, then thrust a candle into my hand, lit it and bent to lead the way into the tomb.

The roof of the corridor near the opening was so low that I had to stoop as I walked. The air smelled of earth and damp stone and there was such a draft that I had to protect the candle flame with my free hand while the girl clung tightly to my coattails. The corridor was built of great upright boulders and the roof of wide slabs of stone. All the stones were uncut and there was no sign of masonry to be seen upon them. Then the corridor widened into a little cell in which one could almost stand upright. Inside, a smoky lamp spread a weak light, and the nun pointed silently to some stone articles that had been found in the tomb. The most valuable finds were in the museum, or perhaps it is better to say, the things that treasure seekers had left behind when they broke into the tomb perhaps many centuries ago.

The nun looked at the girl standing beside me and, sighing once more, she crossed herself. She was cold after the warm sunshine, so she remained in the central chamber when the girl led me into the darkness of a side corridor. There was another tiny cell whose roof, with its massive stone slabs, was blackened from the candle flames of many visitors. While I was looking at the wall, upon which I thought I saw a crude drawing cut into the stone (the carved stone sunboats in the museum had already attracted my indifferent attention), the girl's foot slipped. In trying to take hold of my hand to steady herself, she knocked the candle to the floor, so that the molten wax splattered scalding drops upon the back of my hand, and suddenly we were standing in pitch-darkness in the interior of the ancient tomb with the heavy smell of earth and damp stone around us.

"Oh," exclaimed the girl. But she said it quietly, almost in a whisper, and I imagined I sensed a small, strained laugh in her voice. The weight of two thousand years lay around us together with the chill of the grave, a chill that filled one with an idea of the fleeting nature of human life. But I was not thinking of the picture of the sunboat that I had imagined I had seen carved upon the stone wall. I was not thinking of the hope of eternity, of the tiny fluttering flame in the dawn of history: I was not even thinking of the great silence that enclosed us while the unthinking sun warmed the green surface of the giant hill far above our heads. I could think only of her nearness which sent unfamiliar ripples coursing through my body, as if I were in a dream, and indeed, I longed to sink into one—the only possible solace for my weariness, for my yearning. Then my hesitant mouth found her warm cheek and I squeezed her body clumsily. At first she struggled, then she went quite limp in my arms so that in my alarm I almost let her fall to the ground. She did not say anything, but her breast heaved against my own so that I began to shiver as if I were cold.

I had never experienced youth, and perhaps there was something symbolic in the fact that my first kiss took place in a two-thousand-year-old grave. It is only natural that a person who spends his life working with his mind among his books eventually becomes a stranger to what we call "real" life. But when I touched her lips for the first time and to my surprise they parted a bit, a dangerous power of whose existence I had no knowledge loosed itself within me and I knew that I could throw a flaming torch upon the dusty shelves of the most precious library or could willingly pile wood upon a witch's pyre, and Herostratos' deed no longer puzzled me. In the black darkness I kissed the girl's mocking mouth and felt her breast pressed tormentingly against mine, and the novel, wild ecstasy of that moment is beyond anything I have experienced since.

To her it probably did not mean what it did to me, for my violence surprised her and she began to fumble for the matches in my pocket. She easily freed herself from my arms, as if she were used to such things, and striking a match, picked up the candle from the floor and lit it.

"The candle went out," she said unnecessarily and without the least hint of emotion in her voice. "Come on."

By the candle's fluttering light I crawled back along the corridor to the tomb's entrance. The nun was seated once more at the unpainted wooden table. It was all I could do to stop my knees from knocking together and to avoid her eyes as she pointedly rattled the money-box. I put five francs in it—a large sum for me. Then I glanced at her guiltily, imagining that my flushed face and furtive look could leave no room for doubt in her eyes, which were bright as glass from fasting and privation. Disapproval and satisfaction mingled in her face, and I wondered if my sin were not indeed worth more than five francs. Perhaps she pleaded extenuating circumstances for me as I was a stranger to the district, and passed judgment on the girl—as is the custom of women. But the girl curtsied good-bye innocently and outwardly no signs of disorder were apparent. Not a strand of hair was out of place beneath the reddish scarf, and her breathing was quite normal. As we walked down the hill— at what was probably a suspiciously respectable distance from each other—the girl suddenly began to laugh.

"Fine," I stammered. "Fine."

Her laughter froze. She looked at me and said coldly, "I haven't given you permission to call me Fine. I'm not any pickup that you can call by her Christian name."

The words were like a jet of water upon my face. "Why did you laugh?" I asked, in a hurt and trembling voice.

Pleased with the effect of her words, she glanced at me and once again laughed lightly. "Oh, I'm not laughing at you this time," she said carelessly. "I wasn't even thinking of you. I was thinking of the nun. The poor creature doesn't realize that she's doomed to the fires of Hell. She doesn't even dare eat meat on Fridays, but she'll still go to Hell."

I looked at her in amazement.

"Don't you know?" she asked, obviously surprised at my stupidity. "Hell has already been predetermined for most people. Only a few get to Heaven and it doesn't depend on their actions, but only on God's choice. Ask Father, he can explain it to you."

"I wouldn't have guessed that you were religious, Miss van Brooklyn," I said stiffly.

"Ask Father," she insisted, absentmindedly pulling a stalk of grass from the ground and twisting it around her fingers. She said nothing more, and we walked on in silence. But her indifference quickly overcame all my powers of resistance, seeping like some fatal poison into my being and rendering my legs powerless.

"Fine," I said softly after a while. "Fine!"

She did not turn her head, did not even show that she had heard my whisper, but neither did she notice that once again I had used her Christian name without her permission.

"May I see you again?" I asked in a voice hoarse with emotion.

Without replying she walked on, twisting the stalk of grass in her fingers and staring at the sky, her bare legs very brown against her white skirt. I was annoyed and said no more although emotion ached in my chest. At last she awoke from her daydream and said, "I'm sorry. Did you say something?"

I didn't answer and she continued, "I didn't hear. I was thinking of something else."

Then I hated her so that I could have spanked her as I would any ill-mannered child. But I was powerless and instead walked sulkily on at her side until she stopped at the nettle-bordered gate of the villa.

The French families were returning from the beach in little chattering groups. Their faces were alarmingly sunburned, the fathers were obviously suffering from headaches, the mothers would feebly forbid their children to throw fir cones at the windows of the houses.

Fine van Brooklyn lolled lazily on the garden gate and stared at the pine tops while I stood mutely beside her, my cap held humbly in my hand. Now and then she unsmilingly responded to the greetings of the passersby and I jealously watched how hungrily and eagerly the French youths eyed my companion. Many of them seemed very handsome with their flashing brown eyes and smiling boyish faces. But Fine stood by my side, quite unattainable, regarding the sky above the pines and replying only occasionally and absentmindedly to some greeting or other. Only when the road emptied did she start and smile at me.

"Oh, how absentminded I am," she deplored. "I must go in. Good-bye."

"Good-bye," I answered and took the hand she held out to me. It was like a dead fish.

The gate creaked and she stepped onto the sandy path. Fatefully she was walking out of my life. Helplessly I stretched out my hands to detain her, although I could not utter a word. Then she suddenly touched the collar of her blouse and turned back to me in alarm.

"My brooch," she said. "I've dropped my brooch."

Still facing me, she drew down the side of her blouse and with her hand felt her breast, which gleamed whitely against her sunburned neck. She shook her head in bewilderment and looked at me. "It was a thin gold brooch with a pearl in it—do you remember? It must have fallen somewhere on the road or . . ." She broke off, avoided my eye and blushed. "I must go get it, but Father will be angry if I'm not at home when he returns." She looked at me so beseechingly that joy welled up inside me.

"I'll go and look for it, Miss van Brooklyn," I said hastily. "Don't worry. I'm sure I'll find it."

"How sweet you are," she whispered softly. "Good-bye." And as if made shy by this confession, she ran into the dilapidated villa, the boards of the veranda floor creaking threateningly beneath her feet.

When the last flash of her skirt had vanished I set out along the road we had walked, my temples throbbing and my eyes fixed eagerly on the ground. I found the place where she had fallen into my arms in fright, but there was no brooch to be seen. I walked on along the path, scrutinizing the ground so carefully that my eyes began to ache. The nun was still sitting at the mouth of the shaft, and she looked up from her needlework in friendly curiosity. In asking if I could enter, I thought it best to explain that Miss van Brooklyn had lost her brooch inside the tomb while we had been walking there. A guilty feeling came over me and I was unable to meet the nun's glass-bright gaze openly. To my surprise, however, her expression was amused as she regarded me compassionately and observed that Miss van Brooklyn had had no brooch on her blouse when she had entered the tomb. Nonetheless I asked to go in and she gave me a new candle. Stooping low I examined every inch of the hard trampled ground of the corridor, until I reached the tiny cell in which our candle had gone out. Amid the thousand-year-old smell of stone and mold, I again caught the scent of her skin, light as sunshine, and as the hot wax dripped upon my fingers I stood for a moment staring at the great stone wall, trying to recall her nearness in my mind.

I was alone in the rocky cell and ecstasy still lingered in quivering waves within my body—a sense of youthfulness that I had never before experienced. Wildly and agonizingly I felt a presentiment of the transitoriness of all sensual happiness and when the pulsing in my veins had quieted, the cold doom of the grave crept into my limbs and a discouraging emptiness into my heart. Mechanically I crouched, searching the hard earth floor in the fluttering light of the candle flame and finding nothing except solidified drops of wax. In my mind lingered the brownness of her neck, the whiteness of her breast where the pin shyly held the collar of her blouse, like a metal watchman at the door of virginity.

Exhausted and fed up with the search and with the ache behind my eyes, I crawled back to the plank door at the mouth of the cave—without Fine van Brooklyn's brooch. Silently I handed the remains of the candle to the nun, who prudently placed it in a cardboard box to be used again. She looked at me with her glass-bright colorless Brittany eyes that seemed to look unwaveringly into my innermost being.

"The lady did not have a brooch when she came," she persisted stubbornly. "The lady's recollection was faulty." How mockingly and deliberately she managed to say this. My mouth remained open while the nun, fingering the pearls of her rosary and still not looking at me, continued softly: "Miss van Brooklyn has an evil spirit within her. Her father is a dangerous heretic."

I shook my head as if to show that I did not understand what she meant. Again I walked along the road from start to finish, until overheated and angry, I stopped to rest. Against my will the nun's assurance began to gnaw at my mind like a wicked suspicion. Perhaps the girl really had not had her brooch with her. Perhaps she had made a mistake. The unnecessary bathrobe that I had carried around my shoulders all day like an idiot irritated me so that I would have liked to throw it away. But despite my suspicion, the brooch hung in my mind as a wonderful opportunity to continue our acquaintanceship, for it gave me another excuse to see the girl. So after dinner I returned to the shore though a rest with a book would have been welcome. I walked back and forth along the path, peering at the foot of every tree, kicking the cones from the path as if I imagined I would find the lost brooch beneath them. It was not until dusk that I abandoned this hopeless task and stopped on the stony road to stare gloomily at the dilapidated villa in which she lived. A light shone from a window and I imagined that I could see her shadow walking mockingly across the room. Stunned, I realized that she had made me run around like a clown all evening for nothing, that perhaps she had watched my vain search with secret amusement.

My neck was stiff, but I thrust my head back defiantly and marched back to town. I sat down on an iron bench in front of a little café in the marketplace, and ordered half a bottle of wine without considering the consequences. In my childish hurt I decided to drown my sorrows in the intoxicating juice of French grapes.

5

I had defiantly imagined getting up the next morning with a headache and a heavy conscience after the night's revelry, but to my surprise the sun shone as before and my clothes on the chair were in the same order in which I had punctiliously placed them the night before. A half bottle of wine had given me a deep and healthful sleep instead of my lying tossing about until daybreak, lacerated by love and remorse, as I should doubtless have done without its aid. I disapproved of myself, for this clearly showed how frivolously my feelings swung. I had always imagined I would take a serious, responsible attitude toward love when I found it, as befitted a thinking person.

Now, instead, the sun shone, my mind was alert and the feather eiderdown on top of me so wonderfully light and warm that, contrary to my usual custom, I lay in bed for a long while before rising to dress. I had always thought that lying in bed was a sinful laxity, but my moral sense had decayed and I looked at its ruins with a cold smile and without the least guilt.

For the first time in my life the attraction of evil struck me forcibly. How attractive it was to be bad, to be a person, for example, who had no scruples about drinking a bottle of wine of an evening, or who kissed a strange girl with sensual intent. As a child I had listened terrified as my mother told of people who had played cards in thunderstorms or who had sworn during Sunday church. Now I felt akin to them. The surprising thing was that this feeling awoke such a wild self-confidence in me that while still in bed, I began to plan how I could encounter Fine van Brooklyn and make her introduce me to her father.

The morning passed slowly but I tried to calm my impatience with the thought that I was like a hunter who lies in ambush unhurriedly waiting for his prey. When I came down to breakfast the motherly *patronne* asked me how I was enjoying my stay, and I was able to assure her with a clear conscience that I was enjoying life enormously and that I would probably remain for the whole of my holiday. Judging by the expression on her face this was a pleasant surprise for her, just as if she had found that she had the winning ticket in a lottery, and at table I was waited upon twice as attentively as before.

After the meal, I dutifully went to the beach and had a dip in the warm sea. But there was no sign of Fine van Brooklyn in her faded, skimpy swimming costume, and soon I found the beach too hot and bourgeois for me. I dressed, packed my things, and then smoked a pipe in the shade of the pines, my assurance diminishing minute by minute.

At last I went slowly to the road and stopped at that dilapidated villa, trying to force my paralyzed arm to lift the gate and open it. The gate creaked threateningly and scornfully in my ears, but I manfully closed it behind me, and avoiding a couple of rotten planks, made my way across the veranda to the door. I could not discover a doorbell, so I knocked as bravely as I could. I'm quite certain my knock was not loud, but in the stillness of the afternoon it startled me like a sudden thunderclap. In spite of this nothing happened. Not a sound could be heard within, though with the courage of despair I knocked again.

The house was of course deserted, but as I turned to go I instinctively pressed upon the doorknob and the door opened. It was unlocked. Without pausing to consider the correctness of my behavior I walked in and came to the empty hall. I coughed and turned to look through an open door into an ill-furnished living room.

There lay Fine van Brooklyn, resting on a worn settee. She was engrossed in reading a book which partly hid her face, but her position was so studiedly careless that I suspected her of following my military operations at the gate and on the veranda from the window. As she turned, her white skirt rose well above her bare brown knees and her hair hung down over her shoulders. The whole position evidenced an unconscious desire to charm, so that a more enterprising man than I would certainly have flung himself on the floor beside her and kissed those sunburned, attractive knees. Instead I stood thunderstruck, swallowing and not daring to look at her directly. At last I gave another cough.

She started realistically, the book fell from her hand and hastily she pulled down her skirt. "You! How dare you!" she exclaimed and leaped up with her hands clenched, so that I retreated a step and stammeringly attempted to explain.

"I thought I had better come and tell you I could not find your brooch."

"My brooch?" she echoed inquiringly. Then she understood. "Ah, yes, the brooch . . . I didn't have it with me after all. I'd left it on top of the chest-of-drawers. I'm sorry I troubled you for nothing."

Her shining dark blue eyes clearly gave me to understand that she had known this all along, and that my vain search had given her great amusement. But I did not get angry: I was no longer able to. I only stared hungrily at her voluptuous mouth, at those sharp child's teeth which yesterday I had felt against my lips and today was unable to forget. I stared at her stupidly, my cap in my hand, unable to say a word until she observed:

"Yes, it was very kind of you. Thank you for your trouble."

She could not have dismissed me more mockingly or more effectively. I turned like some exhausted wanderer before the gates of Paradise, and sorrow pressed upon my heart. I was leaving, never to return—that I swore to myself—when in quite a different tone of voice she said indifferently:

"Perhaps you would like to sit down for a while?"

I hardened the manhood that was left to me. "I'm afraid I'm
disturbing you, Miss van Brooklyn. I'm interrupting your reading."

She had come up to me, her forehead level with my chin,
and silently passed me the book. It was a French translation of
Hans Andersen's fairy tales. What a liar she was, right down to
the smallest detail.

"Please sit down," she said softly, as if my nearness had shattered her self-confidence. "I'm all alone in the house. You're
not disturbing me at all." This explanation was like an un-
spoken promise, timidly enticing and sweet. My eyes still held
her dark blue gaze; I sank into a chair by the wall, and then
proceeded to fall full length upon the floor. The chair leg was
broken.

She put her hand to her mouth in dismay and cried out
affectedly, "Oh, dear, I hope you haven't hurt yourself. Our
furniture is very poor and I'm sure that the landlord won't
have it mended."

I scrambled to my feet, my face red with indignation. But
once again I tried to beg for mercy. "You are cruel, Miss van
Brooklyn," I said, appealing humbly. "You're making a fool of
me."

Perhaps this moved her a little and made her feel sorry for
me, for she put both her hands around mine and led me to the
couch. There she remained standing beside me, her hands behind her back, and looked down at me in inquiry. Her hair
hung in reddish waves. "Am I cruel?" she echoed thoughtfully. "But why should I be cruel? What do you want from
me? What sort of person do you think I am?"

Her ability to disarm me made me miserable and I avoided
her gaze, hanging my head like a sulking child. Then I made
a confession for which I can only account by emphasizing my
complete inexperience, and to understand which one must
bear in mind that only the day before had my senses been
awakened for the first time. Besides, such words came easier in
French than in my own tongue.

"Miss van Brooklyn," I said. "Fine, I love you. I love you so I
could die. . . ."

When I had said this I was so embarrassed that I hung my head so as not to have to look at her. An ignoble thought flashed across my mind—had I not drunk so much cider with my breakfast, this scene would never have taken place—just as we always seek to invent excuses to cover our mistakes. The silence seemed to last an eternity. Then she put her hand on my forehead and gently stroked my hair.

"My poor friend," she said, her voice redolent with the experience of a woman of the world. "My poor friend!"

When I raised my head, her eyes drew me as a gray butterfly is drawn to a candle flame and crippled. Still seated, I put my hand on her waist fearfully and drew her nearer until I was able to press my face against her breast, or more correctly, her stomach. I felt her body trembling as if she were crying and this so moved me that my throat grew tight. I do not know for how long we stayed in that uncomfortable position but at last she carefully loosened my arm from her waist and sat down beside me.

"You can't be speaking the truth," she said. "You can't really mean what you say. You think I'm just an inexperienced girl whom you can get around with fine talk. You're taking advantage of my friendship."

These reproaches pricked my heart and I once again assured her vehemently that I loved her, as well as saying other rash things which shame prevents my repeating.

"Can I really believe you?" she whispered softly and continued to stare dreamily at the ceiling, upon whose paper surface the rain had left brown-edged spots. Her face was so close that I could smell her perfume and my abashed eyes caught a glimpse of her white breast beneath her blouse.

I tried to squeeze her in my arms and kiss her but she pushed against my chest and her mouth evaded my lips. "No, no!" she said weakly. "You mustn't." And to her unspeakable surprise, like an ass I let go of her.

"I can't believe you really love me." To my regret she returned to a subject we had already dealt with. "Would you run away with me?" she asked. "Would you take me to Paris? Would you go hungry for me? Would you kill for me?"

I found these questions rather perplexing, for truth to tell I had not planned so far ahead and I saw no immediate reason why I should run off with her, let alone kill anyone.

"Aha! You hesitate!" she cried scornfully. "You're just talking nonsense. I hate you."

Her head sank into her hands and her shoulders began to shake. Alarmed, I lost my head and hastened to swear all sorts of vows—so wildly that I had no time even to wonder how easily they came to my usually tied tongue. I put my hand on her shoulders and vainly sought to draw her around, until suddenly she lifted her head, threw herself on my neck and burst out laughing.

"You're wonderful," she choked. "You're unbelievable. I shall die from laughing. You're just like a big polar bear. Kiss me, you fool."

Her persistent desire to populate my homeland with polar bears hurt me for my country's sake, but I did not think this a suitable moment for geographical explanations. She responded to my embrace and bit my neck so fiercely that passion began to blind my eyes. I kissed her cheek, her chin, her neck, and blushing, the breast which was bared beneath her blouse as she pressed against me. My senses began to live a life of their own quite beyond my reason, and my clouded eyes could see only her closed eyes and hot red-brown cheeks. Yet as I reached that point at which my inexperience fortunately barred the deed, she wrenched herself from my arms as suddenly as she had thrown herself into them, pushed away my uncertain hands and hit me across the ear with all her might.

"You scoundrel," she said bitterly. "How can you . . . Get out. Get out immediately. I never want to see you again!"

My ear rang from the force of the blow and my cheek smarted so that tears trickled from my eyes, while she, quickly adjusting her dress, turned her back upon me to hide the treacherous blush upon her cheeks.

"Didn't you hear me? Get out. . . ." she said in a weak voice, as if she were tired.

"All right," I said, my voice throbbing and tears in my eyes.

"All right, my love. I wouldn't hurt you for the world. I'll never behave like that again."

For it was up to me as a man to accept the responsibility, although it was she who had thrown herself on my neck; it was she who had responded to my embrace so willingly—at least insofar as I was able to judge such things. Perhaps she sought only to excuse herself, feeling ashamed of her passion, and I experienced a strong, masculine satisfaction from the blow that still rang in my ears, for it showed that I was able to arouse such feelings in a girl.

"Get out," she said once more in a faint voice and began to tidy her hair. I do not know how long this impasse would have continued, had I not suddenly and to my considerable alarm heard heavy steps upstairs.

"Aren't you alone?" I asked her, seized by the instinct of a trapped animal to flee through the first open door.

"Of course," she said innocently. "My father has been upstairs sleeping since lunch. He must have just waked up."

I had not even time to determine if my appearance was in order before Mr. van Brooklyn came in, his gray hair uncombed and his clothing rumpled. His gray eyes were sleepy as he examined me disapprovingly and glanced inquiringly at his daughter.

"Oh, Mr. Mr.—say the name yourself—well, he looked in on his way back from the beach to see how I was. He's very nice, Father."

There was not the least sign of agitation or hesitation in her innocent manner. On the contrary, as she spoke she smiled in a faintly superior way, as if her father and she had a clear preunderstanding of their own about me. A silence fell around us.

"Mr. van Brooklyn," I began despairingly, "I want to excuse myself for talking so foolishly about the solar theory when we met."

Did I really see the suspicion of a smile flit across the insensitive face of this stubborn idealist? "Aha," Mr. van Brooklyn said to his daughter, "so this young man has already discarded the solar theory. Why haven't you asked him to sit down, Fine?"

I didn't think that I ought to, Father," Fine van Brooklyn explained promptly, and for a second she rubbed her face against his rumpled sleeve as caressingly as a kitten. At the same time she looked at me, the secret understanding of shared deceit in her eyes. "Please sit down, sir."

Van Brooklyn sat down and lightly touched his knees, which rose sharply and visibly beneath his uncreased trousers. Then he dug out his spectacles, placed them on his narrow nose and examined me carefully.

"And what conclusion have you reached now, my friend?" he asked and tittered quietly to himself, rubbing the palms of his dry hands together. "I would enjoy hearing what you now think about these megalithic memorials. Presumably you also have an opinion as to the many-oared boat that is rowed upon the stone, beneath the eternal sun?"

"Father, Father," said Fine van Brooklyn hopelessly, sighing and settling down comfortably in a corner of the settee with her eyes shut and her hands crosswise upon her breast—that breast which only a few minutes ago my lips had kissed.

This disturbing memory muddled me, but by exerting all my self-control, I was able to pour out the information I had gathered during the last two mornings. However, perhaps I had not prepared my work sufficiently carefully, for van Brooklyn's expression became more and more cold and disagreeable.

At last he could not control himself any longer and interrupted me, banging his bony fist upon the windowsill fiercely: "Just what are you getting at, sir? Are you an archaeologist? Are you trying to steal my ideas?"

Violently I thrust this despicable suspicion aside. I was able to plead my own branch of science, a branch that had no connection with archaeology. Moreover, I was ashamed of the superficiality of my knowledge which would doubtlessly have made the true student laugh. But even a chance tourist could not avoid the impression that this ancient and sacred coast with its megalithic stones held one of mankind's most puzzling riddles in its soil.

While I was speaking, Mr. van Brooklyn examined me suspiciously but he seemed gradually to become mollified. He must now have thought that he had misinterpreted the expression on my face and my confusion, for the glance he turned on his daughter and then on me was only faintly scornful, and soon he sank into his own thoughts. The silence lasted for rather a long while before he stroked his dry forehead with his thin hand and uttered some words whose seriousness could not fail to have their effect upon me:

"Sir, this is a dangerous land. There is a lot of sorcery here. Emotion dims the eye of the seeker and then the demons seize him. Be careful, sir. The smoke of the sacrificial fire lies heavily over the land and the protecting chapel on St. Michel's ridge has existed for but a fleeting moment in the stream of centuries. Remain a summer visitor, young man. Remain a tourist who comes today and departs tomorrow to tell at home of the strange stone statues and to have his photo taken at the foot of a monolith. Be like my daughter here, but do not confuse two things."

I started guiltily and instinctively glanced at Fine, whose eyes were still shut but who had stretched out her straight, bare legs for my admiration. Mr. van Brooklyn stood up as if to indicate that my visit was at an end, but remained to look at his daughter inquiringly. Swallowing hard, I hastened to ask if he would allow me to take his daughter for a walk some day. My question seemed to surprise him.

"To tell the truth, I'm not used to being asked questions like that," he admitted frankly. "My daughter is very stubborn and chooses her own company. You are a serious-minded man and I would certainly like her to learn something from you, but . . ."

He hesitated and looked at Fine sharply.

"But what?" I stammered in disappointment, and my desire and dismay were reflected only too clearly in my face.

"But I fear she will hurt you," Mr. van Brooklyn said gloomily. "When you look at her you would not believe that many people have come to me to tell me that she harms their children. She has brought me many troubles."

"Father," warned Fine van Brooklyn.

"And also many joys," Mr. van Brooklyn hastened to add. "But I am immune to her. You are still young and it is her pleasure to annoy people. But what's the use of talking. . . ."

I took his words as consent and shook his hand warmly, like a thief taking leave of the host and hostess with the family treasure under his coat. Mr. van Brooklyn looked at me pityingly and nodded to himself sadly. Fine accompanied me to the balcony and casually offered me her hand. I held it between my own, trying to soften her.

"When may I see you again, Fine?" I pleaded.

"I've already said that I never want to see you again," she answered coldly and looked past me at the road.

My heart sank and joy died in me. "You are cruel, Fine," I said. "I promise you I'll never again behave like . . ."

She put her hand quickly over my mouth. "I don't want to damage your soul," she said scornfully. I tried to kiss her palm.

"Tonight, Fine? Tomorrow? When are you free?" I watched her expression beseechingly.

"Oh, sometime—perhaps," she said as if tired of my begging.

And as I walked back to the hotel, this half-promise left me feeling as if all my limbs were filled with a gentle fire.

6

It is difficult for me to remember the next few days, for during them I came to know what a bitter price a man must pay for his pleasures and how treacherously passion blinds an intelligent being. Seemingly I was spending the most comfortable of holidays. The days were invariably fine, my room was cool at night and the food at the hotel was plentiful and appetizing. My face soon grew tanned. But the effect of the food, the sea and the hours I spent on the beach merely obscured my true thoughts and my body was still in a torment which kept me from concentrating upon my studies, which at any other time would have had my undivided attention. After I had read but

a few lines, my thoughts began to drift and the mocking face
of Fine van Brooklyn peered up at me from the pages of the
book. As I walked yet once more that long route I had followed the first day, my imagination summoned up her image
against my will, fleeing frightened from my grasp amid the
deserted columns, while I walked restlessly on and the evening
grew cool. My senses were awakened and nothing had any
value to me without her. Yet each time I encountered her, I
returned to the loneliness of my room, scorched and surging
with resentment.

For I saw her just often enough to perpetuate my lack of
confidence. She would come walking along the road toward
me with some adolescent French boy, and when she saw me
she would casually put her hand in his arm, chatting away so
animatedly that she hardly noticed my greeting. Sometimes
she stood at the gate as if waiting for me, a smile upon her
face. But when I asked her to come for a walk or to swim,
regretfully she remembered that she had promised her father
to go to the moor with him or else she was going shopping
with Susan. A hundred times after I had sworn bitterly to
myself that I would never try to see her again, she would creep
up on me on the beach unnoticed, throw herself down by my
side, tossing the nearness of her young body like a stake upon a
gaming table. And she overcame me, as the light, careless
touch of her shoulder against my bare skin blinded me, or as
she leaned toward me, bringing her lips close, then moving
suddenly away once she had seen my expression.

Her attitude changed constantly. She was evasive and eluded
my every grasp, so I never knew just what she was getting at
or what she really meant. And all that really happened was
that she looked up at me coyly, pity and amusement mingled
in her glance, until she held my eyes and melted all my resistance. I felt hurt and shame, but I would have liked to have
been wealthy so that I could have given her everything she
desired, have bought her sympathy even briefly and assuaged
my restlessness and pain. She ruled me by my dissatisfaction,
although I could not understand this. Even as a child she had
understood that bitter law that most women never understand

—that no man has ever been held by being satisfied, that only dissatisfaction feeds his passion. When she had enjoyed my embarrassment and humiliation sufficiently she would suddenly pick up some sand and throw it into my eyes. While I groped, blinded, eyes smarting, she would run away from me, leap into the water and swim slowly and contentedly through the big breakers. When at last I overtook her and we swam side by side in the salty water, our bare limbs tormentingly close, she would accuse me of looking at her lasciviously and declare she could not bear it. Losing all control, I imagined the bitter pleasure of holding her arms to her sides and pulling her down with me to the depths, to drown her, to drown myself, breast to breast—although I knew that probably she would have slipped easily out of my hold and laughed at me.

So the days went by and she continued to toy with me, as cruelly irresponsible as a cat that releases the cornered mouse only to place its paw upon it the more firmly, ensuring that it cannot escape. The sun shining monotonously each day began to irk me and sometimes I yearned for the peace of my beautiful winter and the contentment to be found in increasing one's knowledge at a quiet table in a great library. But I despaired when I thought of all this, for work had passed from my thoughts and when I tried to turn my mind to some of its problems or to consider some point that remained unclear to me, I felt a frightening reluctance to speculate upon it quietly.

Only occasionally did I find a peaceful moment when the restlessness within me was stilled. Sometimes as I sat on the quiet bank, my cider bottle drunk dry, my pipe lit, a sense of peace came over me so that without thinking of anything, I enjoyed merely being; or when on a walking trip, my body damp with sweat, I could throw myself down among the thorny plants of the moor and listen to the violent whirring of unseen insects amid the bright red flowers, tiny as the head of a pin. I rested by the side of some uncovered grave and its gray stone surface was hot in the sunlight while the earth beneath the flagstone was blackened from coals burned long ago. My heart too was like those coals and in my dreamy torpor in the warm sunshine, my suffering and sorrow and longing were numbed as though my body were anesthetized. Then from a great distance I could watch myself and wonder at my folly, for Fine van Brooklyn was only a spoiled child, in whose outwardly beautiful body flourished the seeds of corruption and whose cruel behavior should have long since extinguished all feeling in me, had I the least pride or self-respect.

Yet when later I saw her for a moment and she was gracious enough to exchange two words with me and to let me look into those dark blue, innocent yet cruel eyes, everything inside me melted and I was helpless as water, my pride broken. When she left me, my mind was again tormented and fire was in my limbs, and I shut myself in, replying irritatedly to the chance remarks of the guests at the hotel. I was so distraught that I suffered a terrible headache and a sleepless night when one day on the beach she coldly remarked that I was like a hairless white worm. After this I let my skin get scorched and suffered the pain that followed. "Ugh, now you are just as black and uninteresting as those French boys," she said scornfully a couple of days later, and tore a piece of loose skin from my back.

Yet one Saturday she surprised me by standing waiting at the gate for me. "My father invites you to come and see us after dinner this evening," she said coquettishly, turning a fir cone round and round with the point of her shoe. "He thinks that you're lonely and would like you to have a glass of gin with him."

"Fine," I said, "what fiendish trick are you up to now?"

"It's quite true," she answered indignantly. "Come whenever you like this evening, but preferably before nine."

I did not know what to think. Fine did not want to come swimming. She was going to the hairdresser's—that is, insofar as one could get one's hair done in Carnac. I lay for a long time on the beach, trying in vain to think what this surprising invitation meant. And then brighter still a new, dim hope shot into my mind that perhaps . . .

The maid at the hotel kindly pressed my only suit for me and I tried to brush and tidy myself as best I could. I was even so ridiculous as to practice before the mirror, molding my face into different expressions, polite attention, tenderness and others that I foresaw might occur during the evening. The maid busied herself in the stuffy corridor outside my door and got to her feet to say—a little sadly, I thought—"I hope you enjoy yourself tonight, sir." And as I walked downstairs I still felt her sad eyes upon my back, and I thought in passing how monotonous her life must be. It was as if the yearning, melancholy soul of this whole country were revealed in her sad, dark eyes. But her body was like an ironing board and her hands red and rough from scrubbing floors and I wasted no more thought upon her as I walked impatiently toward the shore.

Dusk was falling as I stepped through the creaking gate. Susan opened the door to me and in the sitting room Fine stood looking at me. At first I did not recognize her. Until now I had seen her only in a bathing suit or a blouse and white skirt. Now her hair was combed back from the neck and drawn up from the sides and formed into most attractive waves. All this artifice had changed the shape of her face and made her look very adult. She was wearing a long, full-skirted dress that left her shoulders and throat alluringly bare, and her sheer silk stockings set off her slim ankles. Her high heels and hair style made her noticeably taller than before, so that her forehead was level with my eyes. She had painted her lips a yellowish-red and added a touch of green to the corner of her eyes. In fact she was a strange woman, the sight of whom took my breath away and filled my heart with an uneasy premonition.

Mr. van Brooklyn regarded his beautiful daughter with open admiration. He removed his yellow-tinged glasses before holding out his hand to me and bidding me welcome. On the table there were coffee cups and tulip-shaped glasses, and beside an old-fashioned coffeepot stood an earthen liquor bottle.

There are people who like Dutch gin but since that evening even its smell is horrible to me. However, I sat down carefully on the edge of a chair, feeling that my hands and feet were too big and took up much too much room. Fine was noticeably ill at ease and spent the whole time looking out the window. She had been drinking with her father after dinner and I could smell it upon her breath when she passed by me and, in her instinctively irritating way, leaned toward me and brought her round, brown shoulders close.

"You were very kind to keep me company," said van Brooklyn in a friendly tone. "I think we shall have quite enough to talk about, for in all modesty I am going to tell you what I think about these stones."

I thanked him for this promise and indicated that the pleasure was wholly mine. He was very kind to offer his hospitality to a lonely stranger. The gin made my inexperienced body hot and my eyes remained glued upon Fine, while hope and fear washed in alternate waves around me.

"Actually it was my daughter's idea," added van Brooklyn, and my heart plunged at the next words. "She was afraid that I would feel lonely when she's out so late. . . ."

It was a few seconds before I fully grasped the irony of his words. "Isn't Miss van Brooklyn . . . is Miss van Brooklyn . . ." I stammered in my dismay. Van Brooklyn smiled gloomily and Fine hastened to say innocently:

"I'm going dancing in Quiberon tonight. Didn't I remember to tell you this morning? I'm all dressed. They're coming for me at nine."

At this, a car hooted noisily from the road outside. Deliberately Fine drew a shawl over her hair and kissed her father's cheek lightly. "Bye-bye," she said to me, carelessly waving her arm.

My heart weighed like a lump of stone in my stomach as I stood by van Brooklyn's side peering out through the window at the road. The car was old and dilapidated but in its front seat sat a black-eyed French boy with white teeth that shone like a toothpaste advertisement. A couple of other young people were also in the car.

"That's how she is," said van Brooklyn morosely and shook his head, but in spite of this I could not help noticing an unreasonably fatherly pride in his voice.

"Who are they?" I tried to ask the question scornfully, although my voice shook.

"I don't know," said van Brooklyn simply. "I've never seen

them before. My daughter picks up people in the oddest ways."

The remark applied to me too, but I tried to go on. "Don't you . . . well, aren't you . . . I mean, don't you ever worry about her? Strange company can be . . ."

Van Brooklyn looked at me in quizzical inquiry and shrugged his shoulders.

"Nothing can hurt my daughter," he said somberly. "Haven't you noticed that yet?" He put his lean hand upon my shoulder and shook me gently. "Tut, you're blind." At the same time he stepped back to the table and casually filled my glass. Without thinking I emptied it, my throat burning and tears in my eyes.

After a while I was able to say, "I don't understand what you mean. Why can nothing harm your daughter?"

I looked at him defiantly, the strong drink burning my guts and on my tongue a thousand bitter words which politeness alone prevented my uttering. My depression was giving way to anger and I peered at my host in the dusky room as cross as a flustered owl.

"Fire cannot burn her, water will not drown her," said van Brooklyn slowly, and seemingly seriously. "She will never be old and her skin will never become ugly with wrinkles, for she has been given the power to trouble all without being troubled herself. I do fear for her but there is nothing I can do for her. She has been sent to try the righteous and to bring the impious to ruin. Her spirit is older than the religion that has delivered us, as old as the hills around us and the tree of the knowledge of good and evil that is in the hearts of men."

I touched my head gingerly for it felt curiously thick and there was a booming within it. Mr. van Brooklyn looked at me compassionately and continued:

"I see you don't understand what I am talking about at all. You think I am an old fool whose head has become confused by too many complex ideas. But don't you realize that from the very beginning of time there have always been people who have brought grief and torment to others? They cannot change, cannot help themselves in any way. I have realized this clearly this summer as I've watched her becoming a woman."

He looked at me thoughtfully, as if deliberating whether I was really worth such confidence. With a note of warning he continued:

"I hope you won't mention any of this to her. When she was a small girl she was saved from a fire in the Hague in a very strange fashion—a fire, incidentally, in which three adults died. Everyone who has befriended her has found himself in trouble in one way or another. . . ."

"That's ridiculous," I said scornfully. But van Brooklyn continued imperturbably.

"We had a pretty servant girl once. Fine liked to get into bed with her when it was too cold in her own. Quite by accident the girl got a jet of boiling water in her face. Lost her looks and was half blinded. Fine may not realize it herself, but there have always been people whose mere presence brings misfortune. Sailors are aware of this even today."

"That's nothing but primitive superstition," I said in surprise. "I thought you . . ." Politeness forced me to interrupt my sentence. Van Brooklyn smiled in faint disdain and glanced pityingly at me.

"People have been cast into the sea from ships about to founder," he continued in all seriousness. "People were burned at the stake as witches or have fled to the woods and deserts, when people were more sensitive to the intermediaries who unwittingly unleash evil powers. This land radiates evil but it cannot harm us if there is no medium to direct it at us."

I stared at my host in amazement but his face exhibited no sign of any emotion.

"It's the truth," he finished simply. "An elementary truth which our age has forgotten, just as it has forgotten the healing powers of the earth and stars."

He got up and quietly lit the oil lamp, pausing to look at its leaping flame.

"Then, too, it may well be," he said, "that I comfort myself with such ideas in order to lessen my own guilt, for it is true that I have brought her up badly. Please sample the gin, my friend. Let us laugh together at that which we cannot alter."

After a while he began quietly to explain his theory about the Carnac stones. Insofar as I understood him correctly, he thought that long ago, perhaps a thousand years before the birth of Christ, some Egyptian war vessel had been shipwrecked upon this dangerous coast while venturing far beyond the then known world. Some unlettered mariner had grafted upon the local stone-age religion such stray wisps of knowledge as he could recall. That engraven sunboat with the rowers was obviously Raa, the sailor of the firmaments. The monoliths were inspired by the Obelisks, and his theory concerning the lines of stones was so foolish and confused that it has escaped my memory: for as I listened to his monotonous voice, my thoughts wandered to Fine, who was enjoying herself in Quiberon. For I was, of course, certain that she was enjoying herself.

Time passed, the oil lamp flickered cozily on the table and darkness fell behind the windows. The gin set my mind to imagining what Fine could be doing at this moment and brought every detail of her sharply to my memory, as van Brooklyn's dreary voice turned to speak of sunken Atlantis and of the fragments of its civilization which were to be found in Carnac—fragments that had been misunderstood by the barbarians of the Stone Age and were disguised as the strangest forms. Gradually, due probably to the gin, his wizened forehead became flushed. His voice rose several tones higher and he began to mix more and more Dutch words into his speech.

I was already perfectly clear about van Brooklyn. He was an old man who had become more and more peculiar the older he had got, who was now fanatically set in his opinions and who, like most amateurs without any real knowledge, imagined he could divert science to new paths. A religious fanatic, he had fused to his Calvinism quite a few pagan ideas which he had quite unknowingly extracted from the literature of theology. He bored me, for I was used to a bright world of knowledge that employed fewer big words.

It was nearly midnight when Susan came in and, without asking, cleared away the gin bottle and glasses. Van Brooklyn quickly lowered his voice and soon began to yawn demonstratively, as I sat stubbornly in my chair.

"I thank you for this evening, my friend," he said, rising at last. "You are a good listener. At first I thought you were bored, for you grinned so strangely. But then I realized that it was apparently only a tedious habit of yours. Try to stop it. I mean this only for your own good."

I was dumbfounded, but I arose, holding fast to the table edge. I had been silent for so long that my tongue would not work for a moment or two and I stammered in a most confused fashion: "Mr. van Book . . . Mr. van Rook . . . Mr. van Brr . . ."

He gestured to me kindly and soothingly with his hand. Straining all my powers of concentration I understood that by the word "grinning" he apparently meant my expression of studiously polite attention. Wounded, I assured myself that I had no need to care about a carrot-head like him, and the image of a carrot-head was so vivid that I burst out laughing.

"Mr. van Brooklyn," I stammered, laughing with tears streaming from my eyes, "I thank you from the bottom of my heart for this carrot-head, I mean, as we say . . . for the gin, if you'll pardon the allusion . . . I mean . . . I beg your pardon . . ."

The wall seemed to be collapsing on top of me in a rather surprising fashion, so I held on to the doorjamb.

I really must be ill, I said to myself in alarm, and summoned all my willpower to bring the room in focus once again.

"Do you think you'll be able to get home alone?" van Brooklyn asked anxiously and supported me by the shoulder. "I didn't imagine you were so inexperienced. I've heard that in the north even the children drink. . . ." I pulled myself free from his protecting grasp and burst into gloomy laughter.

"I am sick—sick with love for your daughter, Mr. van Brooklyn," I said, interrupting him. "My intentions are honorable but what's this infernal stuff you've poured into me?"

Susan came to the door, a nightcap on her head above a

faded brown nightdress. I fell silent when I saw her, and bidding them good night in as clear a voice as I could, I stepped out into the night, which so befuddled me by its blackness that I stumbled into the porch rail. The shock cleared my muddled brain. I felt sick, sick from love and betrayal as I groped my way along the path to the gate.

It did not occur to me that I was drunk for the first time in my life. Instead I resolved that I absolutely could not go to sleep before seeing Fine arrive happily home.

I stumbled forward a few steps and sat down beside a pine tree standing by a dry ditch. Gradually my eyes became accustomed to the midnight darkness. The stars shone above me and the road seemed lighter against the dark shadow of the woods. From the shore I heard the sigh of the surf and its sound mingled with the sickness that murmured in my head. Carefully I picked a stone as big as my fist from the ground. With this squeezed tightly in my hand, I sat waiting, fully determined to batter it upon the head of the French boy with the toothpaste advertisement smile. The night was warm, and gradually a sense of sweet satisfaction came over me, for after long anxiety and uncertainty a sure decision frees a man.

7

I do not know how long I sat there by the dry ditch with my head throbbing gently. It had been about midnight when I left van Brooklyn's, and when I heard the car arriving, a pale sunrise had crept unnoticed into the sky.

I thought about many things during those few hours so they did not seem long to me. My relaxed condition had enabled me to sit without stirring in the same position without my limbs stiffening. The thoughts that swept through my mind were of a bright steely quality and many things that had puzzled my mind became as clear as daylight. Unfortunately they were all confused the next day, but I know I did not sleep at all, say what you will, for asleep one cannot think. Yet I do not want to deny absolutely the possibility that I may have dozed off for a minute or two, for the bleak dawn of morning did surprise me.

A remark of van Brooklyn's returned to comfort me while I sat there. He had said that not far from Carnac a curious event had taken place, and at the end of the last century too, when they had pierced, with a knife kept for the purpose, the head of a child who was born lame. Van Brooklyn had compared this with the primitive Egyptian custom of as a last resort performing an operation in which the skull was pierced with a stone knife, after which the hardiest patient rarely survived for more than three days and nights.

This symbolic deed especially attracted my broken mind as I sat in the darkness in unspeakable loneliness. Overwhelmed by self-pity, I thought how much better it would have been if my head too had been pierced with a stone knife the day I was born, so that I would not have had to live through these evil days. It is easy to smile afterwards, but I assure you that my dejection was all too real that night.

As our subconscious often awakens us from sleep, so I awoke from my reverie just before the car came, and had time to be startled by the dawn, that most comfortless time of the day when our vitality is at its lowest, hope is nonexistent and morning seems eons away. Following directly upon my earlier thoughts, a terrifying sense of purposelessness overwhelmed me. My limbs were stiff, my face stubbled and I felt a terrible thirst, as if my tongue were some strange form in my mouth.

Ashamed, I let the stone fall from my fist, the stone that I had held so tightly for so long that I could hardly straighten my fingers. I was oppressed by a painful sense of self-contempt. Had I really deteriorated to the extent that I was actually prepared to commit the most frightful deeds and chance the most unpleasant complications, echoes of which would travel speedily to my own country, all because of a heartless chit of a girl? For the first time it occurred to me that I had been drunk, drunk as a lord.

At that instant I heard the car coming. Its motor backfired a couple of times at the turn of the road, then its hum roared in my ears like the trumpets of Judgment Day, so that I expected the entire neighborhood to leap to its feet. However, nothing happened. The car stopped at Fine's door with a squeal of brakes and I heard Fine's laugh, a laugh that electrified me and made me forget everything else.

The villa's sloping fence with its nettle bushes sheltered me, so that neither of them noticed me. The car was only twenty yards away and the sky was now so light that I could easily follow their every move. It obviously did not occur to either of them that anyone could still be awake, for they were completely engrossed in each other.

They were sitting in the front seat, and as Fine was apparently to descend to the road, the French boy threw his arm around her and bent toward her breasts. "No, no!" said Fine in that low voice I knew so well. Then they embraced, Fine pushing at the boy's chest with her hands, pretending to hold him off. They sat clutched together for a long time, while I stared at them loathingly from behind the nettle bush. Then Fine nimbly freed herself, got the car door open and went to the gate of the villa, as if intending to gain its shelter. Her fingers, however, spent too long groping for a handle which did not exist, so that the boy easily caught her and held her prisoner in his arms. Here Fine remained twisting about, her dress skillfully slipping from a shoulder that was bared seductively to the sweet border of her breasts. The French boy's face grew red and he breathed so chokingly that even in my terrible jealousy I could sympathize with him. They whispered passionately but so softly that I was unable to make out a word; but the arrogant set of Fine's neck and the way her body stiffened spoke most eloquently of the gist of their conversation: "Go away, what do you think I am? I never want to see you again."

The French boy laughed softly and his hands slid over that slim, attractive body. He was not so foolish as I, nor so inexperienced, for after a minute they were embracing each other fiercely against the gate, Fine's arms around the boy's neck and his mouth on her shoulder and breast. I could not look at them any longer but bent my head forward with my eyes so wide that they ached, until the gravel crunched and the gate squeaked; and when I looked up, Fine was standing on the other side of the gate, keeping it shut between them and evading the boy's hands. Her breath came calmly as she fixed her dress, and I felt as if her dark blue eyes would have cut through the pale dawn to me, kindling a hot flame that melted my frozen breast and stiffened limbs and made tears well in my throat. How graceful was her every gesture, despite its apparent casualness, how slim those ankles in their wispy stockings, how round and tanned that naked shoulder. But now I saw her as a dangerous beast at play, a too handsome animal that bewitched the careless watcher into drawing too near. I did not doubt her future. I did not doubt that she would easily get everything that she wanted from life; but I was equally certain that ruin would mark her trail and that all green and living things would wither as she passed.

They talked for a while longer and the boy's amorous desires weakened and his face was pale in the bleak morning light. Then Fine went in, stepping lightly as if on air. She turned for a moment on the porch, raised her hand almost casually and smiled, a shining, dark blue glance which literally glowed with the loveliness of virginity. Thus her image remained in my mind! Thus it still regards me from across the years, never dimming, still as plaguing today as ever. She went in and after that, I never saw her again.

The boy stood at the gate looking after her. Then sleepily rubbing his eyes, he lit a cigarette and stepped out of sight to the other side of the car. There he passed water, then got into the car and drove right past me without noticing me, the cigarette drooping in the corner of his mouth and the brightness of his black eyes clouded with a gray film. He was no longer smiling.

When the car had disappeared, I descended to the road and began to walk stiffly back to the hotel, thirst once more burning my mouth. Only one desire was left—to find shelter, to hide my face, to be able to cease thinking of my shame. The hotel door was locked and I had to knock for a long time before the maid came to open it. She had thrown her dark dress over her nightdress but its hem showed beneath the skirt and the warm flush of sleep showed in her serious face, making it surprisingly tender in the bitter morning light.

I was ashamed at disturbing her and wanted to apologize but was able only to slur some unclear syllables. She looked at me pityingly with her sad eyes and another's sympathy was too much for my overwrought feelings. Tears came into my eyes and all inside me was like an open wound, so that every movement hurt.

"But, sir, sir, dear sir . . . you're ill . . ." stammered the maid in alarm and gently took hold of my arm as if afraid that I would fall. I wiped my eyes with the back of my hand and sleeve, but tears of annoyance trickled down my cheeks, blinding me and falling onto my collar and jacket. Carefully, almost like a mother, the maid led me to my room, warning me in a whisper of the steps, so that I should not stumble. She led me to shelter as a mother an irritable child and her sympathy wrung my heart.

She came into my room leaving the door ajar, and sat down beside me on the bed. She warmed my cold hands between her rough ones and stroked my hair lightly with her palm and at the same time she quietly whispered some words in a strange language, words which I did not understand but which fell consolingly onto my mind like bright dew. She was so kind to me that little by little I grew calm and was able to ask her to awaken me in the morning so that I could leave by the first train.

Sadly—and it seemed to me, disappointedly—she looked at me, but she did not try to persuade me to alter my decision, merely nodding her head to show that she had understood. After I had calmed down, her presence began to annoy me (it was too heavy a load on my self-contempt), and when she noticed this she whispered good night and went away. The flush of sleep had left her face and it was again bony and sad.

I looked at my face in the mirror. The inflamed skin, the tangled hair and the stubble on the chin accentuated its strained look. I detested that image more than anything in the world and asked myself if I was really becoming like that? For from the mirror a libertine gazed at me; a drunkard who had disappointed in his promise and in whose features the marks of incipient degeneration were painfully obvious. Then I had fallen so far, and could only thank fate that my eyes had been opened in time and I could still draw back from the edge of the abyss. I was not yet destroyed. I could still marshal my willpower and build something from the ruins. But there was only one decision possible and with the tears still smarting in my eyes, I began to stuff my few belongings into the suitcase.

It was still some hours before the train left, so I undressed and went to bed as soon as I had packed my things, although I knew that I would not be able to close my eyes. In the bright light of morning, my heart ached with emptiness. More clearly with each passing hour were the dangers of this development revealed to me. I saw how I had fallen, indeed watched it as a stranger on a mountain peak observes the landscape spread before him. It had already begun by the time I arrived in Paris in November and enjoyed the sweet sense that no one was observing where I went or what I did. Childishly trusting in my own feeling of responsibility, I had gradually allowed myself to drift with the current. Everything in that great, gay city accelerated the gradual weakening of my powers of resistance —the unrestrained gestures, the loud way of speaking, the brightly lit bars set one after the other along the great streets, even the lighthearted language itself which lent ambiguity to and made even the most morally dangerous thoughts seem innocent. The new surroundings with their attractions and deceitful tang of freedom had released in me energy which I had never known I possessed. But the feeling of accomplishment and the dangerous self-confidence that it lent had hastened my escape from the accustomed habit with which before I had been bound and upon which one can build a normal and worth-while life. It had all begun with slight, scarcely noticed lapses, until ultimately I even felt curiously favorable toward the open kissing in the streets and the colorful pictures of naked girls on the covers of magazines. I had sunk so low that I had even replied to unknown women who spoke to me at street corners, and what is worse, had yielded to the temptations of drink, beginning each evening with a so-seemingly innocent glass of beer. So I was ripe for it, ready and willing to fall into the trap which the depraved girl set for me. Yes, I was so blinded that I had been ready to commit any stupidity, perhaps ruin my life, just to gratify this worthless sexual urge. What I had become was clearly visible in the mirror.

Having reached this point in my thoughts, I buried my face in the pillow and drew the eiderdown over my head, as if to bury myself in the darkness of deepest self-loathing. I may have slept like this, for I awoke to the maid's cautious knock as though climbing from lead-heavy mud. She brought me my morning coffee and on the tray beside it was my bill. Her voice no longer had the same cheerful ring when she greeted me. She examined me curiously with her sad eyes and I felt myself blush to the roots of my hair so that I had to turn from her gaze. Once more I saw the framed lithograph on the wall with the Child in His mother's arms, purple as if the embodiment of a bad conscience.

For the last time I ate the gray, soft bread of Brittany, but it had lost all flavor in my dry mouth, and I felt ill when I looked at the butter. I understood now just how the first man must have felt when he tasted from the tree of good and evil, for daylight hurt my eyes, the flowers had lost their color and the sky its blue. Instead of being glad to be alive I felt quarrelsome, and impatient to criticize all before me.

Already I had to hurry to catch the train. Outside in the corridor I shook hands and said good-bye to the maid, avoiding her eye but nevertheless feeling a pale ripple of gratitude for her kindness in my mind. I paid my bill and left. I have not been back.

For had I returned—as in weak moments I have considered doing—it would not seem the same to me now. The houses would appear small and gloomy, the hotel too large and uncomfortable, the beach tiny and filled with seaweed. I should perspire too much as I walked, would suffer from palpitations of the heart, the strange food would trouble my stomach, and I would not again find here that youth which once flamed in me for so brief a moment.

I do not doubt the sincerity of the moral reaction in which

my belated youth so quickly expired, but age and experience must surely have lessened the violence of feelings, for while writing this I have often (with all the signs of an obviously bad conscience) been surprised to find myself wondering what might have happened had my reaction not been so abrupt and so violent. I also feel rather unkindly about old van Brooklyn's gin. Its effect was so sudden and calamitous that I am afraid it acted as some kind of *deus ex machina* in the events of that fateful night. But it is better like this, for I have kept my memories secret, first overcoming the greatest remorse and self-loathing: but as the years steadied me they faded and sealed the gulf of what I should like to call criminally sweet memories, memories which have at last attained their true perspective form. By writing this I have exorcised all my spiritual embarrassment, I can look at the affair dispassionately, as though at a paper-thin flower that I have found (to my displeasure) pressed between the pages of some book, all fragrance gone.

In any case, it is obvious that this brief experience clearly aided my development before the flesh mercifully enveloped the bullet and sealed it off so it no longer tortured my body. Once I had written this, I fully understood from what deep source my misogyny arises.

When I began this little book of memories I was in a most nervous and irritable frame of mind, but I am completing it in peace and rare good humor. I can even say that I have experienced some sort of literary pleasure in this trivial passing of time.

To be consistent I may as well say a few words about my subsequent life. I arrived back in Paris after an uncomfortable journey on a hard seat of a jolting third-class carriage. The smiling landscape and gentle hills of France were not for me and I regarded the destructive vineyards with the deepest moral indignation. It was late when I arrived and I hated every bright light that glowed in the August evening, each low laugh and cheerful human voice. I cloistered myself with my work, although this was difficult when the heat of the streets reflected scorchingly in one's face and the asphalt sank softly beneath one's heels. I established the most rigorous rules for myself and night and day I disciplined my rebellious body with a shower. This did not, however, improve my peace of mind, for the water was unfortunately warm.

I completed my work, although at the time I could no longer feel any appreciable enthusiasm toward it. I returned to my own country, tormented by an unspeakable homesickness, and nervous and harsh both to myself and others. As the years went by the eternal circle of study, documents and the library shelves had become ever more rigid. Perhaps my spirit has begun to decay in the same way as my body, from too little exercise and too rich food. I surprised myself by dishonestly fishing for compliments, like a dog begging for a piece of sugar, and I hasten to point out that I am aware of the significance of my work, and even prepared to emphasize it when my colleages sometimes seem to forget it.

It is perhaps better that I end my story with the first snow of November that autumn, just one year after I set forth on my journey.

I walked through the old park in front of the Knights' House on my way from my temporary lodgings to the University. The first snow had fallen that morning, covering the black ground in a thin layer. The scent of the snow stopped me in my tracks and from the clean whiteness Fine van Brooklyn's face looked up at me. Piquantly, cruelly, it was as if I had sensed in my nostrils the scent of sunshine in her hair and skin. The illusion was shockingly clear and alive and, overcome with a poignancy which this first snow had awakened in me, I could not avoid the thought that somewhere, in some warm room in a small Dutch town, she, at that very moment, spared me a passing thought or spoke my name in her laughing voice. To my surprise I no longer felt contempt for or anger toward her. Time had passed and I was moving toward my first success, success that fills all that is empty, fills the grave and heals all wounds. My anger had burned out and to my surprise I felt affection stir within me. The early snow had fallen over the black earth of my heart, but beneath the earth my love still lived its own unreal, shadowy existence. The thought that somewhere, far off in a strange land, she spoke my name, awakened it and brought it back to life.

Well, Fine van Brooklyn, my spoiled and naughty child, if I were to meet you now, still just as you were, I would tweak your ear mercilessly and give that pretty bottom of yours a fatherly spanking. Yet all the same I would avoid those dark blue eyes of yours.

SOMETHING IN PEOPLE

Translated by Paul Sjöblom

1

SHE was different from the others. At least to me she was different. Her name was Osmi. It was an unusual name. On the street and in the schoolyard the other children would run after her, pointing at her and repeating tauntingly, "Osmi, Osmi, Osmi!"

What could have prompted her mother to give her daughter a name which even as a child set her apart from others? Her mother was the same kind of poor man's wife as the other women on our block. She was in no way superior to them—quite the contrary, for her husband was a sewer cleaner and it was smelly work, even if he did perhaps earn more than some of the other men. My father was a machinist on a battleship. When Osmi was thirteen and I fourteen, the World War broke out. In August, 1914, my father was shipped far off to the shores of the Black Sea and from there he wrote of lying under a tree in the hot sun and eating pomegranates every day.

Perhaps there was a bit of the dreamer in Osmi's mother and perhaps she wove or had woven all kinds of poetic meanings into the name Osmi. But Osmi developed into a timid child who walked by herself and played by herself, and whenever I passed her I simply had to snatch her doll and fling it against a wall or kick over her toy house. Whenever she was playing alone in the yard I had to pass her may times until at last she would begin to cry and go home. This is how it was when we were still children. But by the time I was fourteen, we were no longer really children for she no longer played with dolls and I had stolen my first money.

When Osmi was thirteen, she no longer cried as easily as

before and she had eyes which were different from those of other girls and very red lips, though she was poorly, even carelessly dressed. She still went to public school, but after graduation she was supposed to get a job as a messenger girl somewhere to earn a living. As for me, my mother had sent me to high school, even though I did not want to go; and I was spending another year in the same grade and, since I wanted to leave school, picking fights between classes so that I got bad marks in deportment. I envied Hanski, who was my age and did nothing and yet had bought a pair of brown shoes and always had cigarettes and money in his pockets. There were a number of us boys who did everything Hanski ordered, and I never seemed to have time to read my lessons, not that I wanted to, and during the spring term I started to play truant.

One day during the spring Osmi's father was working near the harbor next to the gasworks and at noon Osmi took his lunch to him in a basket covered with a gray cloth. Something made me walk behind Osmi and watch her; and the next day I was by the shore at the same place, throwing stones into the water, so that she had to pass me. The spot was deserted save for the piles of sand and junk and overturned boats.

"Osmi!" I said to her as she went by. But she did not answer me, walking quickly past without even looking in my direction. Perhaps she thought I only wanted to make fun of her, for she was ashamed of her sewer-cleaner father and disliked having to carry his food to him. Perhaps I did only want to make fun of her and spoke to her only for that reason, but she did not answer me or even look at me.

She was still small, but her eyes were different from those of other girls and were framed by short, very black lashes, and her mouth was large and red.

The next day, too, I shoved my schoolbooks down through the cellar window in the morning and found Hanski waiting for me at a street corner. I told him that there were piles of cables and other junk along the shore by the gasworks and we might be able to find something salable there.

We went to the shore and rummaged in the junk piles and then lay basking in the sun on a sandpile. The snow had already melted and the boats smelled of fresh paint, and in the distance a new bridge was being built across the bay. We smoked Hanski's cigarettes until my head swam and my mouth began to smart, and he told me about deals he had made with Russian soldiers and drew a handful of silver Finnish and Russian coins from his pocket and showed them to me. We lay on the sandpile and all the snow had already melted and Hanski asked whether I had played such and such with girls. I was curious and he told me all kinds of things and I thought he was lying.

Then about noon Hanski raised his head and said, "Look, there comes Osmi."

I raised my head, too, and saw Osmi coming with the lunch basket under her arm; and her hair was braided and the end of the braid was tied with a worn, red silk ribbon.

"Yes, there comes Osmi!" I repeated, and we watched her from behind the sandpile; and I don't think she noticed us, for she smiled to herself as she walked and gazed at the sky, and she had never smiled at me. I looked at her and my mouth was dry and my hands clenched into fists.

I was fourteen and I think that I was still but a child, though I had already stolen with Hanski. But Hanksi looked at me slyly and said: "We could grab her and tease her a bit!"

"No," I said, "she's bringing her father his lunch. Her old man's working next to the gasworks today."

"Sewer rat!" said Hanksi. "Her father is a sewer rat!"

I laughed, for Osmi had already passed and we could no longer have caught her even had we tried.

We lay on our backs on the sandpile and smoked cigarettes until Hanski started to laugh to himself. He glanced at me and asked: "Is she coming back this way?"

"Who?" I asked, though I knew whom Hanksi meant. And a black wave washed over my head, even though the sun shone bright and I saw the water and every particle of dirt floating on its surface and the houses on the cliffs across the bay.

"Osmi," said Hanski, stretching his legs. "Did you notice how she looked?"

"Let's go!" I said and my tongue felt so swollen I could hardly speak. I sat up and prepared to leave.

"Are you afraid of a girl?" asked Hanski, lifting his eyebrows as only he was able to do. That made me angry and my jaws began to clench as they always do when I lose my temper.

"God Almighty!" I said, "I'm not afraid of anybody in the world. But I just don't feel like it."

"You don't dare," Hanski challenged and thrust his face close to mine. "I bet you don't even know what girls are like."

"Someone might see," I said.

"We won't hurt her," said Hanski and chuckled to himself. "We'll just tease her some. We'll take her to the shore and tease her some."

The day before, I had spoken to Osmi but she had not answered me or even looked at me.

"She's coming," said Hanski. "Come on! Let's walk over toward her and grab her."

"No," I said. "I'll grab her!" For I did not want Hanski to touch her.

Osmi came along the shore toward us, and we got up and hid ourselves beside the sandpile; and when she came near, we stepped out and approached her.

She had the empty basket in her hand and swung it as she walked along, smiling and humming softly to herself. But at the sight of us she stopped and looked back and then stepped to one side and tried to dodge past us. And she no longer smiled but looked at me as though she hated me. Yet I felt she had no reason to hate me, for I had not teased her in a long while and the day before she at least could have answered me when I spoke to her.

I grabbed at her when she tried to dodge past us, but my movement was so clumsy that she could have easily twisted loose and run away. But my hand was stronger than I was, and when it touched her I caught hold tightly, so that she stumbled to her knees and dropped her basket. She struggled to tear herself free, until Hanski grabbed her other arm and jerked her head backwards by her braid, loosening her red ribbon, which fell to the ground.

"No," I said, "don't touch her! I caught her."

"No," Hanski said, grinning, "let's have fun together."

Osmi did not cry out. She knew both of us. After all, I lived in the same yard. She did not cry out, but she struggled to get free and I felt her slim body beneath my hands. But she was not as strong as we were and Hanski knocked her down right away.

"Hold her hands!" Hanksi said through clenched teeth and without looking at me. Osmi lay on the ground and I pressed her hands to the ground with both of mine so that she could not move them. But she did not cry out. And Hanski sat on her legs and his hands moved over her body. But she did not cry out.

"What are you doing?" I said, staring at Hanski's hands.

But Osmi kept her eyes shut tight and her lashes were like two black streaks across her face; and she did not cry out, though I hoped she would scream so that I would have an excuse to let her go and run away. Perhaps I might have let her go anyway and run away, but I did not want to leave her alone in Hanski's hands.

At last Hanski looked at me and rose. I rose too, releasing Osmi's hands, and she sat up and looked at us. Her face was white and her eyes were large and very black, and to me the worst of it was that she did not cry out or say anything to us. I could not look at her and did not want to look at Hanski, but I was no longer shaking, for we had not really done Osmi any harm, only teased her.

"Go on now!" said Hanski impatiently and gave her a push when she remained sitting on the ground looking at us. "Now we know what you're like," he added tauntingly and gave Osmi another push.

"For God's sake, stop kicking her around," I said quickly, and with my foot shoved the basket she had dropped across to Osmi.

Osmi arose, picked her basket and ribbon off the ground and went on her way. She limped as she walked, for she had hurt her knee when I had thrown her to the ground.

"What did you do to her?" I asked when Osmi was out of

sight. Hanski did not answer, but his face flushed and he spat on the ground in front of him. I hated him then, though he was my best friend and though he had taught me all the bad things I knew.

"What's the matter with you?" Hanski said and tried to laugh. "Now maybe you know what girls are like?"

I had a vision of Osmi's face, eyes shut tight and lashes pressed together into two black streaks. I grabbed a broken metal pipe off the ground and hit Hanski across the face with it. He sank to a sitting position on the ground, and blood started to run into his eyes from a cut on his forehead. He groped at his head, got his hand full of blood, and started to yell.

I had hit Hanski without thinking, and on seeing him sitting on the ground with the blood dripping between his fingers and onto his clothes, I began to run, wailing as I ran, until I found a dark alley where I lay in the dirt and rubbish for many hours. I did not understand why I had hit Hanski, and I felt as if I myself had been hit so violently that I could not keep my thoughts together. Having lain a long time in the alley, I went over to the other side of town and joined a bunch of tramps who were loafing on the cliffs, and I went to buy them liquor and followed them into the woods of Eläintarha Park. For three days I did not dare to go home and I slept in various places, for the nights were already mild.

Then, dirty and hungry, I returned home. My mother whipped me and my older brother beat me, but they had been worried about me and I was not punished as severely as I had feared. I heard that the cut on Hanski's forehead had been stitched at the hospital and that he had told a story about falling into a scrap heap. Osmi had not said anything at home, but her mother, I heard, was complaining that the girl was acting strangely and refused to take her father's food to him where he worked.

That spring I remained in school and avoided Hanski, going indoors whenever I saw him in the street. I even tried to study my lessons and get ahead at school, but it was too late. I was left back in the same grade for the second time and thus was expelled from school. Then I was entered as an apprentice in a workshop for the summer, and in the beginning of June we moved, so that I did not see Osmi for a long time.

2

As long as the work was new to me, I got along at it; but I did not like having everybody order me around, and when I thought how it would take years before I could become a skilled worker and earn real wages, everything began to go against my grain. It seemed senseless to work nine and ten hours a day just to eke out a bare living when other people made money without working at all. One had to be strong and smart to succeed in this world, and I wanted to make lots of money so as to be able to go to the movies and cafés and cabarets, where there was music and dancing and where Russian officers and war profiteers got drunk.

That is why I did not stay in the workshop long but looked for other jobs or loafed. You see, there was still food and a bed for me at home, even if I did not work, for Father regularly sent his pay home from the shores of the Black Sea and Mother had savings in the bank, too. Mother hoped the war would last a long time, but I figured nobody had ever got rich by saving, and steady work from morning to night every day, year after year, struck me as idiotic. It was only for dunces; and I thought I was smart when on dark nights I unscrewed brass knobs off doors and sold them as junk or stole electric bulbs from hallways and earned more that way in a single night than in an entire week of work, for in wartime it was a good way of making money.

Two or three years passed thusly, until I was seventeen. I was strong for my age and knew plenty of good tricks in fighting, so that I was not afraid of anybody. I was strong all right and the world was in a mess all around me and not once had I been caught at anything, although the detectives had twice fetched me from home for questioning. The war contin-

ued and the streets were lit at night by blue lamps, and
windows were blacked out, and to me it was dangerous and
exciting to be alive.

Then I saw Osmi again and immediately recognized her as
she approached me on the street. She was grown up and beautiful.

"Osmi," I greeted her in astonishment and smiled at her, no
longer remembering why I had once avoided her. I only remembered that we had lived in the same yard, and I was
happy at seeing her.

She looked at me but did not greet me, walking past me as
though she had not seen me. I intended to seize her by the
hand and turn her around to ask what she meant, but just then
I remembered just what had happened. But then we had been
mere children and I could not understand how she could still
hold a grudge against me on account of a silly prank. I
thought she had failed to recognize me, for I had grown, and I
intended to follow her and speak to her. Yet I neither followed
her nor spoke to her.

But at night I saw her in my mind as she had come toward
me on the street. She had not been well dressed and I guessed
that they were still quite poor. But her body was slim and her
hands were small and her eyes were different from those of
other girls and her mouth pretty and red like before. It made
me restless to think of her, and I wondered how it was possible
she did not recognize me. So the next day I went to the old yard
where I had not gone for three years, and I offered the janitor
a cigarette and hung around there until I heard that Osmi's
family still lived there and she had a job at a downtown florist's.

This news gave me a strange feeling, for to me she was
beautiful and she was already a young woman, and at a downtown florist's she was bound to meet people different from us
and maybe some fine gentleman would offer her money and
invite her over to his place, for I certainly knew what fine
gentlemen were like. That is why I waited on the street until
evening, until she returned home from work, so that I might
meet her again. But when she came, my knees grew weak and

I could not think of anything to say to her, though normally I was never at a loss for words.

"Osmi!" I said when she came by and I tipped my hat to her, and I hated myself for doing it even though she was only a girl who worked at a florist's. After all, I was a big-shot on my block.

She looked at me again with her dark eyes, pressed her lips tight together and tried to step past me, but I blocked her path and seized her arm, tried to smile and said: "Osmi, don't you know me? I'm Kauko!"

She tore her arm free, stepped back and stood facing me, breathing heavily. "Ahaa, Kauko!" she said, and looked at me as though I were vermin.

"Of course, and how are you and what are you doing nowadays?" I said lightly and again tried to smile, though my stomach felt as heavy as lead.

"Bum!" she said, spitting the word in my face, and her eyes narrowed and her cheeks grew red. I stood stunned, for I could not understand what she meant. I was well dressed, at least better than she was. I wore a pair of brown shoes. I knew how to affect good manners. I brushed my teeth every day. I had money in my pocket. In my own opinion I was far from a bum. And in my confusion she slipped by me and into the hallway and so escaped from my hands.

I was too dumbfounded even to feel angry with her. I started to laugh and I got to thinking that she was quite a girl. If anybody else—even a girl—had spoken to me like that, he would have got a black eye. But she was not afraid of me and it was beyond me where she had gotten it into her head that I was a bum. I felt I had to tell her that, on the contrary, I was stronger and smarter than many others. She was beautiful and in touching her arm I felt such a desire for her that I would have given anything if she had offered me her hand and spoken to me and walked with me.

For this reason I took up with her brother, who already went to work with his father and thought of himself as a man. He was a dull, sullen lad who always smelled of the sewer, but I overcame my dislike for him and pretended to be his friend and taught him a couple of card tricks, until one day he invited me over to their place. Their home consisted of one room and a kitchen; brother and sister slept in the kitchen, and when we went into it, I asked which bed was Osmi's and sat on its edge. I talked about all kinds of things with the boy, and as I spoke I stroked the covers with my hand and thought of Osmi sleeping in that bed, her head on that pillow. Feigning fatigue, I stretched out, pressed my cheek against the pillow and discovered in it the scent of her hair.

But all the time I waited for Osmi to come home so I could speak with her. I felt I just had to talk to her, and hot waves surged through my body as I thought of her. I despised her home, for it was poor and dirty and the boy's stinking workclothes hung from a nail, and I thought I would like to dress Osmi in beautiful clothes and live with her in a bright room with expensive furniture. Such were my childish thoughts as I waited for her to come home, and I tried to tell the boy all kinds of things so that he would not get tired of my lingering there.

Then the door opened and Osmi entered. She took off her overcoat, revealing a short-sleeved dress. "Well, Kauko!" she said, and in her eyes as she looked at me I saw hate and triumph and something puzzling that I could not comprehend.

"You know Kauko?" her brother asked dully.

"Of course I know Kauko," said Osmi. "What are you doing nowadays, Kauko?" Her voice was normal and quite friendly, and her brother didn't notice anything.

"Oh, all kinds of things!" I said in embarrassment, for she had put her question well. At the time I had no regular job. "One always gets along," I tried to add in a superior way, and I hungrily watched her smallish breasts, which were prominently revealed beneath her tight-fitting dress.

"Yes, your mother supports you, I've heard," Osmi said, still in a deceptively friendly tone. "So you haven't learned a trade? Just as you were too dumb for school. You're the same bum as before."

Again she used that word, used it so mildly and calmly that

even her brother was baffled and looked on mopishly, not understanding what she really meant.

"That's not true," I said helplessly. But when I sought to
explain that I was not a bum, I found I had nothing to say.
My mother did indeed support me and I had not finished my
schooling and I had not stuck to any regular job.

"Oh, no?" Osmi said knowingly, and her mouth was red
and proud and pretty.

That stung my pride and I thought it was beneath my dig-
nity to quarrel with the wench. I certainly had no desire to
force myself on Osmi if I was not good enough for her as I
was. There were plenty of other girls in the world, and better
ones too.

"Go to blazes, both of you!" I said and grabbed my hat and
left, for my face was as hot as a stove.

But by the time I got home, I was depressed and nothing
seemed to matter anymore. I was nothing but a small-time
thief who would never get rich, and if I went on the way I was
going I would soon be a prime prospect for jail. It was only a
question of time, for my mother was bound to throw me out of
the house; and when I thought about life and everything having to do with it, it was like biting into stale bread or tasting
something sour.

Then through some friend of my father's my mother found
a job for me as an electrician's apprentice and for months I
worked steadily, took part of my pay home and avoided my
former companions. Instead, I began to visit the library and
read all kinds of books. Electricians made good money and I
thought that some day I might even open my own shop. So
that winter passed, but the work was fun only as long as it was
new and with the coming of spring I grew restless. The books
I read at night began to bore me. I saw lots of tempting things
and began to dream up ways to make money fast. But nothing
happened; I continued to go to work each morning and at
night I was irritable and restless. And once again I felt the
need to see Osmi, but this time I went downtown to meet her
and waited near the florist's, planning to accompany her home.

"Hello, Osmi," I said when she came. "Are you going home?"

She did not answer me, but in spite of this I fell in step by her side. She was high-strung and as hard as an iron spike, and when my sleeve brushed against her as we walked, she started and drew away, until she was walking against the very walls of the houses and could no longer avoid my sleeve.

"Osmi," I said, "I've got a job now. I'm going to become an electrician."

"Oh, are you?" she said in a voice that was friendly enough.

But she said it in such a way that I realized I would never become an electrician. I could not fool her by going to work and acting like others. There was a wildness in my blood, and she knew it and despised and hated me for it. But now I wanted only to walk by her side and so I pretended not to understand the implication of her question and tried to talk to her lightly, just as if she were any girl to whom I had taken a fancy.

"Do you want to go to the movies with me tonight?" I asked. "Or to a dance Saturday?"

"Ahaa," was all she said and she looked at me sideways and smiled queerly with her eyes and red mouth.

I felt hot all over.

"You've become a very pretty girl, Osmi," I said and tried to touch her arm with my hand.

But she drew back and in doing so encountered the wall, so that she was forced to stand still. She was pale now and her dark eyes had a hard glint as she said, "Keep your hands off me!"

People passed to and fro. They looked at me and made as if to laugh, but they did not laugh. They avoided coming too close to us and some even crossed to the other side of the street. They must have thought I was drunk. Indeed, maybe I was drunk and dangerous-looking, but if I was, it was only because of Osmi and her words.

"Why the devil are you making a scene?" I said and wept inside me because I was unable to say the things to her I wanted to or explain how I felt.

"Stop following me," she said. "Don't speak to me! I'm

ashamed to have people see you talking to me and think that I have anything to do with you. It makes me sick when even your sleeve touches me. Go away!"

"Osmi!" I said and stretched out my hand, but she went and I did not try to follow her.

But still I simply had to see her, and I often waited for her near her house or hung around the streets along which she had to walk home. But I only watched her from afar without speaking to her, and I thought she didn't notice me. And every time I saw her I yearned more strongly for her, and many times I thought I would die when I watched her pass by. That is how insane I was. And I could no longer eat anything and bad dreams disturbed my sleep. At the workshop I quarreled with everybody and deliberately did everything wrong, but for a time nobody dared say anything to me, for mine was wild blood and I was only seeking an excuse to pick a fight.

Perhaps she saw me following her at a distance, for once she was escorted home from work. Her escort was a young gentleman, older than I, and they stood in the street in front of Osmi's house and laughed in the spring evening, while the sky above the city flamed blood-red. After that she was often escorted part of the way home, and she used to go out at night dressed in her best clothes. When she walked alone she smiled mysteriously, and a new expression was in her eyes, and she walked with an ever lighter step. She challenged me with her every movement and gesture and her eyes, her mouth, her face, so that I could not think of anything except her; and I started to stay away from work when I didn't have the strength to get up mornings, after staying up all night.

Then one night I hid between a couple of ashcans in her yard and waited until she came home. A man brought her home in a taxi, but he sent the taxi off and escorted her throught the entrance into the yard and I could not see their faces, but could only hear their voices. When they stopped talking and I could only hear their breathing, I could not bear it; so I went right up to them and beamed my flashlight on them, so that they drew apart and stood blinking.

"Ahaa," I said, holding my flashlight in their faces so they could not see me.

"Who is it?" Osmi said, breathing heavily, but unafraid. I thought she knew it was I standing there holding the light on her and watching her moist lips and heaving bosom, for the man had unbuttoned her overcoat and his hands were around her beneath it. For that reason alone I considered how I could best kill that man without getting caught.

"Get out of here!" I told the man, trying to make my voice unrecognizable.

"It's only the janitor," Osmi said quickly to her escort. "I'm going in now. That's the way it is here. Good night."

She brushed the man's hand with her own and walked to her door. I walked back to the entrance with him, showing him the way with the light, and as I walked beside him I thought that I would surely get caught if I hit him then so that he would fall and I could kick him in the face.

"Sorry for the disturbance," the man said and groped in the dark for my hand and laid a coin in it. It was a silver markka, old, good money, but when he went whistling on his way along the street, I flung the coin after him and swore and went back into the yard.

Hearing my footsteps, Osmi opened the door and came back out. I did not shine my flashlight again, and I felt rather than saw her as she approached me.

"Osmi," I said, "why do you do things like that? You know what comes of it. Gentlemen aren't for you."

"Oh, no?" she said sarcastically. "But what if I got a good price for myself?"

I stretched my hand out in the dark and seized her arm. She twisted and turned, but I did not release my hold and finally she stood still, her body as rigid as iron.

"I've got to," she said, her voice soft. "Since you won't stop chasing me around, I want to move away from here to some place where you can't follow me. To do it I need money and good clothes. I can't be happy any longer living in a backyard."

"I haven't been chasing you," I said and thought she only wanted to tease me.

"You've sneaked behind me every day," she said, her temper rising so that she was no longer able to maintain her friendly pose. "I feel sick every time I see your face. Next time I'll go and spend the night with that gentleman if you won't let me come home in peace."

Her voice was as tight as a pair of tweezers.

"But why aren't I good enough for you?" I said and squeezed her arm. "I can get money for you too, and I can dress you up in fine clothes."

"Can you really?" she said in a triumphant tone of voice. "No," she went on, "I'll sell myself to anybody who comes along just so I won't have to see you! I'd rather sleep with a Russian than let you touch me."

"You're crazy," I said, "even crazier than I am!"

I put my arm around her beneath her coat and pulled her toward me. She rested against me just long enough for me to feel how young she was and to imagine what it would be like to hold her close. But her left hand was free and she hit me across the face with it. She must have picked a rock from the ground while I was escorting her young gentleman out into the street, for I heard the cartilage in my nose crack and felt the warm blood ooze from my mouth and run down my chin. While I stood there, blinded by pain, she left. She went home but she did not run, for she was not afraid of me. That was the worst part of it: she was not afraid of me.

My nose was scarred for life that night and I had to stay indoors for a few days because I was too ugly a sight to go to work. But while I lay at home, I found an old file and sharpened it to while away the time, and then set it into a wooden handle. I made it very sharp and afterwards put a cork on its point so it would not tear a hole in my pocket. When I was well again, I waited a couple of nights on the street in front of her house, and late the third night Osmi came home with a man. They came arm in arm, pressed very close together, and they laughed as they walked. Osmi raised her face toward the man and in the blue light of the streetlamp I caught another glimpse of her features. I did not even know whether it was the same man I had encountered in the yard, but I walked up to them and plunged the sharpened file into the man's breast. I aimed at his heart, but he managed to turn so that the blade only pierced his shoulder. It went right through his clothes and shoulder. The man staggered backwards from the force of the blow, so that I left the file sticking in him and ran.

Only much later did I hear that the man had not died. The police investigated the case and came looking for me where I worked and at home, and Osmi's name was printed in the newspapers so that she lost her job at the florist's. But by that time I was already on my way to Russia to work on fortifications.

3

A lot of us had let ourselves be recruited for fortification work, and we had been promised all sorts of things, good pay and good food; and it was not necessary to show any papers, for they gave us a certificate in the recruiting office to show we were traveling to Russia to build fortifications. We were transported from St. Petersburg to fortify a town so near the front that in good weather we could easily hear the rumble of the guns. But the food was not fit even for pigs and the Russian foremen stole our pay; and we slept in barracks dug into the ground, and the men who lived in them were the scum of the earth. That is why I soon got disgusted and cursed the whole business, and many in the barracks fell sick with bloody dysentery, and everybody stole from everybody else, so that it was impossible to leave anything around.

But even worse was to come: we were told we could go to hell, that we were no longer needed, since Russia had made a treaty with China and three million Chinamen were coming to work on the fortifications from the Balkans up to Finland.

They refused to give us our pay, and when we tried to beg food the people only screamed and ran away.

My friend said to me, "Let's try to get back to Finland, even if the Devil himself tries to stop us." We had no money to pay the fare, but we got on a train; and when, after riding a couple of stations, we were thrown off it, we waited for the next train and boarded it. Everybody was traveling that way those days, and in a few days we reached St. Petersburg. En route we were not badly off, for I could manage a few words of Russian and was able to beg food for us from those who had any.

In St. Petersburg we slept on the beach, where scows were being loaded, or under a bridge. And every day we went to the Finland station and walked around it. One day we saw an old countrywoman leave the station with a heavy basket under her arm and stand peering about her. I walked up to her and said, "What have you got in the basket, old woman?" She dropped her basket and started to run, with my friend after her as if he was trying to catch her. When we opened the basket we found a number of bottles of home-distilled vodka and three big loaves of Russian rye bread. Vodka fetched a good price in those days because it was against the law to sell it. So we went into the station and began to approach the soldiers who were there, asking: "Do you want to buy some vodka?" We sold drinks between some freight cars standing behind the station, and we ourselves drank and ate bread and drank some more. When I awoke I felt terrible and everything I possessed had been stolen from me. My coat was gone, my shoes had been pulled off my feet, and my friend had vanished, although I knew it was not he who had robbed me. Rather I feared that he had gotten into a fight and been arrested by the police. Anyway I never did see him again.

I was only eighteen and young-looking besides and eventually a businessman took pity on me, bought me a railway ticket and took me along with him to Finland. But when I got off the train at Terijoki, I was sick and running a fever, and the businessman left me with some war refugees in an abandoned villa after giving them some money to nurse me. I had already been so sick in St. Petersburg when I met him that later I could not remember his face. My illness turned out to be spotted fever, which I had undoubtedly got from fleas, and when I recovered I was so weak I could not stay on my feet, and my gray complexion together with the furrows around my mouth and my smashed nose made me an ugly sight.

I had changed, too. The spirit had been knocked out of me and I had no ambition at all; I just sat around and smoked cigarettes and talked with all kinds of people. The war was still going on and people in Terijoki were making money hand over fist. I could have made plenty by joining the smugglers, but I was not interested.

After I was thrown out of the villa—the money the businessman had left for my care having long since been exhausted —I did all kinds of menial jobs that came along. So the autumn passed and Christmas came. I was alone on Christmas Day, lying in an attic next to the chimney under a pile of sacks to keep warm. I had no ambition to do anything; yet sometimes I thought about Osmi and wondered what had become of her.

But things could not go on like that forever, so I started to mix with the smugglers and soon was crossing the border regularly on trips down to St. Petersburg. I learned to make my way through the woods at night carrying heavy loads. I also learned to spend money again, and I bought myself a sturdy suit and a pair of shiny boots. That winter I also met a Russian housewife who lived in a villa with her children and two servants. I passed the villa many times; it was surrounded by dark spruce trees and in the yard there was a snow-covered fountain. But one day the lady came to the gate and laughed and asked me, "Are you lonely?" Then she said, "Would you like to live here and guard the house? It's dangerous for a woman to be alone."

That is how I came to move into her house to live, and as I guessed what she wanted from me, I slept with her. I lived with her until I got so fed up I hated the sight of her and despised myself as well. One day when she was out I took all her money and her earrings and rings from her jewel box and started off. But in the yard I met her and she asked, "Where are you going?"

"I'm leaving," I said. "I'm tired of looking at you!"

"First show me what you have in your pocket," she said. "I know your kind."

I showed her her jewels and she shook her head and said, "You can keep them if you promise to come back."

"I'll be back soon," I lied, and she believed me because she wanted to believe and in any case could not stop me.

I sold the jewels in Viipuri for a lot of money and I thought that now I had so much money I could do whatever I liked. About this time the revolution broke out and the Russian soldiers started to shoot their officers and wave red flags. Even the locomotives were decorated with red banners when I got to Helsinki, and I thought the world had gone mad and everybody could do whatever he pleased.

I had not thought much about my mother, but when it grew dark I pulled my cap over my eyes and went to see her. At first she did not recognize me, for my illness had changed me and I was very thin and my face was heavily lined.

"I'm Kauko," I said, and attempted to laugh.

"My son, so it's you," my mother said and started to cry. "You're an old man already. What has become of you?"

"Something at least," I said, "so don't be afraid on my account, Mamma." And to comfort her I told her all sorts of lies, saying I had been a tradesman's assistant in Russia and I would return there soon and earn lots of money. While I was talking I wanted to believe it was true myself, and I mentioned to her the names of people and places and said that the businessman in St. Petersburg who had given me a job had taken a liking to me and that I had an apartment of my own there and that I would soon get married and in time become a rich man. To convince her that it was true I gave her some money and told her to buy something for herself.

But all the while I was so restless I could hardly sit still, and finally I said I had to leave. I put on my cap and only after I had reached the hallway, where my mother could no longer see my face, did I pretend to remember something and asked, "Do you know anything about Osmi, Mamma?"

Immediately my mother began to call Osmi all kinds of names. She said Osmi had left home and had lost her job, and that, young as she was, she was living off men. But where she actually was living my mother did not know. I went to see Osmi's family; they still lived in the same yard, but her mother was dead and her father had taken to drink and he told me to go to blazes and threatened to turn me over to the police when he recognized me. I looked at him and thought what it would be like to be an old man whose wife had died and whose daughter had become a whore, so I did not get mad at him. His hair, gray and messy, hung in his eyes when he cursed at me, and he had not taken off his working clothes, so that the hallway smelled like a sewer.

For many days I searched for Osmi, but she was not yet listed in the police books. I looked high and low, until I found out she was living with a woman who ran a tobacco shop. I went to the address given me and rang the doorbell, and Osmi came to open the door and so I came to see her again. She had grown thin and pale, but her eyes were larger and darker than ever and her mouth was still red and beautiful. She recognized me right away, even though my mother had not, and she said, "Why, it's Kauko!"

"Osmi," I said, and it was wonderful to say her name aloud. "May I come in?"

"Why?" she said and shook her head. "Do you need help? Have you come to borrow money?"

"I heard you could buy a bottle of vodka and drink it here, if you paid enough for it," I said, "I have money. May I come in?"

I did not think she would let me inside, but she led me into a room with red plush chairs and a pink hanging basket of a night lamp on the ceiling. A fat woman sat at a table playing solitaire with torn cards.

"Have you any vodka in the house, Auntie?" Osmi asked.

"This fellow would like to buy a bottle to drink here. He says he has plenty of money."

"Ahaa, so he has money," said the woman. "Give him a bottle of punch. But it costs fifty markkas."

I laid fifty markkas in good, old-time money on the table. Osmi brought a bottle of punch, put it on the table and smiled at me. She was no longer a child. Her breasts had matured and from the way she moved her body, I sensed that she was willing to serve me. The blood pounded in my head and my hands began to tremble.

"Have you anything else to sell, Osmi?" I asked.

"It depends on the man," Osmi said and laughed irritatingly, as women have a way of laughing. She turned to the fat woman, who had gone back to playing solitaire at the table.

"Think of it, Auntie," she said. "This man is in love with me. One time he knifed a man who escorted me home, so that nobody wanted to walk home with me anymore and I lost my job and became what I am now. That's how much he loves me."

"I didn't use a knife," I said and took a drink of the punch.

The fat woman laughed and put the cards away and drank some punch from my glass without asking permission.

"Has he really got money?" she asked and looked at me.

"I don't think he's got enough for me," said Osmi. "I don't think he's even got enough for me to let him touch my little finger."

I thought she was going to surprise me, that everything was as it ought to be. I had been drinking, so I put all my money on the table, proudly piling up the bills; and I looked at Osmi and said, "I'll bet there isn't a girl in all Helsinki I couldn't buy with this money."

I had been thinking of buying an electricity business and beginning to live a decent life, and it was quite a bit of money that I laid on the table. The fat woman looked at the money and at Osmi and laughed hoarsely.

But Osmi glanced at the money and shook her head and said, "It isn't enough!"

"Are you crazy?" I said, astonished.

"There are men who could have me for less," said Osmi, undulating her body slightly. "Yes, for other men I could be had for a lot less. But for you . . . it's not enough!"

She shook her head and smiled with her red mouth, and the fat woman looked at her as though proud of her and nodded her head, emptied my glass down her gullet and smacked her lips.

"Well, what will you give me for this?" I asked, trying to be sarcastic, but she was unlike anyone else and her eyes were different from the eyes of others, so that my sarcasm fell flat and my money, and in fact my entire life, seemed meaningless without her.

Osmi looked at the money and, coldly and calculatingly, at me. "Oh, I could give you one kiss for that price," she said and haughtily tossed her head. "You could have a kiss, if you think it's worth it."

"Osmi," I said and felt the taste of blood in my mouth. "Maybe I've wronged you. You can have the money. You don't have to give me anything for it."

"Business is business," Osmi said and walked over to me. "I won't accept anything from you as a gift. But I need money, I need lots of money."

She came lightly into my arms and slipped her hands around my neck. I felt her breasts against my chest and her hips against my loins, and she opened her lips for me as I kissed her and the touch of her hands burned my neck. I thought of all the men in whose arms she had lain, but so insane was I that the thought only made her more desirable to me. But having kissed me she slipped out of my grasp and went to the other side of the table and kept her hands behind her back and looked at me with her black eyes filled with hate.

"Now you know what I'm like again," she said. "And take your money! I don't need it. If you come back here, I'll have the police on you!"

But the fat woman quickly put her hands on the money and looked reproachfully at Osmi.

"No!" said Osmi. "He's only a crazy bum. He's dangerous. We can't take his money."

I took my hat and groped my way to the door. I did not take my money and my eyes were so blinded that I had to feel my way with my hands. I shut the outer door and walked down the stairs. Then Osmi came to the door and threw my money after me, so that the bills lay all over the stairs. Without saying a word she threw the money and shut the door.

I was not so crazy that I did not pick up the money. With the taste of blood in my mouth I crawled around the hallway and gathered the bills and stuffed them in my pocket. But I did not buy an electricity business, for at the hotel I encountered a couple of men who were playing cards. I joined the game and we drank brandy and vodka and played all night and all the following day. I thought I knew how to play cards, but they played better, and when I woke up I had not a penny left, and I had gambled away my extra suit and my overcoat and even my watch, so that I had to start all over again from scratch.

Times were restless and everything seemed to be going to the devil, though there were those who thought the kingdom of heaven was at hand. I tried all sorts of ways to make money and joined a gang that carried on a black-market trade with Russian sailors. But nothing turned out right, and in the end I found myself again at a fortification site near town. Nobody worked there any longer and nobody paid any wages, but the old man who guarded the equipment let me sleep in his hut. I spent the summer of 1917 with him and his dog, and the world was still at war and there was unrest in the country, and the bums I met scampered about as though there were hot coals underfoot and threatened all kinds of things. But I did not believe them.

The old man was crazy. He had made a lot of money during the building of the fortifications by selling tools over and over again, in cahoots with the cashiers. But he was such a miser he could hardly bear even to eat, and kept his money hidden beneath a floorboard behind his bed. He thought I did not know about the money, that nobody knew about it; but I discovered his hiding place by spying on him, and I felt that an old man like that had no use for money. Besides, he was crazy; but in a way I liked him, and I liked the dog, too. And there was no place else where I could stay, because I did not want to go home after having told my mother how well I was getting along.

All summer long I racked my brains to decide what I could do and why I existed at all. I thought about Osmi too, but I did not want to see her because my suit was torn and I didn't even have any socks or decent shoes. Besides, I thought she would indeed have the police on my neck if I tried to see her, and there were plenty of reasons why I did not want to have anything to do with the police. So I let the old man keep his money, nor envied him for it.

But there were others who knew that the old man had money. And one fall night when I came into the hut with a loaf of rye bread under my arm, the light was burning and the whole place was turned topsy-turvy. The old man lay on the floor with his head split open, his body already cold. The dog had been stabbed with a bayonet and had crawled under the bench to die. My guess was that some Russian soldiers who knew the old man had come in search of his money, and I lifted the bed out of place and noticed that the floor was intact. I had liked the old man and his dog, too, and I thought that if I should ever meet one of the soldiers who had loafed around the hut and stood guard there, I would kill him at the first opportunity. But a corpse had no use for money, so I tore up the floor and found eight thousand markkas and a lot of rubles, and I took it but left everything else alone, thinking that the police would suppose the murderers had found the money. So I fled with the money and went back to town.

But I should have been smarter; instead of leaving town and going into hiding, I bought myself a new suit and a watch and a ring; and I thought that now I could go and see Osmi again. Osmi was not at home, but the fat woman let me in and sold me some wine and brandy, which she said she had bought from a Russian hospital ship. She treated me politely and we spoke about Osmi and only then did I learn that Osmi had a job and in fact had had one all the time. She had never been on the police books and had nothing to do with the men who constantly flocked after her. This the fat woman told me while I waited and she complained how impossible Osmi was and how much money she could have made if only she had been "nicer." But Osmi had behaved toward everybody else just as she had toward me, and now she had some railroad worker who came to see her and wanted to marry her. But I was not supposed to care about this, I was only supposed to sip brandy while I waited for Osmi, because I had the money. I did not believe everything she told me, but she drank with me and spoke to me as to a human being and I was so fed up and unhappy that I could have wept when that pudgy, ugly woman spoke to me in a friendly voice.

Then Osmi came home, came gaily and out of breath, and she looked beautiful in my eyes—until she saw me. Then she started and her face paled, and she asked the old woman why she had let me in.

"Don't you remember what I said when you were here last?" she said to me.

"He has money again, he has even more money than last time," said the fat woman and looked meaningfully at Osmi.

"Is that so?" Osmi said, and abruptly her agitation left her and she sat down at my side by the table and poured me a drink.

"Drink, then!" she said.

I was already drunk and got drunker than ever when she sat beside me.

"You kissed me last time, Osmi," I said. "Do it again, I haven't forgotten it."

"I'd kiss a snake, if the price were good enough," Osmi said and smiled calculatingly at me, poured out some more brandy intended for wounded Russian soldiers and added: "Drink it now!"

That is why I thought she was only fooling, as strange and mad as she was. "I grow wild when I drink," I told her, "but I'll drink gladly if you tell me to. Besides, you lie when you speak of a price. I know you don't sell yourself. Why do you lie like that to me?"

"Drink!" she said and poured some more brandy into my glass. "Maybe I'll even kiss you—later."

She smiled and looked at me with her dark, cold eyes. The fat woman looked at her, then at me, and shrank back from the table and her face took on a frightened look.

"That railroad clerk of yours is coming tonight," she reminded Osmi.

"I'm going to telephone him not to come tonight," Osmi said. "But first I want to look at Kauko, because I guess I won't be seeing him again for a long time."

"Why do you hate him so much?" the fat woman asked, her eyes seeking first the door, then the window. But I was already so drunk I could not understand what she meant.

"Osmi," I said, "I've been waiting for you for years. I've gone hungry and been cursed for your sake. I've waited for you for years, and when you smile at me I think that all the things my old mother has said about heaven are true."

Yes, I was so drunk that I said such things. Osmi looked at me and smiled and her red lips parted, showing her teeth, so that she seemed to be mocking me.

"Drink!" she said softly, but I did not feel like drinking any more. I shoved the bottle away from me; I started to cry with desire and tried to embrace her.

"In a while," she said, "in a while! First I've got to telephone my friend, for you might stab him too if he came while you were here. That would be too bad, because he's a good man, much better than you, and I intend to marry him."

But I thought she was only teasing me, and I forgot everything when she put her arms around my neck for a moment and let her hand steal under my shirt and touched my bare breast with her fingers.

"You must be very strong, Kauko," she said admiringly. "But now I must go, and soon, very soon I'll be back."

She left and stayed away quite a long time, for she stood in the hallway waiting for the police, after telephoning to them, and came back only when they had arrived. I was so drunk and they rushed at me so suddenly, I did not even have time to stand up, and they twisted my arms behind my back and clamped handcuffs on my wrists before I could do anything.

"Good," said the commissioner, who out of curiosity had come along himself. "We've been looking for this fellow. He murdered the watchman at the fortifications and stole the old man's savings. He lived with him all summer to spy out the place where he had his money. He's a clever one, but we're smarter and he won't be bothering you for a long time."

But I only looked at Osmi, and I was still looking at her when they shoved my hat on my head and dragged me away. Down the stairs they pushed me, beating me when I held back, but I kept my eyes shut to preserve the image of Osmi as she stood before me, for I guessed that many years would pass before I would see her again. But at the same time I swore that I would see her once more, and I relished the thought of how much time I would have to plan what I would do to her when we met.

4

So I was brought up for questioning. But no matter how they pressed me I would not confess. I told them to question the soldiers who had been on guard at the fortifications, and they admitted that the dog had been killed with a bayonet and they asked where I had hidden the bayonet. Maybe they finally began to doubt my guilt themselves, but the times were unsettled and it was difficult and dangerous to imprison Russian soldiers, although they were becoming wilder day by day. They had found the money on me and I had lived with the old man all summer, but in the end they did not convict me of murder but only manslaughter and burglary. They said, "You got off easy as the devil, young fellow!" And they said, "You're going to give us plenty of trouble yet." In their minds I was a holy terror, but they also thought they were smarter than I was.

So it was that I was set to counting bricks and breaking rocks and other heavy labor. The food was bad and got worse day by day, until my face was gray and I staggered rather than walked. Only as an echo from a mountain we heard how the world was progressing toward the kingdom of heaven on earth, when all the big-shots would be executed and the money divided among the common people. Many a cellmate of mine listened to such talk with eyes agleam and mouth awater, but none were freed.

Not until April, 1918, when the thunder of German guns began to be heard from Huopalahti, did they come for us and open our cells and cry: "Come on out, comrades!" In the prison yard, rifles were shoved into our hands, and we were told: "Chase the Germans back, then you'll be set free and pardoned for everything!"

The comrades marched us to the top of Watertower Hill and behind the lines on the cliffs, and watching carefully to make certain that nobody slipped away, said, "Anybody who tries to run away will get a bullet in his head. Now fight for your freedom, lads!" And cigarettes were passed out to us and girls brought us pea soup in buckets.

But the Germans were already bombarding the Turku barracks across the bay and their ships were shelling the main Russian garrison next to the bridge at Katajanokka. They also aimed their guns at the new bridge connecting the workers' quarter with the rest of the city so that great chunks of granite were knocked off the balustrade. But I was thinking of Osmi, and when night fell and the flames of burning houses lit the town I reasoned that I was bound to die sometime and at the moment it made no difference whether the comrades shot me or the Germans. So I slipped away into the darkness of the cliffs, though our officers were behind us to prevent anybody from fleeing back into town. I fled down the hill and they fired after me and shouted, "What damned coward is that?" But I held on to my rifle so I would have a weapon. In the darkness all was confusion as I ran along the streets and I was shot at many times from the dark, for the firing went on all night all over the town, and the fires lit up the sky and I thought that this was the end of the world. That is why I wanted to find Osmi.

At last I found the house and broke in the downstairs door with the butt of my rifle, and ran upstairs so out of breath that I wheezed and grunted as I ran. Sobbing breathlessly I rang the doorbell and pounded on the door with my rifle butt. The house remained pitch-dark, so I lighted up the door with matches as people began to cry out from behind other doors on hearing the pounding of my rifle butt. At last the fat old woman came to open the door for me, only she was no longer fat; she was thin and bent and had shrunken away almost to nothing. I rushed into the hallway and shoved her against the wall and panted at her: "Osmi, where is Osmi?"

"I don't know!" she said. "She hasn't been here for months. What kind of bum are you to chase after girls on a night like this?"

Then I put my bayonet against her breast and I pressed her against the wall and demanded, "Where's Osmi? Tell me or I'll kill you, you old hag!"

"Even if you kill me, I wouldn't know!" she screamed, and fell on her knees on the floor when I released her. "Osmi is married," she said, "didn't you know that? She doesn't even live in the city, because she hasn't come to see me."

"All right," I said, "I'll find her one day. Tell her that when you see her! And I won't die yet, if that's what you're hoping. I'm going to find her first, so wish her lots of luck from me, because I'm not going to die yet."

But my head was like a black well as I went down the stairs, for I was convinced I would die. So I pounded my chest with my fists and cursed as I went down the stairs. And I thought that if there was such a thing as Fate or Providence it was pretty smart, smarter than I. For if I had got my hands on Osmi that night I might have killed her and we would have died together. Such was the state of my world that night.

As I reached the street a couple of comrades wandered by, waving their rifles excitedly, and they said in frightened voices: "Come along, comrade! What unit do you belong to? There were three of us, but our third man disappeared back there when we were sent out to cross the bridge to see how far the Germans have got."

"All right," I said and suddenly started to laugh, and all the while as we crossed the bridge I laughed in the darkness and held my head high, though the other two crept along on the ground in the cover of the balustrade and tried to hush me up.

On the other bank, men wearing the hats and with the white bands of the Civil Guard on their sleeves came out of the surrounding dark and shot at us, the flames spurting out of their rifles, and they shouted, "Hands up!"

We threw our rifles away, for we were even more afraid of them than they were afraid of us, and we raised our hands in the air and were taken into a schoolhouse and thrown in with a crowd of other prisoners. Some of them were wounded, and there were even a few girls there, but everyone was very subdued and kept silent even though no one got food or water all the next day and night. Everyone kept his mouth sealed tight and said nothing, thinking that was the best way of preserving his life.

So I was again locked up in the penitentiary, and there was hunger and disease and many died, but I did not die and I thought that maybe I would not die after all before I saw Osmi; and I became uncertain and puzzled over what I would do to her, for the mere thought that I might see her again was like a gift to me.

My old mother did not come to see me in jail, and I was glad of it, but I did get one letter from her, in which she wrote that my father was dead. He had been thrown overboard from the battleship and the Bolshevik sailors had made a game of shooting at his head until they hit him. The money Mother had saved from his wages was now worthless, but my older brother had a job and they got along somehow. She did not write again and I was glad because I would not have answered even if I had been allowed to write. I had nothing to write about.

But in jail I got a chance to read a lot of books again and I read as many as I was allowed to take out of the prison library. The prison chaplain was kind to me, and at times I thought that perhaps one day when I was let free I would get myself a job and read a lot of books and live with my old mother and lead a peaceful life and say nothing bad about anybody. But my blood was still untamed and there were days when I only swore and talked with hardened criminals kept in our common cell. They advised me on the best way to commit a burglary and how to hit to kill and how to soften the blow when one only wanted to knock the other fellow unconscious. They taught me their own jargon and the signs by which they recognized each other and what to tell the police under cross-examination and what one could confess and what should never be admitted. And they said to me: "A wolf is always a wolf and can never baa with the sheep." They recalled everything they had ever done and planned what they would do before they landed back in jail again, if ever they were set free. And as they spoke about these things their eyes gleamed and I listened to them.

But in jail, each day is like all the others. And neither cursing nor weeping helps. I read lots of books at night and on Sundays and I learned the carpenter's trade, and unlike many of the others I played no tricks, because I did not think them worth while. So four more years passed and then I was freed when I no longer expected it. I left with a few markkas in my pocket, and I had grown so much in jail that the clothes I had worn when I arrived no longer fit me. For I was a grown man at last, although my face was gray and my back was bent and I could no longer look people in the eye.

That is how I went free and I had to rediscover myself and what I would become and what I intended to do. I still had some vague plans, but four years and a half of a fifth had fled by and I was no longer in any hurry.

5

That is why I humbled myself and went straight from jail to my mother's. But she had moved and for a while I could not find her, but at last I found her in a hole-in-a-wall of a kitchen, where she lived with my older brother.

"Is that you, Kauko?" she said. "I didn't think I'd ever see you again, so you might have spared me this sorrow."

But I was bull-headed and hung my hat on a nail and just sat in a chair and waited until my mother sighed and dished me out some food. In the evening when my older brother came home he told me to go to blazes, because he had no desire to support a thief and a murderer. So much time had passed that I had forgotten what I had been and what I had done and I pictured myself only as I thought of myself now, which is why I became angry. But so smart had I become that I did not show it; instead I humbled myself and asked to be allowed to remain a few nights until I could find a job which would enable me to make a living.

For I had to find out where Osmi was, whom she had married, and the kind of person she had become. All this I wanted to know before I saw her, even if it took time; and above all I did not want to get caught before I found her, though afterwards nothing would matter to me. That is why I humbled myself and slept under the kitchen table and ate as little as possible, so I would not be in the way and irritate my brother or put my mother to any trouble.

But I could not get a job, no matter how I begged and prayed for one, because my reputation held me to be dangerous and everyone was afraid of me. Some days I collected rags and some days I sawed logs for firewood in the lumberyard, until I met Hanski.

"Well, if it isn't Kauko!" said Hanski and he wore a good suit and carried a gold watch with a gold chain in his vest pocket. But he still had the reddish scar on his forehead where I had once hit him. He pretended not to remember this but offered me a cigarette and told me to come down to the harbor in the morning and he would get me a job. He did indeed get me a job at the harbor, but it was heavy work and I had to work so hard my fingers started to bleed and my knees gave way under me, for I was still weak from my stay in prison. Occasionally Hanski walked by in his polished shoes, the scar glaring on his forehead, smoking a cigar and saying, "Toil away, toil away, Kauko! Or have you had enough, already?" And he laughed at me and went over to look at his motorboat, which he kept openly by the shore, a long gray affair with a powerful motor of the sort that liquor smugglers used in those days.

"Wait," I told him, "maybe I'll have had enough before long."

After a few weeks I had saved enough to get myself some decent clothes. So I scraped the dirt off my hands and went to the barber's and set out to follow Osmi's trail. And soon I learned her new name. Her husband worked for the railroad at a station near Helsinki and they had a house near the station. Having cleared up this matter, I went to see Hanski and said, "How about lending me your revolver tonight?"

"Have you had enough?" Hanski said and laughed in my face. "Why don't you join me and make loads of money? I'm going out to sea again tomorrow if it's cloudy."

"That's fine with me," I lied and he gave me a revolver and some bullets. I went into the woods just outside town and put a cigarette box on top of a tree stump and shot at it a few times from close range. Then I waited for a train at Pasila and when the train came I boarded it and at the right station I went to the baggage office and asked whether such and such goods had arrived for such and such a person, because I wanted to see what kind of man Osmi had married.

He paged through his books and said no goods such as I had described had arrived, but I refused to accept his word until he went through all his books once more and promised to clear up the matter. He was a small, fair man, shorter than I was, with light blue eyes, white eyebrows and reddish freckles. He spoke to me in a friendly manner, stuttering a bit as he talked, and I ended up laughing so hard at him that my hands and knees shook. At that he became frightened, gathered up his books and went away from the window muttering: "Lunatic!"

But I walked whistling down the road and asked for the house where Osmi lived. It was a small, new house with a sandy path leading up to the door, and it was painted yellow except for the window frames and the corners, which were white. Trees and bushes had been planted in the garden although they were still leafless, as it was early spring. I went in through the gate, and since the door was not locked I went inside. Osmi stood by the oven, her sleeves rolled up, and a baby crawled on the floor by her feet, sucking on a dirty block of wood.

"Osmi," I said, and my hands and knees began to tremble. "I've come back, as you see."

She looked at me as if I were a stranger, and then her face grew pale and she dropped the ladle from her hand and, her eyes on me constantly, stumbled backwards against the side wall so that the baby was left crawling on the floor between us.

"So it's Kauko," she said in a voice that cracked, and she swallowed.

I looked at her and the revolver was heavy in my pocket. She had put on weight since I had last seen her. She was a mature woman now, beautiful and tempting. Her arms were very white and her eyes still large and dark, but they seemed gentler than before and so frightened when she looked at me that I felt exultant.

"So you've got a baby, too," I said.

"Yes, I have a boy," she answered and continued to stare at me, her back still pressed against the wall. My eyes went over her body insolently, taking in every inch of her, until she turned her face away and her breath began to come unevenly.

"I guess you didn't expect me to turn up again," I said and tried to laugh, for the revolver weighed heavily in my pocket.

"I don't know," she said softly and looked at me and grew pale again.

"The boy looks like your husband," I said and looked at the baby, who was still sucking on the dirty block of wood on the floor. "He'll stutter and stammer too when he gets bigger and he'll have the same kind of white eyebrows."

"Have you seen my husband?" she exclaimed, her voice rising. "What have you done to my husband?" she cried and stretched out her hands toward me, her fingers arched like the claws of a cat.

"I haven't done anything to him. He isn't worth the trouble," I said easily. "But you recognized him from my description, and of course you're very happy?"

"He's a good man," Osmi said more calmly. "I've borne him a son."

"You're very happy?" I asked again, raising my voice in turn. "You're very happy?" I cried and my hands and knees trembled.

"I am quite happy," Osmi said in a dull, dead voice and her eyes which gazed at me evenly were hard. "But you came back and when I look at you I know that I can't be happy until you are dead, that I can never find peace until you are dead. Are you satisfied now?"

"You kissed me once and I know what you are like," I said and the blood rose to my head. There was a fire in the stove and she lifted the kettle off of it. I shoved my hand into the fire and pulled out one of the red-hot gridirons and held it in my trembling hand until it had burned a white track across my palm and no longer hurt. Then I dropped it on the floor and I showed my hand to her and said: "This is what you do to me!"

She came nearer to me and pressed her hands together and whispered to herself: "Yes, yes, you won't give me peace until you are dead." And she looked at me and her eyes flashed and she too began to tremble.

"I came to kill you," I said, "but it's not worth the trouble since you're so happy. You have a good husband and a son as well, but I have nothing. So I guess it's best I leave, and now you can be certain you're rid of me, because in Helsinki they're recruiting men for the war in Karelia* and they'll take me into the army even if I'm not fit for anything else. So don't worry about me anymore, because this time I won't come back."

"I hope you don't come back," she said and looked at me and trembled and breathed heavily. "I hope you don't come back," she repeated as she followed me to the door. "Every night I'll pray you'll be shot," she said and stood on the steps,

* Russian: Olonets, southern East Carelia.

her trembling hand extended. "I'll thank heaven on my knees when I hear you're dead," she said.

That is all said to me in farewell, and when I got back to town I went straight to the place where they were recruiting men for war. I wrote my name on the papers and in that way I got to go to Karelia.

6

In 1920 they did not ask who and what you were, just as long as they got men who were not afraid. There were some like me who had rotted in jail and who had nobody to care what happened to them. But most had been soldiers in the war, although some were only college students and even schoolboys who had run away from home to fight. We talked of how we would be given land in Karelia when we had won, land on which we could live, for it was said that there was game in the woods and fish in the lakes and even pearls in the rivers. But it did not matter to me where and how I died and I lay in my billet and thought about my father who had been thrown overboard from a battleship as a target for the Russian soldiers on deck.

That is why it was easy to go to war, although it was a bitter war in which no prisoners were taken; which did not matter to us since nobody wanted to fall into the hands of the Bolsheviks alive. It was exhausting marching over the bad roads and wilderness cowpaths, and the schoolboys with us grew thin and pale until only their eyes glowed in their exhausted faces. Some of them began to be frightened and tried to get sent home, and a few deserted, fleeing back across the border into Finland or falling into the hands of Bolshevik patrols in the woods.

The mere boys aroused my pity and sometimes I carried two or even three rifles when they became exhausted. I was used to foraging as I went so I did not go hungry, even though I divided my spoils with the others. And because nothing mattered to me any longer, the captain said I was a brave fellow. But I was not brave, for many a time, when the sky was blue and red above the Karelian wilds, I yearned for death so strongly that death seemed like a friend or home or the warmth of a good bed on a freezing night.

But fate was smarter than I, and finally we lay on a ridge thick with heather and fired down upon a village in which the houses had high gables and walls built of logs. The captain ran along our line and jumped into the hole in which I was lying. After resting he lit a cigarette and gave it to me and smiling, said, "We're attacking right away!" He was a Jäger and he wore the Jäger's green uniform, although it had become worn and faded in the sun and rain.

"Why are you friendly with me, Captain?" I asked. "You probably don't know what kind of a man I am?"

"You are what you are," he said. "I don't ask to see your birth certificate! I've watched you and know that you're a good man."

"I've been in jail," I said, "and if we get back alive, there's no place for me to go."

"When we've won," he said, "you'll be given land here and you can stay and live in Karelia." And again he began to talk about the game in the woods and the pearl clams in the rivers.

"I know," I said, "I'll get a plot of land six feet long and three wide, like the others, because we can't win, and you know it, Captain!"

To this he said nothing, because I was not a child like so many of the others and he knew better than to try to convince me.

But after a while he said, "My parents have a big farm and if we get back to Finland I'll take you with me if you don't find anything else."

"Shake hands on it, Captain," I said and laughed, for I had not imagined that he, too, was afraid. But now I admired him all the more, for he was a real man.

Then we attacked for the last time, and as we ran down the ridge toward the village I was hit in the leg by a machine-gun bullet and the captain was shot through the head, so that he never saw his parents' big estate again. My leg was broken and I was transported by sleigh along a forest road to the Finnish border and to a hospital. The journey took many days, but I did not die and my leg was not even amputated. But that is how I became lame for life.

It was a long time before I was able to walk again. By then everybody had come back home across the border; that is, everybody who was able to come back. Their fight had been for nothing, and they scattered over the country, each to his home locality. When I was better I was asked where I wanted to go. "I don't know," I said. So I was given a little money and was allowed to keep my uniform and my boots as well.

Trying to regain the full use of my legs I limped along various roads, roaming from place to place as long as I had money. It troubled me that even death had no use for me, even though I had made it my goal. Eventually I sold my uniform and boots, for I found the uniform a hindrance when it came to finding a job. But even so, it was impossible for me to find work, for I was still lame, and if I said I had been wounded in the Karelian war, nobody dared to give me work, and even if I had found a job, my fellow workers would have chased me away, for hatred ruled the country in those days.

So in the end I found myself again in Helsinki doing all kinds of odd jobs and even a little begging when no policeman was looking. Then one day I met one of the men who had recruited me and I asked him for a job. He gave me some money and said, "I've heard you were in jail once."

"So I was," I said, "but you did not ask me that before."

"No," he admitted, "but a lot of bad things are being said about the volunteers' army now that we've lost. And it would be better that they don't get any more ideas."

"You needn't worry about that," I said and I gave him back the service certificate I had been given when I was discharged. After that I hesitated no longer but sought out Hanski and told him that I was ready to take orders from him. So all autumn I smuggled liquor with the islanders. Hanski paid me well, but he had bought himself a brick house in the Töölö quarter of town and no longer went to sea, letting others do the work for him. Money came and money went. I spent my free time drinking and playing cards and on the police books there was a mark beside my name, for I was lame and could not flee trouble as readily as the others. That is why I always kept a gun with me.

All this time I had not seen Osmi but tried not to think about her. But my blood would not subside and the dangerous life at sea hardened me, so that I began to see many things differently than before. I especially began to understand women better than I had and it often occurred to me that I was a fool for still thinking about Osmi. She was another man's wife and she had a son and she had said she was happy. Why should I bother her anymore?

But in the winter it was quiet and I could not look at other women, and if I spent a night with a girl, I beat her in the morning. Liquor did not appeal to me anymore, so that I lay and moped and bit my fists and thought that I was going mad. And when I thought of the future I saw nothing to hope for, because I knew that one day I would be stabbed or would drown at sea or there would be some other trouble and I would land in jail again. That is what seemed to happen to everyone like me sooner or later.

At last I could stand it no longer and decided to go and see her. At the station there was no train leaving for a while, but having made up my mind, I was so impatient I took a taxi. As I paid for my ride before her house, I saw a boy playing in the snow in the yard. He came over to watch the taxi.

"Here, boy, go buy some candy," I said and gave him some money and went in through the gate. But the door was locked and nobody came to open it.

"Open the door, Osmi," I shouted through the door, "or I'll break the windows."

But she did not come to the door, so I broke a pane of glass with my fist, and the blood started to run down my hand. Then at last she opened the door.

"What do you want, Kauko?" she asked. "Are you drunk?"

But she let me inside, closing the door behind me and standing with her back against it.

"So you're not dead after all," she said, "even though I've prayed you were!"

"I'm not dead," I said and the blood dripped off my hand and onto the floor. "No, I'm not dead, but I've lost a leg and my back is bent. That ought to make you glad!"

"Yes, that makes me glad," she said softly. And she did not avoid me when I went to her and seized her by the arms. She did not cry out when I kissed her. She bit me but she did not cry out.

I touched her face with my hand and she no longer bit me when I kissed her. Her eyes were closed and her face flushed at my touch and her breath came hoarsely. She was beautiful as she put her arms around my neck and her lips against my cheek.

"Your son has grown," I said.

"So he has," Osmi said. "He stammers like his father already. And he has white eyebrows like his father."

"You are very happy, of course," I said, "with a good husband and a son and a house of your own."

"This was not meant for me," Osmi said. "At first I thought it was, but it wasn't. My father was a sewer rat and I grew up in the backyard with you, Kauko. That time when you hit me and knocked me down, I knew that I would follow you to hell."

She wrung her hands together, and her eyes were wild as she said, "I can't help it! You're stronger than I am. I can't get rid of you. I've prayed that you'd come back, you've been in my dreams every night and when my husband makes love to me I keep my eyes closed and cry out for him to hit me so that I might think of you."

"You're mad," I said, "you're even madder than I am!"

But she began to gather her clothes together, emptying her drawers. She took some money and silverware from a closet and she flung her clothes on the floor and made a bundle out of them.

"Some day I'm going to get a knife in my back," I said, "or a bullet in my head or be thrown in jail. That's no life for you, Osmi!"

"I'll follow you to hell, Kauko," she said from where she squatted on her knees on the floor, tying up her bundle of clothes. "I can't live without you any longer, for I've cursed each day you've been away and I've trembled at every letter and watched every passerby from the window hoping it might be you."

Her arms went around my legs and she wept bitterly. She was different from all the others and her eyes glowed at me and I cannot describe how beautiful she could be as she knelt there with her breasts pressing against my knees and her arms around me.

"Then come with me," I said, "then come with me, as long as you don't cry afterwards."

So I took her with me and she never saw her home again. I took her with me to hunger, crime and misery, and from that day we lived together, until she died and I became what I am now.